The Mayflower Bride

The Mayflower Bride

The
Daughters
of the
Mayflower

KIMBERLEY WOODHOUSE

BARBOUR BOOKS

An Imprint of Barbour Publishing, Inc.

©2018 by Kimberley Woodhouse

Print ISBN 978-1-68322-419-8

eBook Editions:
Adobe Digital Edition (.epub) 978-1-68322-421-1
Kindle and MobiPocket Edition (.prc) 978-1-68322-420-4

This book is a work of fiction. Names, characters, places, and incidents are either products of the author's imagination or used fictitiously. Any similarity to actual people, organizations, and/or events is purely coincidental.

Cover Photograph: Lee Avison/Trevillion Images

Published by Barbour Books, an imprint of Barbour Publishing, Inc., 1810 Barbour Drive, Uhrichsville, Ohio 44683, www.barbourbooks.com

Our mission is to inspire the world with the life-changing message of the Bible.

Member of the
Evangelical Christian
Publishers Association

Printed in the United States of America.

DEDICATION

This book is lovingly dedicated to my fellow "super-pants" wearer: Tracie Peterson.

For two decades you have taught, mentored, loved, and cheered me on. Now, umpteen published books later, I hope you know how much you are appreciated.

Without you, I wouldn't be where I am, and I know it's to God that the glory be given—not only for this gift of story and publication, but for the gift of you. You are my dearest friend other than my precious husband—and sometimes I wonder how or why you ever put up with me. But you do. Through thick and thin. And I'm so very grateful.

Precious lady—my prayer and Bible study partner, accountability partner, and listening ear. I love all the opportunities to learn from you, teach with you, write with you, and laugh with you. What a privilege it is to have you in my life.

Thank you for telling me I was a storyteller all those years ago and encouraging me to keep working at it. I also need to thank Jim. Without his encouragement, consistent help, and prayers—and let's not forget all the bunny stories—I would be lost. Give him a hug for me.

This dedication could never encompass my heart of gratitude for you, Tracie. So I will leave you with these simple words: Thank you. For everything.

DEAR READER

What an awesome joy and privilege to write the first book in the **Daughters of the *Mayflower*** series. It has been a delight to research such a monumental moment and to present to you this work of fiction based on the real events.

Writing historical novels is a passion of mine, and I must admit I got caught up in the research. But this is a first for me—most of the time as an author I get to make up the majority of my characters and then sprinkle in real people from the time period. This time was different. With historical events surrounding the *Mayflower* and her passengers, I had to research each person on the ship and then bring aboard only a few fictional people.

But just so you are aware, the main characters—William, Mary Elizabeth (along with her father and brother), and Dorothy's family—weren't real people on the *Mayflower*. Nor was the character Peter. I did that for a reason. I didn't want to take anything away from the ones who lived the true story and live on in history. Rest assured the remaining characters were true *Mayflower* travelers. I pray I've done them justice in this story.

To keep this book enjoyable for today's reader, I have written *The Mayflower Bride* with both modern English and spellings (i.e., I didn't use *thee* and *thou* in the characters' speech. After I trudged through all the historical documents and journals, my eyes and brain were exhausted just from trying to figure out what they were saying, so this decision was for your benefit. You can thank me later). English of the day didn't have common spelling, so a lot of it was phonetic, with spelling changing from person to person. A sample of the way things were written in 1620 is the handwritten copy of the

Mayflower Compact from William Bradford's book. Here is a small sample of it so you can experience the spelling and language:

> *Haueing vndertaken, for ye glorie of God, and aduance-*
> *mente of ye christian faith and honour of our king & countrie, a*
> *voyage to plant ye first colonie in ye Northerne parts of Virginia·*
> *doe by these presents solemnly & mutualy in ye presence of God,*
> *and one of another, couenant, & combine our selues togeather into*
> *a ciuill body politick; for ye our better ordering, & preseruation &*
> *furtherance of ye ends aforesaid; and by vertue hearof, to en-*
> *acte, constitute, and frame shuch just & equall lawes, ordinances,*
> *Acts, constitutions, & offices, from time to time, as shall be*
> *thought most meete & conuenient for ye generall good of ye colo-*
> *nie: vnto which we promise all due submission and obedience.*

Notice the various uses of *u* and *v*. If you try to read an original copy of the Geneva Bible, which the Separatists used, in addition to the interesting spellings and language of the day, you'll see the *s* that looks like an *f* without the cross bar.

I used scans of an original Geneva Bible (1560) for the Biblical quotations throughout this novel, but again, because spelling wasn't modernized yet, I modernized some of the spelling to make it easier to read. It's a beautiful piece of work—the original Geneva Bible—and there are two copies believed to have come over on the *Mayflower* in the Pilgrim Hall Museum. And while the King James Version would have come out by the time the Separatists journeyed to the New World, they would *not* have had anything to do with it because it was authorized by the Church of England and their persecution for many years had come directly from the King whose name the new version held.

Many readers may equate this period with Puritans, but remember that these brave souls, the Separatists, were different. The Puritans wanted to change the Church of England from within and thus fully reform it, while the Separatists wanted to completely separate themselves from the Church of England.

Another important thing to note is the timeline. Back in 1620, the Julian calendar was still used by the English and the colonists. That meant that the new year didn't start until March 25. To try to keep this novel as historically accurate as possible—and yet still understandable for you, the reader—I've time-stamped the dates from January 1 until March 24 with the year notation 1620/1. To the passengers, these events happened in 1620, but we would now think of them as taking place in 1621.

You'll notice throughout the book that there are variations on the spelling of "Plymouth." Modern spellings of both the US destination and England are "Plymouth." But to keep things as accurate as possible and yet clear to you, I used "Plymouth" for Plymouth, England, "Plimouth" to depict how Captain John Smith has this area labeled on his map of New England from 1614 which the travelers used on their journey, and then "Plimoth" for the original settlement. Plimoth Plantation is a fabulous place to visit at the original location.

While a lot of different conversations have taken place about the details of the *Mayflower* and its passengers, many particulars aren't known as fact. I did extensive research, but as always, this is a work of fiction. In trying to stay true to the historical story, I may have made a choice here or there that was based on opinion or supposition because the facts weren't clearly known. Please check the note at the end for more details. Any mistakes are purely my own.

Hopefully, this story will give you a glimpse into the lives of people who sacrificed everything for a better future almost four centuries ago—and were the beginnings of our great country. If you have a passion to read more about this historical time period, might I suggest the following nonfiction books: *Of Plymouth Plantation* by William Bradford (the true account/journal written by one of the passengers of the *Mayflower* and the eventual governor of the area—the edited version by *Mayflower* historian Caleb Johnson is phenomenal with footnotes and other journals included); *Here Shall I Die Ashore* by Caleb Johnson; *Plymouth Colony* by Eugene Aubrey Stratton; *Thanksgiving* by Glenn Alan Cheney; and *Mayflower* by Nathaniel Philbrick.

My favorite website was MayflowerHistory.com by Caleb Johnson.

I pray you enjoy this series full of fascinating history from our incredible country.

It is a joy to give you *The Mayflower Bride*.

Enjoy the journey,
Kimberley Woodhouse

Glossary of Terms

Aback: wind from wrong side of sails

Alee: in the direction in which the wind is blowing

Aft: near or in stern of ship

At hull: to lay at drift with the wind

Battens: Narrow strips of wood used for several purposes on ships. One of the main uses was to fasten down the hatches—thus the phrase "batten down the hatches."

Bow: front of ship

Bulwark: The planks that made up the "sides" of the top deck to keep crew and passengers from being washed overboard (what today we might think of as the *railing*)

Caulk: The pushing or driving of fibrous materials into seams to make them water-tight. Not to be confused with modern caulk compounds.

Companionway: staircase/ladder between decks

Gangway: The long, narrow board used as a walkway onto ships. Most times it had smaller strips of wood across the width of it to aid in climbing onto the ship without slipping. The term changed to *gangplank* in the 1700s.

Gun deck: Where the passengers lived on the *Mayflower* and *Speedwell*. So named because in time of conflict, the guns—or cannons—would be brought out of the gun room to fire out of the gun ports. The gun ports were open only during a conflict or during nice weather to provide light and allow air to circulate.

Hold, the: cargo hold, bottom level of the ship

Larboard: left side of ship, changed to *port* officially in 1844

Masts and sails:

>   **Fore mast** (front) held the fore-course sail and a bonnet sail

>   **Main mast** (midship) held the main sail and a bonnet sail

>   **Mizzen mast** (aft) held the lateen-rigged mizzen (a triangular sail on diagonal)

>   **Spritsail** came up off the bowsprit (a long diagonal-looking mast that hung well over the sea past the bow of the ship)

Poop deck: deck above cabin of the ship master on the aft castle—highest level above the stern

Shallop: Also known as a *tender*, the shallop is a vessel used to ferry supplies and people between the shore and the ship.

Shoal: submerged natural ridge or bar that can be very dangerous to a ship

Steerboard: right side of ship, changed over time to *starboard*

Stern: rear of ship

Thatch: dried plant material such as straw, reeds, grass, and leaves

Ton or tonnage: Does not refer to the weight measurement we use today. Back then it was used to show the cargo capacity of a ship. A ton referred to a wine or beer barrel that was used for food stuffs, as well. So the *Mayflower* was listed as a 180-ton ship. That meant she could carry 180 barrels, each holding an equivalent to about 250 US gallons today.

Whipstaff: Device used to steer the ship. (The large wheel that we think of for steering large sailing vessels hadn't come into use yet.)

Cast of Characters

Saints from the Leyden Congregation:
Fictional:
Mary Elizabeth Chapman
Robert Chapman, Mary Elizabeth's father
Elizabeth Chapman, Mary Elizabeth's mother, deceased
David Chapman, Mary Elizabeth's little brother
Dorothy Raynsford, Mary Elizabeth's best friend
Dorothy's mother and father, Mr. and Mr. Raynsford
Historical *Speedwell/Mayflower* passengers:
Isaac and Mary Allerton and their children: Bartholomew, Remember, Mary
William and Dorothy Bradford
William and Mary Brewster and their children: Love and Wrestling. William was head of the congregation because Pastor Robinson stayed in Holland.
John and Katherine Carver; their ward, Desire Minter; and their servant, Dorothy
James and Susanna Chilton and their daughter, Mary
Francis Cooke and his son, John
John Crackstone and his son, John Jr.
Moses Fletcher
Edward Fuller, his wife, Anna, and son Samuel, about twelve years old
Samuel Fuller (eventually the colony doctor) and his servant, William Butten. Fuller's wife, Bridget, stayed behind and arrived in 1623.
Degory Priest
Thomas Rogers and his son, Joseph

John and Joan Tilley and their daughter, Elizabeth
Thomas Tinker and his wife and son
John Turner and his two young sons
William and Susanna White and their son, Resolved (approx. five years old). She was pregnant when they left England.
Thomas Williams
Edward and Elizabeth Winslow
(Myles and Rose Standish also left with the Leyden congregation from Holland, but they were not part of the congregation. He was a military man hired to be the colonists' militia captain. But he appeared to have strong Separatist leanings.)

Strangers from England who joined the Saints on the venture:
John Alden, hired to be the ship's cooper and given the choice to stay at the colony or return with the ship to England
John Allerton
John and Elinor Billington and their children, John and Francis
Richard Britteridge
Peter Brown
Robert Carter
Richard Clarke
Edward Doty
Francis and Sarah Eaton and their son, Samuel
Mr. Ely
Richard Gardiner
John Goodman
William Holbeck
John Hooke
Stephen and Elizabeth Hopkins and their children, Constance, Giles, and Damaris. Elizabeth was pregnant when they left.
John Howland, manservant to John Carver
John Langmore
William Latham
Edward Lester

William Lytton (fictional)

Edmund Margesson

Christopher and Marie Martin and her son, Solomon Prower

Ellen, Jasper, Richard, and Mary More: four children aged four to eight, who were sent without parents

William and Alice Mullins and their children, Joseph and Priscilla

John and Alice Rigsdale

George Soule

Elias Story

Edward Thompson

Edward and Agnes Tilley with their nephew Henry Samson and niece Humility Cooper

William Trevor

Richard Warren

Roger Wilder

Gilbert Winslow

Crew of the *Mayflower* (about thirty men, but we know the names of only those listed):

John Alden, cooper (barrel maker)

John Clarke, ship's pilot and master's mate

Robert Coppin, master's mate

Giles Heale, ship's surgeon

Christopher Jones, master (captain)

Other crew members:

Boatswain: responsible for all the ship's rigging and sails, along with the anchors and longboat

Leadsman: kept track of the depth of the waters around them, could have had another crew title, as well

Master gunner: responsible for the ship's guns, cannon, etc.

Quartermasters (four): maintained the shifts and watch hours, in charge of the cargo hold, and responsible for fishing and maintaining lines

Ship's carpenter: responsible for fixing leaks and anything else ship related

Ship's cook: responsible for feeding the crew

Other sailors climbed masts, worked the sails, and performed other duties

Native Americans:

Massasoit: sachem (chief) of the Wampanoag in the area

Samoset: native from Mohegan

Tisquantum (the English nicknamed him "Squanto"): from Patuxet, which was the native village that had been where Plymouth is located

But here I cannot but stay, and make a pause, and stand half amazed at this poor people's present condition; and so I think will the reader, too, when he well considers the same. Being thus passed the vast ocean, and a sea of troubles before in their preparation (as may be remembered by that which went before) they had now no friends to welcome them, nor inns to entertain, or refresh their weather-beaten bodies, no houses, or much less towns to repair to, to seek for succor.
–William Bradford, *Of Plymouth Plantation*

PROLOGUE

Monday, 12 June 1620
Leyden, Holland

A splinter of wood pierced Mary Elizabeth Chapman's thumb as she crept behind her lifelong friend Dorothy Raynsford. Resisting the urge to cry out, she stuck the offending appendage in her mouth and tasted blood. Adults weren't supposed to sneak around in the rafters. Why she ever agreed to follow her friend on this escapade, she'd never know.

Well, she did know. She was as curious as Dorothy, just not as brave. The thought of the elders below hearing and catching them? It was enough to make Mary Elizabeth want to faint. But she pressed on behind her bold friend and crawled like a small child up in the attic of the meeting room. The smell of hay filled her nose as fear crept up her throat. This meeting would decide her people's fate. And Mary Elizabeth wasn't sure she was prepared to hear the answers.

Dorothy stopped a few feet ahead of her and laid flat on her stomach, peeking over the edge of the rafters. Placing a finger over her lips, she waved to Mary Elizabeth.

As Mary Elizabeth reached the lookout spot, voices from the room below became clearer.

Pastor John Robinson spoke to a room full of their congregation's elders. "It's clear that the time has come. With the patent from the Virginia Company for a colony, and with the investments of the Merchants and Adventurers, I believe a small contingent can go on ahead and begin the settlement. Within a few years, we should have our whole congregation there and our debts to the investors for the trip paid in full."

Murmurs resounded throughout the room.

"Can these Strangers be trusted?" A voice from the back put words to Mary Elizabeth's own thoughts. She'd grown up with the stories of how their congregation had fled England and King James' religious persecution. The first attempt had been thwarted by a ship's captain who swindled all the passengers and turned them in to the King's sheriffs. When they tried again, a number of families were separated for a year as one ship deserted them, leaving many behind.

But that hadn't deterred them. Eventually, they'd all made it to Holland.

Labeled as Separatists because they wanted to separate themselves from the Church of England—which didn't exactly please the King since he was the "head" of the church—everyone outside of their small group became known as Strangers. Their longing not to abide by the church produced persecution they endured and that was almost as bad as when Bloody Mary reigned.

It was no wonder several folks voiced their concerns about trust this evening.

Twelve years had passed, and here they were again. Discussing a way to leave. This time, not so much to flee persecution, but to secure a better future. The memories of dishonest people, though, were still fresh to all who remembered. No one wanted to go through those atrocities again. They'd lost everything.

Pastor Robinson spoke in a soothing tone. "While no man is without sin, I do believe we can trust them. The investment is sound, and the contracts are binding. We all know the worries that have arisen. It's getting harder to make a living, and our children are being influenced too much by the culture around them. Sin and evil abound. If we stay, we risk losing the future generations to a dangerous course."

Nods accompanied many affirmations.

Mary Elizabeth tuned out the conversation. How would they even survive? Stories of tragedy abounded for those who had ventured across the ocean. And to start a whole new colony? There wouldn't be stores or supplies or. . .anything.

A shiver raced up her spine. Even though they were often looked down upon by the Dutch because they were outsiders and resolved to live out their faith in ways that went against the norm, she'd felt at home in Leyden. To be honest, it was the only home she remembered. But her people had worked menial jobs and longer hours to support their families, and times *were* getting tougher.

A poke to her shoulder made her look at Dorothy.

Her friend's face lit up in an exuberant smile. She raised her eyebrows. "Can you imagine the adventure?" The words floated toward Mary Elizabeth in a soft whisper.

"What?" Had she missed something important?

Their pastor's voice echoed through the room. "It's decided then. We have chosen the first group to go."

As they waited for the room to clear, Dorothy filled her in on the families who would venture to the New World. Dorothy's family—which made her even more animated than usual as she talked with her hands—and the Chapmans, Mary Elizabeth's family, were part of the group.

Mary Elizabeth went numb. She didn't register anything more that Dorothy said. Even as they walked home, her heart couldn't make any sense out of the jumble of words.

Dorothy must have recognized something was wrong and followed Mary Elizabeth home. "Mary Elizabeth. What is going on in that head of yours?"

Lifting the latch to the door of her home, Mary Elizabeth clamped her mouth shut.

"Don't shut me out. Aren't you excited about all this?"

She turned and stared at her friend's eyes. Eyes that sparkled with excitement and joy. Why couldn't *she* feel that way?

Dorothy's warm hand reached out and covered her own. "Come. Let's get some tea and discuss what you're thinking. My parents aren't expecting me home—I told them I was staying over with you—and as long as I am there to milk Polly in the morning and feed the chickens, I should be able to stay as long as you need me."

All Mary Elizabeth could manage was a nod. They entered the door to the small rooms she called home. Familiar smells greeted her. Running a hand over a chair her father had carved, she let the feel of it seep into her soul. How could they leave all of this behind?

Heavy footsteps sounded on the stairs, causing Mary Elizabeth to jump and put a hand to her chest. "Father." Releasing a sigh, she looked down at the floor. He didn't know where she had gone—did he?

"I need you to stay with David." His face was alight with anticipation. "I have much to discuss with the elders."

"Is there anything I need to know?"

"Not yet, my dear. But soon. Very soon." He kissed her cheek and strode out the door.

Dorothy pulled out a chair and pointed to it. "Sit. It's time to destroy this fear and doubt that I see etched all over your face."

Tears sprung to Mary Elizabeth's eyes. They burned as they overflowed and ran down her cheeks.

Dorothy stayed up with Mary Elizabeth in the kitchen, talking about the meeting until daylight crept in through the windows. While Dorothy's voice held excitement and wonder, Mary Elizabeth felt only worry and fear. Her friend quoted scripture and hugged her. Told her it would all be all right. God was in control. This was a good thing.

But what would become of them? Too many of their group were elderly and would have to stay behind, and the elders made it clear that only so many could make the journey. That meant only a small fraction of all the people she'd known the whole of her seventeen years would venture across the vast ocean to the unknown land of the New World.

"Mary Elizabeth?" Dorothy placed her hand over Mary Elizabeth's cold one. "Mary Elizabeth, have you heard anything I've said?"

All she could manage was a nod. "I just need some time."

"All right. I'd better get back home. The chores won't get done by themselves." Her cheery voice did nothing to soothe Mary Elizabeth's nerves.

She doubted anything could.

"Mary Elizabeth, may I go play with Jonathan?" Her little brother pleaded the same thing almost every day.

And she always said the same thing in response: "Have you finished your chores?"

He nodded and smiled.

She tousled his hair and handed him his cap. "Be home in an hour."

"I will."

Brushing her hands on her apron, she watched him run down the street. He wouldn't be a little boy much longer, but oh, how she adored him.

"Mary Elizabeth," Father called from the stairs, "I need you to sit down with me for a moment."

"Of course." The flutters of her heart couldn't be stopped, knowing all too well what he would say. She eased herself into a chair across the table from him.

"We've been chosen to go to the New World. Actually, I volunteered." The smile that lit his face was one she hadn't seen since before her mother died. "It will be good to have a fresh start and finally have land to call our own." His gaze went to the window as the smile disappeared. "And there are too many sad memories here."

He turned back to face her and shook his head. "Forgive me." The smile returned. "The journey is soon. It's all very exciting, but we have much to prepare and I need your help."

Odd how the body worked. She remembered forcing herself to nod, trying to look like she was interested in what he had to say, and tamping down all the fear and frustration inside. But she didn't really hear a word after that. So many emotions erupted inside her that she didn't know how to contain them. Before she knew it, Father stood, kissed her cheek, and walked out the door.

A sob choked its way to the surface. Without thinking, she stood and raced out the door.

Mary Elizabeth's heart pounded as her feet thudded against the ground. Running for all she was worth, she didn't care that it was unseemly for a young woman her age to run. How could Papa be so willing to volunteer?

She reached the edge of the cemetery and slowed down. Tears streamed down her cheeks as she opened the gate, walked through, and quietly shut it behind her. There always seemed to be a hushed reverence in this small plot of graves surrounded by trees.

Mary Elizabeth walked through a few rows and stopped in front of her mother's grave. The fresh flowers she'd left yesterday were already wilting.

Just like her heart.

She fell to her knees in the grass and sobbed harder. "Mother, I don't know what to do! Father has agreed for us to go to the New World. . . ." She couldn't even finish her thoughts.

This place—this hallowed ground—had been her sanctuary in the year since her mother had died. When she had no words to express her thoughts, she came here. And her heart spilled out.

How could she leave behind her mother?

Oh, she knew that her mother no longer resided in the body buried beneath the place where she knelt, but it still felt wrong.

It meant she'd have no refuge. No place to come and hash out her thoughts and questions.

Mother had been the only one to truly understand her. Dorothy was a dear friend, but she couldn't fill the hole left by the woman who'd given Mary Elizabeth life. The one who'd kissed her head good night every evening and sung her awake every morning. No matter how scared Mary Elizabeth had been about trying something new, her mother had always been there to encourage her and tell her she could do it.

Could she do *this*?

No. It wasn't possible.

But the elders had decided. Father had readily agreed.

The reality of the situation sank into her stomach like a rock.

Leaning back on her heels, she cried like she had when her mother had died. "Mother. . .I can't do this. I can't."

CHAPTER 1

Saturday, 22 July 1620
Delfthaven, Holland

Gentle waves rocked the *Speedwell* as the vessel left behind the only home Mary Elizabeth remembered. Salty air stung her nose, and the breeze tugged at wisps of her hair—threatening to loosen them from under her confining cornet.

Standing as close to the stern of the ship as she could without bothering the crew on the poop deck, Mary Elizabeth inhaled deeply. If only the crisp air could clear her mind like it cleared her lungs. Breathing out a prayer for courage, she clung to the bulwark. Courage had never been her strength. The past few weeks had confirmed that indeed it was all happening. And here she stood. On a ship.

Could she do this? Truly?

She'd armed herself with her prized possessions: her mother's red cape draped comfortingly around her shoulders; treasured receipts from generations prior sat safely tucked into the pockets tied around her waist; and the memory of the woman who loved her and modeled what it meant to be a godly wife and mother resided, always and forever, in her heart. Reaching her hand behind her apron, she slipped it through the slit in her skirt and found the string of pockets tied around her waist. The one with the receipts hung in the middle. She ran her fingers over the edges of the worn papers. Grandmother's savory egg-and-spinach pie receipt, a boiled pudding receipt from her mother, and her favorite—Mother's rye-and-barley bread—were among them.

If only mother were still alive. Maybe this journey wouldn't be so difficult.

Even though their time in Holland had been full of difficult stretches, God had been good to Mary Elizabeth there. She'd had her family, her dear friend Dorothy, and plenty of work to keep her busy. Besides that, it was familiar. Safe.

But no more. The land she knew had drifted out of her sight hours before. Never to be seen again.

The Saints, as they preferred to call themselves, had left England twelve years before while under persecution from the King and the Church of England. When they left for Holland, they wished only to separate themselves from England's church so they could study the scripture more and follow the state's rules and taxations less. They believed only what the Bible told them, so they considered all the man-made rules and traditions of the Church of England to be wrong.

She didn't remember England. But Holland would remain forged in her mind for the rest of her days.

Now it all seemed surreal. Listening in the rafters that night had been the beginning for her, but the group's preparation had been going on for years.

Correspondence to grant the Saints permission to start a colony in the New World had gone back and forth to England. And then John Carver and Robert Cushman were sent to London to negotiate an agreement.

Finally, permission from the King had been granted. In fact, he seemed to bless the endeavor with his words, "as long as they went peaceably."

Memories of their departure from Leyden washed over her. The rest of the congregation that stayed behind and many of their Dutch neighbors had come to see them off. There had been shedding of tears aplenty. But when Pastor Robinson dropped to his knees, tears streaming down his face, Mary Elizabeth had lost control of her emotions, as well. As he prayed for the Lord's blessing and commended the travelers on their journey, she wanted to gain strength from his words. But she'd only felt weaker and more inadequate.

A spray of salt water hit her face and brought her back to the reality of where she stood. The planning was done. The packing was over. Goodbyes had been said. And now Holland had vanished from sight. She and the others on the ship would reach England soon, and after they met up with the *Mayflower* and her passengers—the other brave souls who would journey to the New World with the Separatists to establish a colony—they would be on their way.

To what, she was unsure.

Squinting, she gazed toward the horizon in the west. What would this New World hold? Papa had regaled her with stories of lush, fertile land. Land unclaimed by anyone else. Land supplying an abundance of food. Land that held no persecution for their faith.

Her faith. It meant everything to her. And the thought of freedom to worship and learn and grow in God's Word thrilled her beyond imagining. It was the one thing that helped her through the past weeks when she'd had to swallow the reality that yes, she was going to the New World. Dorothy helped her to focus on the positive, and Mary Elizabeth clung to the thought of her faith.

Years ago, her father had spent almost a month of wages on a Bible so they could read it themselves. The first time she'd been allowed to hold the volume in her hands, she'd cried. She found it such a privilege to read the Bible, translated in its entirety to her own English language and printed in 1560, and understood why her people—the Saints—longed to separate themselves from England's Church. Why didn't *everyone* long to read the Word as she did? Why were they content to sit in church, pay homage to their country, and listen to passages read from the *Book of Common Prayer* and nothing else? Church was an obligation, a ceremony, a ritual to them. But followers of Christ were called to share the Gospel and be set apart. The difference in thinking didn't make sense to Mary Elizabeth. Especially since so many had been persecuted for it.

The New World held more than just release from persecution. Papa and the other men dreamed of working their own farms with land as far as the eye could see. In Holland, the hard labor they'd all put in for decades had given them nothing of their own.

To think the New World could hold the answer to all their hopes and dreams.

It sounded lovely.

So why did her heart hesitate so? She'd shed enough tears to create a river the past few weeks, and she'd finally told the Lord that enough was enough. The only way she could make it through was with His help. Her new recitation became *I can do this*.

Papa's excitement rubbed off on her younger brother, David, but most of the time she'd had to force a smile. No matter. It wasn't her place to go against Papa, and his mind was made up. They'd been chosen.

Her father had kept himself busy with the plans to go. So much so, she'd hardly seen him in a fortnight. His absence made their departure that much more difficult to bear.

It made her feel. . .alone.

And now she stood on a ship. Going.

She felt lonelier than ever.

She shook her head. She *could* do this. Her mind just needed to stay off these thoughts of loneliness and instead keep occupied.

Papa was engaged in excited conversations with the other men, which would probably be the daily activity for him the entirety of their voyage. So she must find something to keep her mind occupied and off these thoughts of loneliness.

She *could* do this.

But the recited phrase couldn't keep the questions from filling her thoughts: Would the New World be as beautiful as Holland? Would she make friends? Would she find a God-fearing husband?

Or would the savages kill them all in their sleep?

Another tiny shiver raced up her spine. Such thoughts were not appropriate. Papa would have a fit if he knew she'd listened to the sailors' stories. He'd scolded David for repeating the derogatory name *savages*. But what if that's what they were? Were they sailing into their own demise?

"Mary Elizabeth!"

Dorothy's voice drifted across the deck of the ship, and Mary Elizabeth waved and smiled at her friend. She must not allow her foolish doubts to dull Dorothy's enthusiasm for every aspect of this new life.

"I had a feeling I would find you here. Fresh air is always your first choice." Dorothy smiled and leaned on the bulwark as the ship listed to the right. "Your father is teaching David about Jamestown and the New World."

"David is thrilled, to be sure." Mary Elizabeth looked back to the water. She really must swallow this doubt and fear. Far better to grab hold of the thrill and joy she saw on her friend's features.

Dorothy laid a hand on Mary Elizabeth's shoulder. "I've been praying for you. I know this isn't easy, leaving your dear mother behind and all."

All Mary Elizabeth could manage was a nod as an image of the cemetery flitted through her mind.

The gravestone with her mother's name—Elizabeth Chapman—denoted the all-too-short span of the beloved woman's life. It would lay bare now. No flowers. No one to visit.

Even though Mother's memory resided in Mary Elizabeth's heart and mind, leaving behind the grave—the place she visited weekly to pour out her heart and soul—hurt more than the loss of any other physical object in Holland.

"Here." Her friend offered a brown-paper-wrapped package. "I wanted to give it to you on your birthday, but I couldn't wait."

Mary Elizabeth smiled and took her time unwrapping the gift. The brown paper could be saved and used again, and they wouldn't have access to such frivolities—or anything of the sort—for quite some time. As she turned it over in her hands, she found a deep brown leather book with a leather string tied around it. There weren't any words on the cover or spine. "What is it?"

"It's blank pages. For you to write down your thoughts. I thought it would help since you won't be able to visit your mother's grave anymore."

Tears sprang to Mary Elizabeth's eyes. Only Dorothy knew her heart and the lengthy visits to the cemetery and what she did there. She clutched the treasure to her chest. "This must have cost you a small fortune." Paper wasn't a commodity most could afford. Mary Elizabeth looked back down at the precious book. "Thank you so much." The words seemed all too inadequate.

"I know you have a quill and pots of ink with you since I helped pack them"—Dorothy laughed as she patted Mary Elizabeth's arm—"and once we have a settlement and regular shipments coming in, you might want to write even more. You've always had a talent for stringing beautiful phrases together."

Tears flowed down Mary Elizabeth's face. She didn't even want to wipe them away. What a treasure. Not just the book, but the friend.

Dorothy bounced on her toes. "I will be with you, dear Mary Elizabeth. Through every step of this new journey."

Mary Elizabeth smiled through her tears. "I know you will, and I'm very grateful, I am. The journey will just take some getting used to."

"Well, don't take too long. Adventure awaits!" Dorothy's arms stretched out, and she spun around. Her friend's eagerness for the unknown made Mary Elizabeth laugh and wipe the tears off her face.

Mary Elizabeth folded up the brown paper and tucked it into her cloak. God had truly blessed her. With a wonderful family and a delightful friend. She *could* do this.

Courage. Her prayer from before sprang back to her mind.

The pounding of boots behind them made Mary Elizabeth turn and wrap her cloak around her tighter. The sailors weren't the most gentlemanly of sorts.

The ship master emerged from the group and looked straight at them. The weathered man always appeared tense and stern, but today another expression hid behind his eyes. Was it fear? "Go get your men. We need all able-bodied hands on deck. Including the women and children."

Mary Elizabeth nodded and moved to do the ship master's bidding.

But Dorothy tugged on Mary Elizabeth's cloak and stopped. "What's happened, Mr. Reynolds?"

Seeing the other sailors' grim expressions, Mary Elizabeth felt a knot grow in her stomach. She faced the man in charge.

Mr. Reynolds's mouth pressed into a thin line, and he clasped his hands behind his back as he glanced out to the water and then back to Mary Elizabeth and Dorothy. The severe expression grew dim. "It's not the best etiquette to speak to women of such calamity, but since you will carry the message below and there's not a lot of time, I feel it's best to be honest." He took a deep breath. "The ship's been leaking for some time now, and we're taking on a good deal of water. It is far worse than I suspected. If we don't do something about it, we'll sink before we ever reach Southampton."

Tuesday, 1 August 1620
Southampton, England

William Lytton lifted the last crate and his satchel of tools and readied to walk up the gangway of the *Mayflower* one more time. His leg muscles burned from the numerous trips up the steep, narrow walkway, but it was worth it.

The New World.

For years, he'd longed for change—a fresh start. The opportunity before him now presented all his dreams in one nice package. And the *Mayflower* would take him there.

If he could just make it through the weeks at sea, he'd be fine. They would all have to start with nothing. They would have to build or create everything with their own hands. They would be far away from everyone and everything they'd ever known. That was fine. Making a new life took hard work and sacrifice.

He was ready.

In a matter of weeks, he'd be standing on shores across the vast ocean—literally on the other side of the world. The thought made him smile. He might be an orphan, devoid of family or anyone who cared about him, and unworthy of English society's approval, but he was done with all of that. In this new land, in a new settlement, he could be someone else entirely.

A hand on his shoulder made him start and lose his grip on the crate, but he caught it with his knee. The man standing there didn't look like a thief.

"I'm sorry to disturb you, and I don't wish to startle you, but I have a proposition." The more closely William observed, the more he noted why the man's appearance exuded wealth. A shimmer of gold on the man's right hand didn't escape his notice. Only the wealthy donned such adornments.

William nodded. "Sir. Let me set my burden down, and we can discuss whatever is on your mind."

The man glanced around and moved to sit on another crate. As he reached into the pocket of his vest, the embroidery on the man's sleeves caught William's attention. The man must be rich indeed.

The mysterious stranger cleared his throat. "Are you William Lytton?"

Who was this man? The ring and clothing reminded William of royalty, but he'd had little experience with the upper classes, much less royals. "Yes, sir. I am."

The man smiled and motioned for William to move his crate closer. "I don't wish to take a lot of time, nor do I wish to be overheard, so I'll be brief. I'm with the Virginia Company and am also one of the Merchants and Adventurers. You may know that we have heavily invested in all who will be journeying with you to the New World."

It was no secret. The Merchants and Adventurers provided the monetary backing for the trip, and the Planters were the travelers to the New World. Every Planter over the age of sixteen received one share, while the Adventurers could invest and buy as many shares as they wanted. Once all the debts were paid in seven years, the profits would be divided by those shares. A rush of thankfulness hit William's chest. He had two shares when most Planters only had one.

"Yes, sir. I am aware."

The man leaned closer, his voice hushed. "We need to hire a man with integrity to keep records for us."

William felt his brows raise but attempted to keep a plain expression. "Records? What kind of records?"

The man coughed into his fist as another sailor ran up the gangway. When the young man was past, he continued. "A journal of sorts recording all the comings, goings, workings, business—all that takes place at the new settlement. The ten-point agreement we have with you all, the Planters, is to come to fruition in seven years. While seven years seems like it can go by quickly, it is a good length of time, and the New World is a great distance away. We don't have a man available who can pick up and leave his life and family here, so we thought it prudent to find someone who would be a part of the new colony to help us out. Your name was given to me as a recommendation. We wish to see this venture succeed with the utmost honesty and respect."

Respect. If he'd learned nothing else, William had learned the importance of respect in business matters. As for honesty and integrity? Well, as far as he was concerned, there was no other way to act. And it gave him a boost in his confidence to learn that someone had recommended him. He lifted his shoulders and nodded. "How may I help?"

"We would obviously compensate you for your time—as I said, we are seeking to *hire* someone." The man held a small velvet pouch and a leather book out to William. "This would be your first payment. We will send a messenger down on the *Fortune* next year with another hefty sum. After we have reviewed your report and see how the settlement is doing, there will be additional duties and payments. The book is for your record keeping. Details and exact quantities are important. While we will be receiving the wood, salted fish, and other goods made by the Planters to sell, we need to know that they are abiding by the agreement. Four days' work for us. Two for themselves. We believe them all to be honest people, but we also know many who are going are not a part of the Separatist's congregation and do not abide by the same strict moral laws.

"In essence, you will be our representative there, but we don't want to alarm anyone or create any chaos by making that fact known. Far better to keep this information. . .among those who need to know it. Just until the colony is well under way, you understand. Then we may have a higher position there for you since you will have gained everyone's trust."

William took the book and then the bag, a bit startled at the weight of it. The man's logic was sound. Everyone would have to work together if they were to build a lasting colony and survive. He could handle another job like this if it was just keeping records. It was honest. Even if it was a bit secretive. The extra money would definitely help.

Decision made, he nodded. "I would be honored to assist you, sir, the Virginia Company, and the Adventurers."

"Thank you, William." The man stood and turned on his heel. "I will be in touch."

William launched himself at the man and tugged at his cape. "How did you know my name, sir, as I do not know yours?"

The man's face softened with a slight smile. "Your master was a close friend. He spoke highly of you and often." He straightened and nodded at William. "As for me, you may call me Mr. Crawford."

As Crawford walked away, a tiny pang of grief hit William's chest. *His master.* The only kind person William had ever known. Twenty years ago, he'd been abandoned as a baby and left on a family member's doorstep. They'd barely clothed him and fed him occasionally. But he would have taken those conditions over what happened next. At the tender age of nine, he'd been kicked out and told to find his own way.

Many other orphans his age had been out on the streets, but William soon learned to work as many odd jobs as possible so he could put bread in his stomach.

Then one day—after years of misery, filth, and almost starvation—this man appeared. His master, Paul Brookshire. The man who'd taken him in at thirteen, taught him the valuable trade of carpentry, and given him hope for life. The man who'd loved him like a son for seven wonderful years when no one else wanted him. The man who bought an extra share for William—costing almost an entire year's worth of earnings—before he made his apprentice promise to make the most of his life, throw off the baggage of the past, and seek God.

William never had much of a use for God. The thought of a loving heavenly Father was foreign to a boy orphaned and shown contempt in the streets of London. But his master? He'd started to change William's mind.

Questions he'd longed to ask would go unanswered. Alas, his master died.

William had cared for the man until he took his last breath and had kept up with all the orders for their shop by working into the night. The day he buried Paul—his master and friend—was the hardest day of his life. Harder than living with a family that did nothing but show him contempt. Harder than living on the streets of London. Because he'd lost the only person who ever cared—the one who had. . .*loved* him.

If he were to be honest, no one else knew William—not even his customers—because he'd never given anyone else a chance.

A scuffle on deck of the ship made William look back toward the gangway. He shook his head. These thoughts were best left for a later time. He had work to do and a long journey ahead.

Tucking the bag inside his shirt, William breathed deeply. The grief that often hit in waves needed to be tucked down into his heart, away from probing eyes.

William Lytton was on a journey to a new life. The old had to be left behind.

CHAPTER 2

Peter watched Mr. Crawford walk away from that lousy carpenter. Anger bubbled up in his gut. That should have been *his* job—*his* money. As he'd followed Crawford to the dock this morning, his hopes were that all the pieces were falling into place. Apparently, he hadn't thought through the fact that they might hire someone else. All the times he'd gotten an invitation to meetings or gatherings, all the times he'd spoken to Crawford and offered to help the venture in any way that he could. His cousin had told him he'd made a good impression. Not that it did any good. Not now.

Venturing forth from his hiding place behind a large crate, he squinted toward William Lytton. Why had the Merchants and Adventurers chosen a carpenter, of all people? What did he know about business dealings?

All the work Peter had done to get a look at the contracts and plan for this were now for naught. His piddly savings were depleted. He'd counted on getting hired for the endeavor ever since his cousin had told him about the plan. Now he was stuck going to the New World with no foreseeable income.

His dreams of being established as a respectable and honored person in the new colony were dashed.

Unless. . .

He tilted his head and let the thoughts grow into fullness. It wasn't the craziest idea. Maybe it would work.

Maybe there was another way to earn trust—and to obtain the job he desired.

After more than a week of repairs dockside to reinforce the patching done at sea, the master of the *Speedwell* declared her seaworthy once again. While several of the crew had left the ship as their ship master released them during the repair work, all of Mary Elizabeth's congregation stayed on board. Not wishing to risk any mishap or reason for the King to change his mind, the elders had thought it best to stay out of sight.

But now as they left the port, Mary Elizabeth longed to stand on dry ground rather than on the deck of this ship. This very *small* ship—where the confining spaces threatened to trap her. Panic rose in her throat. She did her best to swallow it down, but it reached prickly fingers into her mind.

Would this be the last time she'd see land? What if they didn't make it to the New World? What if they got lost and ran out of supplies?

Shifting her gaze to the north, she forced her thoughts elsewhere. Across a small expanse of sea, the *Mayflower*'s crew worked her sails as the ship cut through the water beside them. The ship was much larger than the *Speedwell* and carried the rest of their supplies for the New World as well as many other colonists.

It was wondrous to behold and gave her a calming thought. They wouldn't be journeying alone. The panic subsided a bit.

But a sense of foreboding replaced it in full force.

"Good morning, Mary Elizabeth." Dorothy's voice pierced through the black fog threatening to overtake her.

Mary Elizabeth took a breath and then another. "Good morning." The smell of fish and salty sea air filled her senses.

Dorothy came alongside her and grabbed her arm. "What's

wrong? You're whiter than the sails."

Shaking her head, Mary Elizabeth closed her eyes. "It's nothing. I just had a wee bit of fear as we left."

"It doesn't look like it's 'nothing.'" Dorothy placed her hands on her hips and raised her eyebrows. "I've a good mind to go get your father."

"No. Please." Mary Elizabeth raised a hand in protest. "He doesn't need anything else to worry about. Besides, he's too busy with plans and meetings with the elders. I'm very well. I just need to breathe through it." Maybe her facade of bravery would appease her friend. But the niggle of fear that something bad would happen made her heart race. What had come over her?

"You may try and fool me, Mary Elizabeth Chapman, but I can see you are struggling." Dorothy grabbed her hand and squeezed. "Why don't we recite the Twenty-Third Psalm together?"

Mary Elizabeth nodded and kept trying to breathe, but the shallow breaths weren't giving her enough air. This couldn't be happening. Not now. After all she'd overcome. But the deep sense of foreboding wouldn't leave her. Why?

Courage, she just needed courage. Why was that her constant prayer now? And why was she so weak when everyone else around her appeared to be strong?

Dorothy started quoting from the scripture, "The Lord is my shepherd, I shall not want."

Mary Elizabeth let the words flow over her. She inhaled deeper and joined in the recitation. "He maketh me to rest in green pastures, & leadeth me by the still waters." Breathing came easier. In. Out. In. Out.

"He restoreth my soul, & leadeth me in the paths of righteousness for his Name's sake.

"Yea, though I should walk through the valley of the shadow of death, I will fear no evil: for thou art with me: thy rod and thy staff, they comfort me." Mary Elizabeth's voice grew stronger with every word.

"Thou doest prepare a table before me in the sight of mine adversaries. Thou doest anoint mine head with oil, & my cup runneth over." Her breaths calmed to a regular pace.

"Doubtless kindness & mercy shall follow me all the days of my life, & I shall remain a long season in the house of the Lord."

Dorothy smiled. "Now, don't you feel better? The color in your cheeks is back."

"Yes." The honest statement surprised her. It was true. The simple quoting of her favorite passage brought calm to her spirit. Mary Elizabeth hugged her friend. "I feel like our Lord has banished the fear from me."

"Wonderful." Dorothy bounced on her toes—a habit that she'd had since childhood.

Mary Elizabeth faced the west and grabbed onto the bulwark. Water as far as the eye could see.

"Isn't it wonderful?" Her friend's exuberant voice bubbled up and spilled out, making Mary Elizabeth feel foolish for her anxious thoughts. "Like I said, adventure awaits. New land. New home. New life. New. . .everything!"

A small laugh escaped her lips. She'd never tire of Dorothy's positive outlook. "Yes, God is so very good to us." And He was. She knew that. She would conquer this fear and doubt with His help. The fear was because of her doubt and worry—neither of which was honoring to God. She'd have to work on those areas of her life. If she was going to become a Godly woman like her mother, she had a long way to go.

"I'm proud of you."

Mary Elizabeth furrowed her brow. "Whatever for?"

"I can see the determination on your face. It's a brave thing you've done, Lizzy." She covered her mouth after the nickname from their childhood came out. "Sorry, it slipped. I know we're not children anymore."

Mary Elizabeth hooked arms with her lifelong friend and smiled. "It's all right. You're the only one I'd allow to call me that, and I think you have the privilege after all this time." She lowered her voice to a whisper. "Just don't use it in front of David. He'll start calling me that again, and Papa would have a fit. He said it's not becoming for a young lady and implies ill character." She took another deep breath as they took a few, slow steps to the other side of the ship. "Thank you for thinking that I'm brave, but I'm not near as strong as you are."

"That's rubbish." Dorothy put her other hand on her hip and turned toward her. "It's extremely brave. Everything you've done and had to endure. This was a huge step. . .walking into the unknown. It takes a lot more courage when you're not one prone to adventure."

"Like you."

Dorothy giggled. "My other friends in Leyden thought me daft. Always excited about something new. But you never ridiculed me for my unusual and impetuous spirit. I'm very grateful for that. You're the steady, compassionate, dependable one. I'm the—"

"Good morning, ladies."

Mary Elizabeth turned around and noticed Myles Standish, the adviser and guide they'd hired in Holland. "Good morning, Mr. Standish."

"Good morning," Dorothy echoed and grabbed Mary Elizabeth's arm again.

"It's a wonderful day to set sail, isn't it?" Standish stood at the bulwark with his feet spread wide and his hands clasped behind his back. He obviously was accustomed to the rolling seas and was confident in his stance.

Mary Elizabeth studied him and moved her boots apart under her heavy skirt and petticoats while Dorothy chattered. Surely she could hide the unladylike carriage underneath all the layers she wore. It was awkward, but if a wider posture helped her stay steady on the ship, she'd learn. Wouldn't Dorothy be proud and get a laugh out of this later? With a grin, Mary Elizabeth imagined how that conversation might go—and how she could prove she was at least trying to be courageous.

"Mr. Standish." Dorothy's tone brought Mary Elizabeth back to the talk around her. Her friend moved toward the man. "I hear you have copies of Captain Smith's writings and maps."

"Indeed I do, Miss Raynsford."

"Might we see the map of where we hope to land?" Dorothy had tried ever since they'd left Holland to speak to the man, but there'd never been an opportune time. Now her chance had come. And Dorothy was one who never passed up a fortuitous situation like this.

"Of course. Let's find a place below where we can be out of the wind. I don't want to risk anything blowing away." Mr. Standish stretched out his arm, indicating the girls should precede him.

Her friend clasped her hands together. "Thank you very much, Mr. Standish, I'm quite excited to see them."

As they navigated the narrow companionway to the deck below, Mary Elizabeth felt some of Dorothy's excitement. She'd always been a bit fascinated by Captain John Smith and his adventures in the New World, but his reputation as a swashbuckling braggart and his quoted prices to lead their expedition had made the elders search out another adviser.

Now to get a glimpse of the maps thrilled her. Maybe she had a bit more of an adventurous spirit than she thought. Maybe all those prayers for courage were being answered with an affirmation from above.

When Mr. Standish opened the book and pulled out several folded pieces of paper, he became very serious. "Please don't touch the maps—they are tedious to reproduce. I'm sure you understand."

"Of course." Dorothy's head bobbed up and down in a vigorous nod.

"Yes, sir." Mary Elizabeth knew the man was serious about his duties. And ruining a map they needed would be disastrous for their whole colony.

An English soldier who had also been living in Holland, Myles Standish's reputation was pristine. He seemed to be a good and knowledgeable man and agreed to the Saints' rules.

Carefully unfolding a large square, Mr. Standish cleared his throat and held it up so the light from the door above would shine on the paper. "Now this is the map of Virginia."

Dorothy scooted in closer. "And where will the new colony be?"

He pointed to the most northern section of the map and then went off the map farther. "Somewhere in here. Right at the mouth of the Hudson River."

"That's a good deal north of Jamestown." Dorothy pointed and tilted her head.

"Yes, it is. But that is where our patent lies. It will be beautiful and have plenty of water."

Mary Elizabeth studied the detailed map. It must have taken Captain Smith days upon days—possibly even months—to explore all that territory and coastline. The hours invested made her shake her head in wonder. The map itself was exquisite in its detail. "Is there anything else north of Virginia?" She hadn't paid a lot of attention to the discussions about the New World because they seemed to cause her a lot of stress, but now she was fascinated. All she remembered was that Florida was somewhere south of Virginia.

"Yes, there is an entire region Captain Smith named New England." Mr. Standish folded the Virginia map and pulled out another paper. He opened it up. "All of this is north of Virginia and a good deal north of where we are destined. But we won't be headed that far up the coastline. Maybe one day you'll get to explore that area. I hear it's quite beautiful."

"Look, Mary Elizabeth." Dorothy pointed. "There's a place here on the map called 'Plimouth.' Oh, and one named 'Oxford.' And there's even a 'London.'" She giggled and turned to Mr. Standish. "Are there actually settlements or cities there?"

"No. It's barely been explored, although the fishing waters in that area are quite good and many vessels are familiar with the bays and harbors. Captain Smith took the liberty—with Prince Charles's help—to name locations, harbors, points, and such after good strong English names. Thus the title: New England."

"This area is named Cape James?" Mary Elizabeth studied the hook-shaped piece of land at the bottom of the map.

"Indeed. Although another captain named it Cape Cod quite a while before Smith. I think most of the sailors still think of it as Cape Cod because of the abundance of the fish."

"What about the section in between? Do you have a map of that?" Mary Elizabeth's curiosity was piqued. Between the two maps, she could almost picture the coastline of the New World—and instead of inciting fear, it created a new excitement.

"Well, that part is uncharted so far. There are dangerous shoals and other areas that ships have had to avoid."

"I'm terribly glad we're not headed there." Dorothy's light laughter filled the close quarters. "Thank you so much for showing us, Mr. Standish."

"You are quite welcome." He bowed and closed his book. "And don't you worry. We know exactly where we are going."

Wednesday, 9 August 1620

The slight breeze ruffled William's hair as he stood at the bow of the *Mayflower* and watched the *Speedwell* lazily cut through the water. They needed more wind if they were going to make any headway. Their ship master—Christopher Jones—had been ordering the crew to work the sails all morning.

"William!" John Alden's voice made him turn around.

"Afternoon, John." William greeted his new friend.

This was new ground for him. Actually having a friend his own age. Although John was a year past William's own twenty years, they continued to discover how much they had in common.

John had been hired as the cooper—or barrel maker—for the *Mayflower*. An important job, since all the provisions were stored in barrels. His responsibilities were to build, repair, and maintain the hefty number. And since William was a carpenter, they enjoyed working together and discussing shared ideas for building and for working with wood.

"We need some good gusts of wind, don't we?" John patted him on the back.

"That we do." William looked back toward the *Speedwell*. "I'm pretty sure everyone else is having the same thoughts. We're all anxious to get to Virginia."

"Aye. I've got so many things I want to try—my dreams for the future have made my imagination work around the clock." John pulled a small book out of his pocket and looked around them. "I haven't shown this to anyone else, but what do you think? Do you think it will work?"

William studied the drawing of what appeared to be a specialized wood-cutting machine. His friend was much like him. Young and unafraid of the future, William was ready to take on whatever the new settlement might need. He too had lots of ideas for how to improve the way things were done. But he had never shared his ideas with anyone. "I think it's a grand idea. Will you have all the parts to make it?"

"I tried to use only what I knew we would have with us." He turned the page. "But for some of my other ideas, I'll have to wait for the *Fortune* scheduled to arrive next year."

"What about Jamestown?" William eyed the next few drawings. "Do you know what kind of supplies they have?"

"It's such a long way from where we will be. It could take a few days by ship to get there, don't you agree? I don't know if it's worth traveling that distance. I've already requested certain items be sent on each of the next three ships. It was one of my requirements when I hired on."

William nodded. He didn't realize they'd be so far from Jamestown. But it didn't matter. Excited energy built in his heart. There would be a lot of firsts to come. He'd love to be the first one recognized for his craftsmanship in building. He dreamed of building cathedrals and churches as beautiful and elaborate as some of the prized ones in Europe. His mentor and master had shown him several drawings of them. Would his name one day be associated with something beautiful in history?

John's head jerked up from the book and jolted William out of the thought. "What do you think of that?"

William followed John's gaze and watched as the *Speedwell* appeared to be turning around. "I don't know, but it doesn't look like a good thing." He pointed. "Look, there's someone on the bow waving a flag."

Hurried footsteps sounded behind them. William turned.

Master Christopher Jones came toward the bulwark with his spyglass held out. He looked through it.

A small crowd gathered, but silence reigned as everyone watched their captain.

William realized he was holding his breath while he waited for news.

The ship master grimaced then let out a long breath. "Looks like we are headed back to England, chaps. The *Speedwell* has sprung a leak."

Thursday, 10 August 1620

The bucket sloshed as Mary Elizabeth climbed up the companionway once again. Prayerfully, her hour of work was almost done because everything ached. Who knew a bucket of water could weigh so much after these many trips?

The shipmaster yelled down from the poop deck. "She's still sittin' too low, lads. We're takin' on too much water!"

Mary Elizabeth looked up to where the man stood. Leaning over the stern of the ship, he shook his head. "Everyone needs to move faster!"

Faster wasn't something she was sure her muscles could take. There weren't enough people to make a bucket line from the bottom to the top, so they all trekked back and forth. Going down with an empty bucket was easier than climbing up with a full one.

Their group of passengers had been divided up into four groups. Men, women, and children were all included. Each group took an hour shift. A brutal hour of going down to the deepest level of the ship, filling up a bucket with the sea water that continually seeped in, climbing up the two levels, and dumping the water back where it belonged. Afterward they'd rest for three hours while the other groups worked and then start right back at it.

The first shift, everyone was passionate about the job. No one wanted to sink. Fear drove them. But after little sleep and hefting and hauling, most had grown silent. They were soaked and weary.

As she threw the water over the bulwark, Mary Elizabeth saw her father bring his bucket up. For the first time in a long while, he looked tired instead of excited about the journey. "Papa, are you doing all right?"

A forced smile lit his features. "As well as I can." He nodded to her bucket. "We best get back down below."

"Yes, Father." She nodded and followed him down the companionway. Her younger brother made it to the steps as she reached the bottom.

He set his bucket down and wiped his brow. Only half full, it was still too much for a small boy to have to carry.

"Let me help you, David." Mary Elizabeth reached for the rope handle.

"No. I can do it. I just needed a breath."

The poor little chap. Trying so hard to be a grown-up. It didn't make sense that the ship master expected the children to assist. But then again, every able hand was helpful.

David headed up the steps, and she turned and went down the other companionway.

At the last step, her boots hit water. Much higher than before.

The master's mate continued to shout orders from the stern where the leak was worst. Mary Elizabeth sloshed her way to the others. Why was there so much more water? How would they ever get it all out?

What met her eyes caused her to gasp.

The crack in the bottom of the ship wasn't just a thin gap—it had grown.

And water poured in.

Chapter 3

Tuesday, 15 August 1620
Dartmouth, England

William bent over his journal with his quill. So far, there hadn't been a lot to report, but he wanted to be honorable and write down everything—to prove that he was a good steward for his new employers.

Now in port at Dartmouth for repairs on the *Speedwell*, he was anxious to get back to sea. Dry land was wonderful, but it couldn't match the thrill of the new life ahead of him. Going backward in his journey hadn't been part of the plan. And he did *not* enjoy deviations from his plans.

He and John took turns going ashore since neither one of them wanted to leave the whole of their worldly possessions to thieves who might try and get aboard while docked. So every time John went into town, William took the time to make notes of all he could remember having seen and heard.

The delay in getting to their destination would mean delay in getting the settlement set up. But it was a miracle the *Speedwell* had made it back to port without sinking. Thanks to the crew and the passengers, they'd kept her afloat.

But as the calendar days moved later into the year, the possibility to arrive early enough to plant anything this year vanished. While everyone tried to stay positive, the unspoken fear was palpable.

The delay also could affect their preparation of the ground to produce food next year. The risk to the Merchants and Adventurers' investment could be costly. But it wasn't his job to speculate. Only to report. Nevertheless, he couldn't help the little niggle of worry that started in the back of his mind. The delay would affect them all. But how much?

John came down the companionway of the *Mayflower* toward him. "What are you working on, my friend?"

"Just a journal." William shrugged and closed the book. "How was your trip to town?"

"It was good to stretch my legs and run, but it's quite boring to not be of use. Ended up offering to help on the *Speedwell* with repairs, and they said they needed another good carpenter—would you be interested?"

"Of course." William stood. "Anything to get us back out to sea faster." Tucking the journal into his trunk, he covered it with a few other items. Then he pulled out a satchel of tools and locked the chest. "Lead the way, my friend."

John nodded and took the steps two at a time. "I've hired a young lad to keep an eye on our belongings."

"Do you know him?"

"Yes. He's actually my cousin, so I know we can trust him."

A gangly young boy appeared at the top of the companionway. "I'll make sure everything is tip-top, John."

"Thank you, Matthew." John tousled the boy's hair. "This is my friend, William Lytton."

"Nice to meet you, Mr. Lytton." A scrawny hand went over his waist as the lad bowed.

William laughed. "How about we just shake hands"—he held out his hand—"like gentlemen."

"Yes, sir." The boy smiled and gave William's hand a hearty shake.

"It looks like everything will be in good hands." William looked to John. "Let's see if we can help get the *Speedwell* seaworthy again."

John took long strides ahead of William—his eagerness to be useful quite apparent. Such an interesting man this new friend. The simplicity of calling someone *friend* was still a bit unusual for William.

But he'd enjoyed the ease of their conversations and the camaraderie. No one on the ship knew that he was an orphan. No one knew his past—being kicked out to fend for himself as a child and being taken in by the man who'd taught him a trade. Instead of an outcast, he was part of a group—the Planters.

This was new territory.

Seemed like everything about the life ahead of him would be new. A completely fresh start.

John looked back to him. "Have you met Stephen Hopkins yet?"

William kept to himself a lot. "No, I can't say that I have."

"Oh, well now. . .there is someone that you simply must meet. He's been to Jamestown, was shipwrecked and stranded on Bermuda. He even attended the wedding of the famous Indian Pocahontas."

"So you know him?" He had to admit the man sounded intriguing.

"He's a passenger on the *Mayflower*, mate!" John chuckled. "He's been telling us these stories the past few nights."

But William had kept to himself and written in his journal while the men stayed top deck to swap stories.

"Maybe it's time you join us." John elbowed him.

"You've asked me every night—"

"And every night you answer the same." One of his friend's eyebrows raised.

"Well, perhaps this time will be different."

"Perhaps it will." John slapped William on the back.

They reached the *Speedwell* in swift time, thanks to John's fast feet. William raced up the gangway behind the cooper and held tight to his tools. Sounded like he needed to meet Mr. Hopkins. As he followed John toward the door to the lower levels, several people walking about the tiny main deck caught William's attention. He'd heard a lot about the Separatists and was curious to meet them and understand them. Anyone devout enough to stand up to the Church of England fascinated him. Not that he had much use for God or any church.

John stopped at the top of the steps. "Good morning, ladies." He tipped his hat, and a broad smile lit his face as he looked down into the mouth of the ship.

A white bonnet appeared at the top of the companionway. Then a knot of brown hair and a blue cloak. "Good morning." The lady nodded to John and turned to William. "Good morning." Her eyes danced as she smiled.

William was fascinated with the joy on her face. "Good morning to you, miss." He hadn't met many women in his line of work. Especially not any close to his age. And if he guessed correctly, this woman was younger than him.

She turned back to the opening. "Mary Elizabeth, hurry up. It appears we have some dashing men to greet us."

John carried on a conversation with the jovial girl, but William's attention was drawn down.

As he looked back to the square hole in the deck, he saw another white cap emerge. This time, blond hair—the color of his own—was tied in a neat knot at the lady's neck, and a red cape covered her form. Her head was lowered—obviously keeping an eye on her steps. William found himself anticipating another joyous expression.

But when she lifted her head, instead of a large smile, her face bore a timid expression. Unsure. And a bit embarrassed? With brisk steps, he strode to John's side and offered a hand down to assist. "Good day to you, miss."

"Good day." She took hold of his hand. "Thank you for your assistance." Shaking her head, she ascended the last few steps. "You would suppose I could be better at that climb by now."

"Not at all, miss." William found himself smiling. Brown eyes searched his. "Ships can be difficult to navigate. Especially for the fairer sex."

Half a smile. She tucked a strand of hair back under her cap.

He bowed slightly. "I'm William Lytton, aboard the *Mayflower*."

The smile that had started now blossomed into something radiant. "Nice to make your acquaintance, Mr. Lytton. I'm Mary Elizabeth Chapman."

It took a moment to gain his bearings. John's chatter went on beside him, but William was mesmerized by the woman in front of him. Was she one of the Separatists? She must be to be on the *Speedwell*.

"Again, thank you very much for your kindness." She turned to her friend. "Dorothy, we need to let these men get to their work."

Mary Elizabeth—in the red cape—tugged at her friend's arm. With a look over her shoulder, she sent William a slight smile.

As they walked toward the bow, he couldn't tear his gaze away.

"William."

A tap on his shoulder.

"William."

Another tap.

"Will–i–am." John slapped him on the shoulder.

He jerked toward the cooper. "I'm sorry. What were you saying?"

His friend's laughter washed over him. "Nothing. I just had to call your name three times. We need to get down to the hold, but I take it a certain lady has caught your attention?"

"What?" William furrowed his brow and shook his head. Couldn't exactly tell his friend that he'd never had much interaction with young ladies, now could he? "No. Of course not. I was just thinking about our journey."

More laughter from John brought a few stares to land in their direction. He slapped William again on the shoulder. "If you repeat that to yourself over and over, maybe you'll believe it."

Heat rushed to William's cheeks, but he couldn't admit to John that he was right. Best to just get to work and attempt to get a vision of Mary Elizabeth in her red cape out of his mind.

"Well. . ." Dorothy clasped her hands—a sure indication she was about to interrogate her subject—and walked backward up the deck in front of Mary Elizabeth.

"Well what?" No matter how hard her friend tried, Mary Elizabeth wasn't about to take the bait.

"You know exactly what I'm asking about, silly."

"Do I?"

Dorothy stopped and placed her hands on her hips. "Don't play games with me, Mary Elizabeth Chapman. I saw how you smiled at Mr. Lytton."

Even using all her energy, Mary Elizabeth couldn't stop a new smile from forming on her face.

"See? Just like that." Dorothy looked around and then grabbed Mary Elizabeth's arm and dragged her to the bulwark. "He's a handsome man, isn't he?"

"Dorothy Raynsford, you need to hush right now. You know he's not part of our congregation—he could be a heathen for all we know—"

"His friend John is a God-fearing man," her friend was quick to interject.

"And you discovered this fact *how*, exactly?"

"While Mr. Lytton assisted you up the companionway, John and I had quite a lively discussion. I found out that he is the cooper on the *Mayflower* and that his friend is a carpenter. And quite skilled, I'm told."

"Oh, I'm sure."

Dorothy huffed. "You are not playing fair. I've never seen you take interest in any young man. Ever. And you would deny me the pleasure of being a part of this—your best friend?"

For a moment, Mary Elizabeth *almost* felt guilty. But that was always Dorothy's way. Granted, Mr. Lytton was indeed a handsome man. But was she ready to admit that out loud? His hair was the same color as her own, but his eyes are what drew her. Blue and piercing. His gaze had been intense.

Dorothy giggled. "You don't even have to say anything. I can read your face. You're thinking of him again."

"Oh gracious, Dorothy, you could try the patience of the Good Lord above." She wrapped her cloak tighter around her and leaned on the bulwark. The scent of salt water was much better than that of unwashed bodies. And to think they still had weeks to go aboard this ship.

"So. . . ?"

Mary Elizabeth shook her head.

"I'm not saying you have to marry the man, but you are taking all the fun out of this. Can't you at least admit to thinking he's handsome?"

"What about Mr. Alden? You spoke with him longer than I did with Mr. Lytton. Am I to assume that you found him handsome?"

"Diverting the focus of our conversation is cruel, Mary Elizabeth. And yes, I found Mr. Alden quite handsome, as well. But please remember, I didn't get to take a man's hand as he assisted me. It's totally different."

Warmth rushed up Mary Elizabeth's arms as she remembered the simple touch of Mr. Lytton's hand. How could the gentlemanly gesture feel so different from him than from any other man? Once again, she couldn't keep from smiling.

"You haven't smiled this much in a long time." Dorothy's elbow poked Mary Elizabeth in the side.

"All right. You've beaten the subject to death. Yes, I found Mr. Lytton handsome. I've never felt anything like I did when we met. Happy?"

"Yes, quite." Her friend laughed and hooked Mary Elizabeth's arm. "Now, let's take a stroll around the deck and discuss what we hope to find in a husband."

For the love of all things good, Mary Elizabeth couldn't decide what was worse—embarrassment of the topic or admitting she found a Stranger handsome.

David sat on his mat and stared at the toy in his lap. The top was one of his favorites normally, but on a ship it wasn't as fun—extra space wasn't known on the small ship, and when they were out to sea, the rocking motion made the top fall over. It would be nice if he had a friend to play with. But all the other children his age were busy.

It was hard growing up. Ever since he'd breeched—at age six—he'd wanted to be like his father.

A man.

He'd gotten to wear the breeches and clothes like a man, but he'd been small. Too small for any real work. And then Mother got sick and died.

Everything changed with Father then.

At eight years old, David was still small, but before they were chosen to go to the New World, he thought he might like to learn the art of weaving. Many of their congregation were very good at the trade. But Father wanted him to study the Bible more instead of learning a trade like most boys his age. While he loved the Bible, he didn't understand. Why was Father treating him differently now that Mother was dead?

His future was uncertain. But he loved his family. He would obey Father and study as much as he could. Maybe when he was stronger and bigger, he could help the family more.

Maybe then, Father wouldn't be so sad. At least he'd shown excitement about the trip. But two nights ago, David found him crying.

They all missed Mother.

Sometimes at night, he wanted to cry too because he missed her so much. His heart often ached with the loss of her. Now they'd left her buried in Holland. And he could barely remember her face.

He shook his head and stood up, the top in his hand. His thoughts weren't honoring to either his father or mother. If he wanted to be a man, he'd just have to start acting like one.

Taking the toy over to the trunk, David opened the lid and dropped it in. He needed to prove that he was growing up. Father would see that his son could work alongside him in the new colony. Maybe then happiness would return on a permanent basis to the Chapman household.

Chapter 4

Monday, 21 August 1620
Dartmouth, England

William watched the *Speedwell* once again cut through the water, this time with a good wind in her sails. Too bad he couldn't see any snippets of a red cape. What could Miss Chapman be doing? How was she? The thoughts had recurred many times over the past week. Too many times.

Shaking his head, he gripped the top plank of the bulwark. It would be weeks before he'd get to see her again, and even then, he wasn't worthy of her attention. Especially since her whole reason for the trip revolved around her faith. Faith which William didn't understand.

Maybe it was time to learn more about it.

"Afternoon, Mr. Lytton."

William turned and saw Robert Coppin—the master's mate. "Afternoon, Mr. Coppin. What can I do for you?"

"Master Jones was hoping you could help him build an idea he has for his cabin."

"Of course, I would love to be of assistance."

"You would be compensated as well." The man's weathered face concealed his age. But he was an imposing presence.

"While it is much appreciated, sir, it isn't necessary."

"Master Jones insists." Mr. Coppin bowed and nodded. "He's heard of your skill as a carpenter and knows that an honest man is worthy of his wages."

"Thank you, sir." William gave a nod of affirmation. "Please lead the way."

Coppin headed toward the stern of the ship where the master's cabin sat on the main deck behind the steerage room. Above the cabin was the poop deck—the highest level of the ship on the aft castle.

William had studied the ship at great length over the last few weeks. The whipstaff inside the steerage room was how they steered the *Mayflower*. The precise movements of the sailors as they worked the sails fascinated William—climbing to and fro on the large masts. Harnessing the wind was indeed a science.

But this would be the first time he'd seen the ship master's quarters.

Coppin opened the door to the cabin, which wasn't much bigger than an eight-foot square—if that.

Master Jones stood by an old cabinet. "Mr. Lytton. Thank you for coming."

"Of course." With all three of them in the room, it felt quite cramped.

The ship master pointed to the cabinet. "I'm hoping you can remake this into more usable space."

Mr. Coppin bowed to the master. "I'll be on the poop deck if you need me, sir."

Jones nodded and turned back to William. "Do you think you can reuse the wood?"

"What do you have in mind, sir?"

"Something a bit more practical." As Jones described what he was hoping for, William measured the wood with the width of his hand.

"I think it can be done and will give it my best effort."

"Thank you, Lytton. I've heard you've earned quite a reputation as a carpenter in London."

"Thank you, sir." The praise made William's heart swell. If only Paul were still alive. His mentor would have loved the adventure of the New World.

"I'll leave you to it, then."

Christopher Jones walked out of the room, an air of authority surrounding him. No doubt years of commanding ships gave him the confidence to be comfortable with the man he'd become.

Maybe one day William would be able to embrace the man *he* was as well. Maybe one day he wouldn't think of himself as an orphan. Maybe one day he could earn the affection of a beautiful woman like Mary Elizabeth.

Monday, 28 August 1620

Mary Elizabeth leaned over the mat where her brother David struggled to breathe. What else could she do? Father had stayed up all night with the boy and now slept next to him. Dorothy tried to convince her to get some air while the seas were calm, but Mary Elizabeth couldn't leave little David. The ship's surgeon—Mr. Smith—was concerned it could be pneumonia.

The only other time she'd heard that term was when a neighbor in Leyden died from the dreaded disease.

Why had he been out in the rain? She put her face in her hands. Ever since they'd all had to walk around in wet boots and stockings to help stop the last leak, David had had a cough. Even with her warning to stay out of the rain, he'd gone out to help with chores on the ship's deck.

The past couple of weeks, David had acted differently—instead of sitting and playing, he'd tried to work with anyone who would let him—and Mary Elizabeth wasn't sure what had prompted the all-fire independence. He'd always been a busy child, but very cooperative and docile. To see him lying still and lifeless. . .

The thought of death sent her into another bout of uncontrollable tears. God understood the appeals from her heart. She knew that. But was she deserving of His grace in this matter?

Oh, Father God, please forgive me for my foolish ways and sinful nature. And please, Lord. . .please. . .spare David.

Her tears soaked into the blanket covering her brother. What would she do without him? What would her father do? Her brother was so small. . . .

Footsteps sounded behind her, and Mary Elizabeth swiped at

her cheeks. Most of the congregation had stayed away because of the fever David couldn't break, but maybe someone approached with help.

The makeshift curtain separating her family's small space swished to the side. "Miss Chapman"—the surgeon's clipped tone held a sense of relief—"Master Reynolds is turning us about. The ship is leaking again, and so we make for Plymouth for repairs."

"How bad is it?"

"Not as bad as the last, I'm told, but I'm thankful for David's sake. He needs more care than I can give on the ship."

The words sunk into her heart. That meant David was worse than she'd imagined. With a swallow, she choked back the tears. "How long will it take us to return to port?"

"A few days. But if we can keep the boy's fever down, we might be able to help him more once we reach land. I'll be back this evening to check on him." The man turned on his heel and left.

While his words were not encouraging, the surgeon did give her a slight reason to hope. God could heal David. Of that she was certain. And even though they would be delayed further, maybe it was Providence that brought them back to England. But what about the leak? Would they be able to keep it from growing like the last? For the third time, their ship would have to limp its way into harbor. Her heart sank as fear built in her mind. She shook her head. The time was needed to be faithful and positive. Not doubting or anxious. *Oh Lord, please help us. I need Your courage to fill me.*

For David.

For her father. He'd already lost so much. Losing David would crush him.

No. She wouldn't allow her thoughts to go there.

Thankfully, they had a surgeon aboard. Mr. Smith appeared very young, and she'd been told that he was betrothed to a young lady back in England—but this wasn't a time to doubt his abilities or to question his experience. From what she could tell, he was very knowledgeable.

Father shifted on his blanket. "Mary Elizabeth?"

"I'm here, Papa."

He swiped a hand down his face and sat up. "Was someone talking? Any news?"

"Mr. Smith came to give us some news—"

"Mary Elizabeth, how is our sweet boy doing?" Dorothy slipped in beside her.

The sound of her best friend's voice soothed her worry. "The surgeon just told me that we have to keep his fever down. We're headed back to England, and we will need to get him help there."

"I just heard Master Reynolds telling the people on deck. People are worried about the delay, but no one wants to be on a sinking ship. Especially after last time. I think we're all still drying out." She smiled and brushed some hair back from David's forehead. "And we can get help for David."

Father got up, his face grim. "I'm going to check on the details of the leak and ask the elders to pray."

Mary Elizabeth nodded and reached up for his hand. But he didn't look at her.

"I'm sure he's just tired." Dorothy took the outstretched hand.

"I wish it were only that. After Mother passed, he went to a very dark place—you know that. Ever since David has gotten sick, I've seen the same look in his eyes, and it scares me."

"Don't let your thoughts go there, Mary Elizabeth. God will get us back to England, and then we can get help for your brother."

Mary Elizabeth nodded. If they could keep him alive until then.

CHAPTER 5

Friday, 1 September 1620

A warm hand touched her own as she peered up into startling blue eyes. *"Good day to you, miss."*

Mary Elizabeth woke with a start. It wasn't the first time she'd dreamed of that day. The day she'd met William Lytton and his friend. The thought of seeing him again made her insides do a little flip. His eyes held such depth—unlike anyone else she'd ever met. Were there secrets hidden behind them? Would she have a chance to speak with him again? At the moment, she'd like nothing more.

David moaned next to her.

She shook her head at her foolish and selfish thoughts. How could she think of her own desires when David struggled with each breath? Good thing Father couldn't know her thoughts. He'd certainly scold her for such behavior.

Unsure of the time of day down on the dim and dreary gun deck where all the passengers resided, Mary Elizabeth wiped the sleep from her eyes. It must be the middle of the day because she'd stayed up all night with David. She'd torn strips from one of her petticoats and soaked them in cool sea water. All night she'd bathed David's forehead and chest, hoping to keep his fever down.

His breathing was quieter now, but what did that mean?

Sitting up, she pulled her knees to her chest. Mother would know what to do. But she wasn't here.

That made Mary Elizabeth long for Leyden and the cemetery. That wasn't a possibility, so she longed to pour all her thoughts into the journal from Dorothy. But now wasn't the time.

Only one thing remained certain—life wasn't easy. And probability ran high that it never would be again.

Every prayer she'd sent heavenward of late asked for courage. Yet here she sat next to her sick brother in the depths of a ship. The future unknown. Everything in tumult.

The *least* thing she felt was courage.

Lord, please help me. I'm weak and little of faith. But I know You are almighty God.

With a deep breath, Mary Elizabeth ran her fingers through her hair and tidied it as best she could. Replacing her cap, she sent another prayer heavenward for David's healing.

"How is he?" Father opened the curtain a slit and peered down at his son.

"He feels a bit cooler now." Hoping her words came across as confident, Mary Elizabeth swallowed her fears.

Father nodded. Dark bags under his eyes portrayed his worry and lack of sleep the past few days. His hunched form appeared weary. "We are almost to port in Plymouth. The surgeon will escort us into town. The ship master knows of another good surgeon there."

Mary Elizabeth stood as best she could, but the ceilings were several inches short for her stature. Wasn't it bad enough there were no windows? They had to walk around all bent and crouched.

"Mary Elizabeth, there's something else you should know. The decision has been made to leave the *Speedwell* behind. No one wants to risk a leaky ship, and Mr. Reynolds has done nothing but complain. The crew will stay behind, as well as some of the passengers. The rest of us will all have to move to the *Mayflower* for the remainder of the voyage."

While a change of scenery would be nice, Mary Elizabeth had gotten used to this particular ship. It also meant that everything needed to be packed. "I'll get our personal belongings put away right now."

Father nodded and knelt beside David. "I'll get the curtain down and help roll up the mats." He touched his son's head. "He does feel cooler. Let's pray the Good Lord sees fit to heal him before we need to depart."

That thought hadn't even crossed Mary Elizabeth's mind until Father put it into words. What would they do if David wasn't strong enough to make the voyage? They'd sold everything to get this far and only had meager possessions on the ship. Everything else was invested in the voyage and venture in Virginia. Besides that, they were Separatists. And without the support of their congregation, how would they deal with the persecution?

"Don't worry, Mary Elizabeth. I can see it on your face." Father's hand rested on her shoulder. "The Lord knows our plight. He will see us through." A thin smile stretched across his weary features. "I have no doubt we will be on the *Mayflower* when she sails."

As he pulled down their small dividing curtain, Mary Elizabeth packed the trunk they'd brought aboard for their necessities. Everything else was below them in the cargo hold. Making quick work of the few items, she felt the ship lurch.

"We must be in the harbor." Father tucked the blanket around David and lifted the small boy into his arms. "I'll meet you on deck with the surgeon."

Urgency filled Mary Elizabeth's heart. Looking around their tiny space that had been their home for all these weeks, she checked to make sure everything was ready.

"Mary Elizabeth. I just saw your father." Dorothy was at her side and hugged her. "I'll make sure it all gets transferred over, and I'll set up your curtains again."

"Thank you."

"Think nothing of it. I'll be waiting for word on my little King David." Dorothy sniffed and wiped at her cheek.

Mary Elizabeth's friend had called him that since he was born. And David loved her for it. As he grew from baby to gangly boy, he often said he wanted to be a man after God's own heart just like the real King David from the scriptures.

"Now go. I'll take care of everything here."

Mary Elizabeth hugged her friend one more time. She took her cloak and raced to the main deck.

Fresh air and bright sunlight greeted her for the first time in several days. Spotting her father, she made her way toward him just as the sailors lowered the gangway.

The walk was steep, but she followed her father's confident steps.

"Look. The *Mayflower* is a good deal larger than the *Speedwell*. The journey should be a good one." He nodded to the ship tying in next to them.

All at once, the reality of the situation hit her. They'd be joining everyone on the *Mayflower*. For the entire journey across the ocean. The *Speedwell* had been full of their congregation and the crew. But now they would join a new ship's crew and many Strangers.

She allowed a smile to ease onto her face as her insides fluttered. David *would* get better and maybe just maybe. . .she'd have that chance to speak with Mr. Lytton again after all.

Monday, 4 September 1620

William watched Miss Chapman's friend walk up the gangway. Obviously resolute in her objective, she took determined steps and placed her hands on her hips when she reached the main deck. Her brow furrowed.

"Looks like Miss Raynsford needs assistance." John patted William's shoulder and headed toward the young woman.

"How did you guess?" William stifled a laugh and followed his friend.

After crossing the deck, John bowed. "Miss Raynsford, how can we be of help?"

"Mr. Alden, Mr. Lytton." She curtseyed, then put a hand over her heart with a sigh. "I can't tell you how glad I am to see you. I need to make accommodations for the Chapman family."

William moved closer to her. Was Mary Elizabeth all right? "I know they've been transferring everything to the cargo hold, but I didn't think they were moving passengers until tomorrow."

"They're not." She clasped her hands under her chin. "That's why I need your help. You see, little David—Mary Elizabeth's brother—took ill, and they are in town at a surgeon's. I need to help move my own family tomorrow, but I promised I would take care of Mary Elizabeth's belongings. She's my dearest friend in the whole world, and I need to make sure they have a good space. Especially for David to recover." She finally took a breath. The pleading in her eyes couldn't be mistaken.

"Mary Elizabeth's not ill, is she?" William couldn't help but question.

A soft smile split Miss Raynsford's face. "No. She's not. But thank you for asking."

John offered the young lady his arm. "We'd be glad to assist. But let's do it quietly so we don't trouble anyone else."

"Do you know where we should set up their things?" Miss Raynsford looked hopeful.

"I'm not certain. . ." John shot William a questioning glance.

Several thoughts passed through William's mind. His spot was one of the choicest, at the stern in a corner. There was less movement of the ship at the stern and less water seepage. There was also a bit more privacy since it was up against the walls of the ship. "They can have my spot." The words were out before he knew it. "It seems we will have to make room for a lot of people, anyway. Let me give my area to the Chapman family."

Miss Chapman's friend covered her heart again. "Mr. Lytton, that is so very generous of you."

"It will be my privilege, Miss Raynsford." William eyed John and noticed his raised eyebrows. "There could be enough space for your family to be next to them as well."

"But where will you go?" Miss Raynsford appeared doubtful.

"I'll just have to find a space near John." He gripped his friend's shoulder.

"We will probably need to share the tiny area I already have." John nodded. "With as many passengers as we need to house, we will have to economize space."

Within minutes, the trio had collected all the Chapmans' belongings and were headed back to the *Mayflower*. When they reached the top of the gangway, William noticed the crew struggling with a large burden on deck.

As soon as he got a better look, he realized what it was. "Look, John. It's a house jack." How exciting that they were bringing this with them to Virginia. From a carpenter's perspective, it was amazing. They'd be able to get houses up a lot faster.

"I've actually never seen one." John stopped and studied the wood-and-iron contraption that resembled a giant screw.

"Gentlemen, I know it's fascinating, but my arms are getting sore." Miss Raynsford shifted her burden.

"Oh, of course. My apologies." William moved ahead. "Follow me."

When he'd first boarded the *Mayflower*, William had been proud of grabbing his accommodations. Never would he have thought that he would so readily give them up for someone else. Of course, he never thought that the passengers and belongings from two ships would be making the journey on one. But at this point, he didn't mind. They hadn't even gotten one hundred leagues past Land's End when the *Speedwell*'s master had turned her about again.

Master Jones wanted to get back under way as soon as they could replenish a few supplies and get loaded. This would make the third trip out from England. First from Southampton, then from Dartmouth, and now from Plymouth. William could only hope they'd make it all the way across the ocean this time.

Ducking into the short space of the gun deck, William steered Miss Raynsford and John to the back corner. "Let me just store all of my belongings and get them out of the way."

"I'll hang their privacy curtains." Dorothy laid her burden down and went to work.

John shuffled over to William. "Hand me whatever is ready to go, and I'll haul it to my quarters."

William made swift work of his packing and had everything out by the time Dorothy had the curtains hung. He moved the Chapmans' things into the tiny space while John carried items across the ship to his area. A sense of pride filled William as he realized he'd been able to help the beautiful Miss Chapman and her family.

Dorothy touched his arm. "Thank you."

"I was honored to do it, miss." Bent over, it was hard to acknowledge her in the proper way, but he sent her a smile.

"Not every man has as much honor as you, Mr. Lytton. You gave up a very agreeable space—for a long journey no less—to perfect strangers."

In his mind, Miss Chapman wasn't a stranger. He'd thought of her and their meeting often. But to the rest of the world, Dorothy made a valid point.

He didn't *know* the Chapman family.

Something he'd like very much to change.

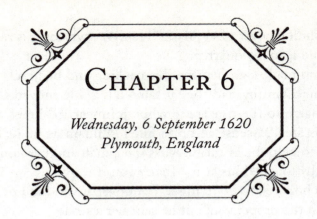

The good alee wind they'd enjoyed leaving Dartmouth seemed to follow them as the *Mayflower* once again left England's shores. William prayed it would be true and not just his fancy as the sails billowed above his head. At this rate, he wasn't sure when they would reach Virginia. As he'd studied all the writings he could find on ships crossing the Atlantic to the New World, everything pointed to a September departure as too late. Disastrous even.

Stephen Hopkins had been telling them of the storms that happened this late in the year, and then of the trouble the colonists at Jamestown had had with the Indians. While the stories were fascinating, William didn't need more doubt entering his mind.

No. He couldn't allow the negative thoughts to reign. He'd overheard enough conversations to know that the entire ship full of people were tired of the trip already. And now they were packed into every inch of space. With over 130 souls aboard, the 180-ton ship was full to brimming.

He thought that in such confined quarters the chance to see Mary Elizabeth Chapman again would be high. But ever since her father carried young David aboard, the pretty Miss Chapman had stayed within their curtained-off area.

Maybe once the boy was doing better, he'd have a chance to speak with her again. His hopes would just have to hang on that thought.

Why was it that for the first time in his life, he was fascinated with a female? Possibly because he'd been so concentrated on learning all he could from Paul in years prior. He tried to be logical about it. Perhaps a lady capable of capturing his attention never before crossed his path. And if he were honest, he knew it was because he found Mary Elizabeth enchanting.

Being an orphan had a profound effect on William. Even the family who took him in as a baby treated him as less than their own child. He was more of a slave. And then to be kicked out at such a young age—forced to live on the streets and beg for food? It was the worst possible scenario in William's mind. No child should have to suffer in such a way. To always be scorned by people. To have things thrown at him. To always be covered in dirt and grime but hoping that someone would see past that and cherish him for who he was.

But no. People had been cruel. He'd slaved for every penny he'd earned. Each twopence, each sixpence—and once he'd worked for weeks and weeks to earn a whole shilling. He thought it would be his lot in life for the rest of his days.

Until Paul Brookshire saw him on the street one day haggling with a merchant over a loaf of bread. By that time, William was hardened to the world. It didn't matter that it was common for families who took in orphans to put them out again at age nine. It didn't matter that once in a great while a stranger would come along and give him a sack of discarded clothing. What mattered? Four years, he'd fought to keep food in his belly. Thirteen years, he'd been treated as less than everyone else.

Paul changed all that. But it took years for William to trust the man.

The years passed. When his mentor tried to convince him to spend time with people his own age, William always refused. Why would anyone see him as anything other than a despised and rejected orphan?

The tangy scent of the sea made him take a deep breath and shake his head. No sense in digging up the anger and hurt of the past. Things were different now. No one knew what he'd been—or where he came from. Now he was a respected and well-trained carpenter. His master had seen to that. William Lytton's name had become known for quality workmanship. And this opportunity to start something brand new, in a setting around the world and away from everything and everyone he'd ever known was *exactly* what he wanted.

Would Mary Elizabeth be able to see him as someone special?

Shaking his head, William knew the thoughts were fruitless. She was a Separatist. And he'd learned in the past couple of days that those who called themselves Saints also thought of everyone else as Strangers.

John had brought up the subject yesterday. He didn't want to be known as a Stranger to the Leyden congregation—his beliefs lined up with the people. But since they'd faced such persecution for so many years, having lost everything on multiple occasions because of betrayers, the lack of trust was understandable.

Something William understood all too well. While he wasn't ready to discuss his background with John quite yet, he found himself respecting the man more each day. But the discussions on God and the Bible—two of John's favorite topics—made William more uncomfortable. For years, he'd hardened his heart, basing his thoughts of God on how the world around him had treated him. But for the first time ever, he was seeing a different side in people.

With the open ocean before him, William looked to the sky. If God existed the way Paul believed—the way Mary Elizabeth and John believed—then maybe it was worth asking questions and educating himself.

Peter watched William with a close eye. The man never seemed to do anything untoward or questionable.

Who was the carpenter, anyway? Maybe there was something in the man's past. Something that would plant a seed of doubt.

Once they were on board from Southampton, Peter had hoped he'd have a chance to go through Lytton's things, but William chose too good of a location for his quarters. Then when he'd given up his spot for that Chapman family, Peter thought maybe he had another chance. With all the people milling about, certainly, he could disappear and look. . .

But no. So far he hadn't had any luck.

Well, he had the whole voyage to put his plan into action. Maybe he just needed to sit back and be patient.

The time would come.

Saturday, 9 September 1620

"The sea is calm, Mary Elizabeth." Father looked down from his crouched position. "As long as you and I have a good hold of David, nothing can happen to him. I think the fresh air will do him some good."

"Please, Mary Elizabeth?" The illness had made her little brother's voice scratchy and weak.

Looking from him to Father made her realize how overprotective she'd become. Maybe this was another chance to show courage. "All right. Let's head up to the main deck together." She stood from her kneeling position and pointed a finger in David's direction. "But you must promise me that you will not let go under any circumstances."

"I promise." The twinkle in his eye lifted her spirit.

She hadn't seen it in a fortnight—or more. "I've been longing for a bit of fresh air myself."

"And sunshine." Father chuckled.

"Yes, and sunshine." Helping David with his shoes, Mary Elizabeth realized how thin he had become. "We need to fatten you up, young man."

"That won't be a problem. I'm starving and could eat a whole loaf of bread by myself." He rubbed his stomach.

"Well, we don't have any loaves of bread, but let's see what we can find." Mary Elizabeth shook her head. Her brother's active personality had often gotten on her nerves before, but now she would be thankful for it. After watching him be almost lifeless for so long, she wouldn't trade his energy for anything in the world.

"I'll meet you at the steps." Father tousled David's hair.

The way to the companionway was dim—another ship with no windows on the gun deck—but her eyes had grown accustomed to the lack of light. When she saw the sun shining down from above, she couldn't get there fast enough.

"Not so fast, Mary Elizabeth." Her little brother tugged at her hand.

Slowing her pace, she smiled. "I'm sorry. Is this better?"

"Yes, much."

"Before long, I won't be able to keep up with you."

"You couldn't keep up with me before I got sick, Mary Elizabeth. It must be because you're a girl."

"I beg your pardon?" Laughter bubbled up. And it felt good.

"You're a lot older too."

"Is that so?"

"Yup, you're more than twice my age. Old people don't move very fast."

"You little imp." She stopped and pulled on his hand so he would face her. "Then I think we need to make a deal."

"What kinda deal?"

Mary Elizabeth tapped her lip with her forefinger. "Hmmm. I think we should see just how 'old' I am when we get to our new home. We'll have a race and see who is faster. But that means you have to eat everything I tell you so you grow big and strong."

His giggles floated around her. "You'll never beat me. I'm too fast."

"We will just have to see about that, now won't we?" Tugging on his hand, she nodded toward the steps. "But no running today, all right? Master Jones said it isn't safe for the children to run up there."

"Yes, Mary Elizabeth."

"Good." The companionways on ships were not much more than a glorified ladder. What with all her petticoats and skirt, climbing up was always a cumbersome chore. If only there was a blue-eyed gentleman named William waiting for her at the top to offer a hand again. She shook her head. She probably needed to repent of all the thoughts she had of Mr. Lytton. Goodness, she'd only met him once.

At the top, she reached down for David. "Come on up, it's a beautiful day."

His ascent was slow but steady, and it thrilled Mary Elizabeth's heart to see him moving so well.

"Hold on to my hand now." She straightened to her full height and squinted in the bright light. Stretching her legs felt better than anything had in a long while. Looking down at David, she caught his smile.

"This is a big ship, isn't it, Mary Elizabeth?"

"It's bigger than the *Speedwell*, yes."

"How much?"

"About three times bigger."

Mary Elizabeth held a hand above her eyes to shield them from the sun. Days without bright light had made her eyes sensitive. Several groups of people stood around the small deck. Master Jones had made sure that everyone knew the rules. If the seas became at all rough, no one but the crew was allowed on the main deck. He didn't want to risk anyone getting washed overboard or getting in the way of the sailors as they did their jobs.

They were fortunate to have beautiful weather right now. It gave them the opportunity to walk around upright and be out in the fresh air.

Father nodded at her and reached for David's other hand. "Let's get some exercise, shall we?"

At eight years old, her brother was still a small boy, but he wouldn't stay that way for long. Mary Elizabeth relished the feel of his small hand in her own. She'd never take for granted the time she was given with him. Not after almost losing him.

And then there was Father.

The stoic man God had blessed her with was beginning to show age that would attest to him being a much older man. The past year since Mother died had taken its toll on him. Gray sprinkled his dark hair, and lines around his eyes gave evidence of his penchant for smil-ing and laughter.

But there hadn't been as much of either since her mother had died. Mary Elizabeth longed to see him return to his jovial self. A new thought struck her—would Father ever remarry?

He definitely wasn't an ancient man beyond marrying—not even forty years of age.

"What are your thoughts, Mary Elizabeth? Your brow is quite quizzical. . ." Father's voice intruded on her thoughts and made the heat rise in her cheeks. Could she tell him?

David laughed and pulled on her hand. "Her face is turning red, Father, look."

Best to tell the truth. She couldn't allow them to think she was thinking anything unworthy. "I was thinking of Mother. . .and if you'd ever marry again."

Father's face softened a bit.

Mary Elizabeth couldn't decipher the emotions that seemed to spread across his features. Her father had always been so strong—and so in love with their mother.

"Your mother was a wonderful woman. No one could ever com-pare." Facing forward, his shoulders stiffened.

"I'm sorry, Father."

No response.

Even David ducked his head and kept his eyes down. Would they ever be able to talk about it without being overtaken by pain and grief?

Silence surrounded their little family as they walked in a slow pace around the deck.

Father looked at her. "It seems David is doing quite well. I need to discuss some things with Elder Brewster."

His desire to depart was all her fault. She'd wounded the man she loved and adored above anyone else. "That is fine, Father." While Elder Brewster was the head of their congregation because Pastor Robinson had stayed in Holland to prepare the others to join them in Virginia, Mary Elizabeth wasn't so sure what could be so important.

Other than avoiding the topic she'd voiced.

"Don't let go of your sister, young man." Father gave his stern look to David.

"No, sir. I won't." The power in David's voice surprised Mary Elizabeth. After just a few short minutes, he already seemed stronger. Or maybe it was just for her benefit—since she knew she'd hurt them both with her words.

"Good, good." Father nodded and walked toward a group of men from their congregation.

Mary Elizabeth tightened her grip on David's hand. Things needed to turn around. "Where would you like to go next?"

"To the front."

"To the bow?"

"Yes." David wasn't overly talkative.

Mary Elizabeth understood, even though her heart ached to hear his happy chatter. Why did she have to bring up Mother?

Taking slow steps, Mary Elizabeth thought of ways to shift David's attention.

While there wasn't a lot of room to meander, Mary Elizabeth enjoyed being outside. The crates of animals were fun to see. Goats, chickens, pigs, and a couple of dogs resided on the main deck. Maybe she could engage David that way.

"Can you make the sound of a pig?" She stopped in front of one particular crate.

Her little brother looked up at her and then back to the animal. "I'm not sure. . .but I can make the sound of a rooster, I think."

"Why don't you give it a try. Let's go see the chickens."

"Maybe it would be better to cluck like the chickens."

"Whatever you want to try." Mary Elizabeth watched as David crouched by the crate.

He clucked at them and giggled at the random noises they made back at him.

She tugged at his hand to resume their walk. At least he'd laughed.

When they reached the bow, Mary Elizabeth spotted two familiar figures. She sucked in a breath.

"Mary Elizabeth, what's wrong?" David's pull at her hand made her look down.

"Not a thing. I'm sorry. I just wanted more fresh air."

But by the time she finished speaking, two pairs of boots entered her vision.

"Good morning, Miss Chapman. Such a pleasure to see you again." Mr. Alden greeted her. "This must be young David that we've heard so much about."

The comment puzzled her. "Good day to you, Mr. Alden. How have you heard about David?"

"Your charming friend—Dorothy—has kept us apprised of the situation."

No doubt she had. Dorothy could regale anyone with her stories. She never seemed to run out of words.

Mr. Lytton stepped closer and looked at her brother. "I'm so thankful to hear you are recovered."

"Thank you, sir." David gave a slight bow. "I'm David Chapman."

"Yes, I know." Mr. Lytton looked up at Mary Elizabeth and smiled before he looked back down at her brother. He put a hand to his chest and bowed. "And I am William Lytton. This is my friend, John Alden, the cooper of the ship."

"Nice to know you both. But what's a...cooper?" David's curiosity energized his voice.

As John answered, Mary Elizabeth enjoyed watching her little brother. He, of course, had more questions, and the men were patient in their answers. But the thrill at seeing William again caused the blood to pound in her ears. A feeling she hadn't had ever before. Everything in her cried out to stare at the man who'd offered his hand the first time they met. But she forced herself to keep her eyes focused on David. And snuck a peek here and there at the handsome man. The racing of her heart only caused her breaths to be short. Why was she so nervous? Maybe they would keep talking until she could calm down and trust herself to speak in a normal manner. Maybe then she could get to know the intriguing Mr. Lytton a little better.

CHAPTER 7

The look on young David's face as John explained his job as a cooper made William smile. But Mary Elizabeth appeared uncomfortable.

"What do *you* do, Mr. Lytton?" The young boy's enthusiasm was contagious.

"I'm a carpenter." William smiled at him and then peeked at Mary Elizabeth.

"So that's how you knew so much about Mr. Alden's job too. You both work with wood and build things." David scrunched up his brow. "I might like to do that when I'm older."

"I'm sure you'd be very good at it." John patted the child's head.

Memories washed over William. He was barely older than this boy when he'd been left on the streets to fend for himself. But seeing the lad hold tight to his sister's hand gave William a thankful heart. His desire would be that no child ever go through what he'd endured.

"William's done beautiful work." John's words cut into his thoughts.

"Mr. Lytton." Mary Elizabeth's soft voice drew his attention upward. "Could you tell us some of the items you've made?"

As he listed off some of his most recent pieces, he watched her face. Deep brown eyes stared into his own. Her skin was quite fair, and he saw a few blond locks of hair attempting to escape her starched linen cap. The red of her woolen cape set off the loveliness of her full, red mouth. If he wasn't careful, he'd be caught staring.

"Have you ever built a ship?" Little David's question made his attention turn back to the boy. The lad twisted and turned under Mary Elizabeth's arm.

"No. Not yet. But my master taught me some of the best techniques."

The younger Chapman swung the hand that held his sister's. Always movement, even though he'd just recovered from sickness. The energy of youth. "Do you think you could build one as big as the ark?"

Mary Elizabeth chuckled at the question and then covered her mouth.

John tapped William's elbow with his own. "We were just discussing the ark this morning, weren't we?"

"Well. . .could ya?" David persisted.

"It's plausible that yes, I could build a ship that size, but I'm not sure what I would use it for—do you have any ideas?" Maybe the way to get to know Mary Elizabeth would be through this boy. William shrugged. It was worth a try.

"It sure would hold a lot more than this ship. So we could bring lots of animals and people to the New World, and we could teach them about the Bible." He rubbed his chin. "But the ark didn't have any sails, so I wonder if it would work."

John knelt in front of David. "You're correct, it didn't have sails, at least from the description in Genesis. And if I understood the passage, they didn't direct where the boat was going—that was God's job. But those are very intelligent thoughts."

"Mr. Alden, would *you* like to build a boat as big as the ark?" The boy never seemed to run out of questions.

"I think that would be a fun project, but remember, it took Noah one hundred years to build the ark, and I would need Mr. Lytton's help. He's better at that kind of work."

William watched Mary Elizabeth as John and David continued to discuss the ark.

She turned to gaze back at him. "Thank you. You are very kind to indulge him." Her voice had lowered in volume.

He moved a step closer so he could hear her better. "He's a wonderful boy. I'm very glad to see he's doing so much better. You must have been pretty worried."

An expression he couldn't decipher flittered across her features as she looked down at her brother and then back into his eyes. "Yes. After we lost our mother last year, I couldn't bear the thought of losing him as well."

"I'm so sorry about your mother."

Tears appeared at the corners of her eyes. The sheen made her eyes all the more beautiful and rich. "Thank you. I fear my father has suffered the worst of it, although losing Mother was the worst thing I've ever been through. But thankfully we have our faith, and the Lord has taken care of us."

What would it be like to have such faith? "It must be very difficult for a husband to lose his wife."

"Yes. He loved her very much." She bit her bottom lip and paused for several moments. "Where are you from, Mr. Lytton?"

"Please, call me William. And I'm from London." Not wishing to give anything away, he kept his answer vague. Lots of people were from London.

"Well, I'm not sure it would be appropriate to be so familiar quite yet to use your Christian name. I haven't known you very long." An attractive blush swept up her cheeks.

"My apologies. I do not wish to offend." How did a man go about getting to know a woman? Paul never gave him any training in courting. He'd made sure his young charge knew the manners of society, but that was the extent of his advice. Besides, Dorothy had insisted that John and William use her Christian name.

"There's nothing to apologize for, Mr. Lytton." She looked down at her hand—still swinging with her brother's. But the boy was engrossed in conversation with John.

What a good friend. Taking the time to talk to a child so William would have the opportunity to talk to Mary Elizabeth. He'd have to thank his friend later. "I'd love to get to know you better, Miss Chapman." The words were out before he could stop them.

The pink in her cheeks deepened. "I'd like that." She cleared her throat. "Did I understand correctly that you and Mr. Alden have been discussing the scriptures?"

The question made his heart sink. How much did he tell her? As one of the Saints, she may look down upon him if he didn't share her beliefs. Choosing to be vague once again, he pasted on a smile. "Yes. It's been very enlightening discussion."

"Do you do that often?"

"Of late, yes. There's more time for it while we are on the ship. But John has been hired to do a job as we sail, so he gets called away often to take care of the barrels."

She nodded and tilted her head to the right. "I see. I know we are all thankful—especially since those barrels hold our food stores." Her bottom lip crept into her mouth again.

William found it very appealing—the way she did that seemed to indicate another question was on its way.

"What made you decide to go to the New World with us?" She smiled.

"It's exciting to me to start something new. To be a part of something bigger than myself." He couldn't risk telling her more, could he? "And I must admit that I admire the passion of your group. It's inspiring—to stand firm on your beliefs."

"I am glad that our little congregation can inspire you, Mr. . . ." A deep voice accompanied a large man in dark breeches and coat. He took several steps and stood next to Mary Elizabeth.

Where had he come from?

"Father. . .I'm so glad you could join us. This is Mr. Lytton and Mr. Alden." Mary Elizabeth's cheeks had turned very red.

William bowed. "Mr. Chapman, it's an honor to meet you."

John bowed as well. "At your service."

The man's stern expression was undecipherable.

"Father, Father, you won't believe what we've been talking about."

David saved the day. "Mr. Alden is a cooper and Mr. Lytton is a carpenter, and they both want to build a boat as big as the ark!"

Mr. Chapman's expression softened as he looked down at the lad. "Is that so?"

"And Mr. Alden says that Mr. Lytton is a master carpenter. The captain even had him build something in his private quarters."

"Do you mean *Master* Jones? Remember, they are only captains when they sail military vessels."

"I forgot that part." David looked back to William and smiled. "Do you think we can see what you built for Mr. Jones?"

William opened his mouth—

"We don't need to take up any more of Mr. Lytton's time." The stern look was back on Mr. Chapman's face. "It was a pleasure to meet you, gentlemen." He bowed.

So much for William's conversation with Mary Elizabeth.

"Thank you, Mr. Alden"—she curtseyed to John—"and Mr. Lytton"—she curtseyed to William—"for helping David with his questions."

"But of course." William bowed, attempting to look as respectful and honorable as possible. He didn't need a reason for Mr. Chapman to keep Mary Elizabeth away from him. But it appeared as if that may have already happened.

As the family walked away, John poked William in the ribs. "Did you have a nice chat with Miss Chapman?"

He couldn't help the smile that sprang onto his face. "I did. But it wasn't long enough."

"Young David sure is inquisitive."

"Weren't we all at that age?"

"You're probably right."

William crossed his arms over his chest. "What did you think of her father?"

"I'll be honest. He didn't seem too fond of us, William. But remember, they are proud people. Steadfast in their beliefs. And they've been hurt multiple times by people outside of their faith." He clapped William on the back. "Give it time."

"What if he doesn't give us any chance to have more time together?" The thought made his stomach churn. How had a woman gotten into his heart and mind so swiftly?

"Then I suggest you pray." John beamed a smile at him. "A lot."

The big boat rocked back and forth under David's feet. Somehow the sickness had made him feel even smaller. How was he supposed to help out and show Father that he was capable of work if he couldn't even navigate the deck?

Mr. Lytton and Mr. Alden sure were nice. Maybe he could ask one of them to take him on as an apprentice. That's what men did when they wanted to learn a trade. The more he thought about it, the more he'd like to be a carpenter.

Jesus was a carpenter.

To him, there couldn't be a better job. But Mary Elizabeth would probably tell him it was dangerous, that he wasn't strong enough after being sick. And Father. . . Well, what if he said no?

Mr. Lytton was so tall and strong. David wanted to be like him.

Perhaps a week or two of gaining his strength back would help them all see that David was serious about learning carpentry.

He would be obedient and help out wherever he could.

Nodding his head, he knew he had a plan.

Father would be proud of him. And one day soon, he'd help build them a house in Virginia.

CHAPTER 8

Tuesday, 12 September 1620

Tightening the strings at the neck of her shift, Mary Elizabeth thought about the last few days. Short walks on deck, entertaining David, and Bible reading with her father. Not once had he brought up Mr. Lytton and Mr. Alden. Which was a great relief, even though he hadn't seemed too happy to meet them.

William.

He'd asked her to call him by his Christian name. And while she already thought of him that way in her mind, she knew it wasn't appropriate until they were better acquainted. Many other young men were aboard the ship, but most of them were sailors with questionable morals and profane mouths.

Not William. He'd been respectful and courteous. A perfect gentleman.

A shiver raced up her spine, and she pulled the blanket around her shoulders tighter. She needed to mend one of her sleeves on her dress—not think about Mr. Lytton. Again.

As she pulled out needle and thread, she focused her thoughts on the task at hand. The constant wear was taking its toll. That and no way to wash clothes. She had one other dress in the trunk that was for Sundays and worship since that was their sacred day. They spent the whole day studying scripture, singing worship to the Lord, and absolutely not working or playing.

Her other clothing was in the hold with the rest of their belongings. Not that she had multiple trunks full of skirts and shirtwaists, but they weren't poor by any means. Mother always insisted that they look their best—because they represented the Lord.

The thought made her smile. Her mother had been such a beautiful lady. Mary Elizabeth hoped she would one day be as fine. She'd inherited her mother's hair, eyes, and coloring. But Elizabeth Chapman had had something else that made her glow.

Might it have been the love she had for Mary Elizabeth's father?

Would Mary Elizabeth have that same glow one day?

The ship rolled and heaved on the waves and almost knocked her over. She'd learned to stand with her feet apart to give her a sturdier stance, and when she sat on the floor in their tiny quarters, she bent her knees and crossed her feet to give her a stabler foundation. But the wind had kicked up this morning. And not in the direction beneficial for their sails. The sailors called it *aback*, and Mary Elizabeth knew the term wasn't good.

Then the rolling began.

With more than one hundred people crammed into the gun deck's small area, families had put up blankets or thin wooden walls to give them privacy. But nothing could take away the sound of retching nor the smell that accompanied it.

She could only hope that the seas would calm and this turbulence would pass.

Even Dorothy had succumbed to the seasickness that troubled so many souls aboard today. But her mother hadn't been well for several days, so Dorothy hadn't gotten any fresh air for a while.

Mary Elizabeth needed to remember to check on her friend tomorrow. The Raynsfords might need her help.

The last stitch in, Mary Elizabeth held the sleeve out to examine it. Not too bad considering the circumstances.

David's deep breathing from the corner was music to her ears. Her precious brother slept better each night, for which she was thankful. She should be sleeping as well, but she hadn't been able to get her mind to obey.

A snore from her father reminded her that she *needed* her sleep.

Tomorrow would be another long day aboard ship. And the day after, and the day after that. Until they reached their destination.

Snuffing her candle inside the lantern, Mary Elizabeth shifted down onto her mat. Life on board the ships had been different. Sleep was harder to come by because she didn't labor as much during the day as she had at home. But a weariness also seemed to affect everyone as the days passed. Whether it was the travel, the constant weeks aboard ships, or the lack of fresh air and exercise—the problem was real.

Then she also dealt with the pesky problem of reining in her thoughts. Sometimes, it seemed to be more than she could bear.

Her dreams of marrying one day still held true. But she'd never imagined marrying someone outside their congregation.

Ever since meeting William Lytton, she couldn't get him out of her mind. Handsome in his green doublet and breeches, he invaded her thoughts and dreams with his blond hair and blue eyes.

He was strong and a hard worker, and he seemed to be very respectable.

But all of his wonderful traits did not change one fact: he was still a Stranger.

One she didn't know much about other than that he came from London and Mr. Alden seemed to think highly of him. Even the ship master must, if he'd hired William to build something for him in his personal quarters.

Father's stormy expression the day he met William was not encouraging. While she couldn't read his thoughts, she'd seen that look before, and it didn't communicate his pleasure.

So what could she do?

Her heart longed to see more of William. Was that wrong? Why did she yearn to spend time with him? These feelings were all so new and exciting. And she was normally the stable and calm one. Mary Elizabeth let out a sigh. Dorothy would be thrilled to know that thoughts of Mr. Lytton kept Mary Elizabeth awake at night. Her father on the other hand would be mortified.

Shoving her face beneath the blankets, she worked to rid her mind of all the spinning thoughts.

But one question continued to haunt her.

Did he believe as she did?

Saturday, 30 September 1620

The rolling seas they'd endured a few weeks ago were nothing compared to the tumultuous seas the last couple of days. Every time Mary Elizabeth didn't think it could get worse, the wind raged and churned up the seas around them.

Many people had battled seasickness from the beginning of their journey, but now almost every passenger aboard had succumbed.

Father was so sick he didn't have the strength to lift his head anymore and slept most of the time. David wasn't sick, but he complained of the awful stench they couldn't eliminate from the stuffy quarters.

"Mary Elizabeth?" Dorothy's voice penetrated the curtain.

"Come in, Dorothy." Mary Elizabeth stood as much as she could without hitting her head on the low ceiling and hugged her friend. "You are a wonderful sight to see."

"I'm much thinner than I was, but at least I'm not sick all the time. My parents aren't so fortunate."

"I'm sorry. We've been taking care of Father, and I should have checked on you."

"That's why I'm here, Mary Elizabeth. A great many people have been in misery for days, with no one to care for them since everyone else is sick. Mr. Jones won't let anyone up on deck for fear that someone will get washed overboard, and I think the lack of fresh air and inability to see the sky is making matters worse."

Mary Elizabeth looked down at Father. He slept. Not unlike the past few days. "I suppose David could look after Father when I'm not here."

"I can do it." David nodded and lifted his shoulders.

Turning back to Dorothy, Mary Elizabeth furrowed her brow. "Do you think you and I would be able to handle *all* of the passengers?"

"I've gone to each family's and person's quarters. Only three others aren't sick, but they have several to look after already. Then there's Elizabeth Hopkins—she looks like she may give birth any day now, and she isn't faring well. We must try to help. It's the Christian thing to do."

Mary Elizabeth nodded. Her friend was right. "Let's start now, shall we?" She tied her apron over her skirt and gave instructions to David. "I need you to be strong now and take care of Father."

"I told you I can do it, Mary Elizabeth. And when he's sleeping for long periods, I can help you." David stood and lifted his chin.

"Of course you can." Dorothy chimed in and gave David a hug. She turned back to Mary Elizabeth. "There's something else I need to tell you."

The tone of her friend's voice reminded her of when someone shared bad news. Breathing deeply, she took Dorothy's hand. "Please, tell me."

"William is very sick. John was taking care of him, but many barrels have been damaged by the rolling of the ship, and he was needed to repair them, so he asked me to check on Mr. Lytton. I'm afraid it's much worse than seasickness. He has a high fever."

The rats had eaten the last of his bread. Right through his sack too. Now he didn't have anything to eat, and he'd have to fashion a new bag as well.

Tears threatened to spill down his cheeks. Why was life so hard? Didn't anybody care?

"Hey, William. Why are you crying?" The taunting voice belonged to one of the older street boys.

"I'm not crying." He sniffed and wiped at his face.

"Look everyone, little William is crying. He can't make it on the streets like us. He's nothing but a baby. A crying little baby."

William grabbed his blanket—the only thing he had to call his own and to ward off the cold at night—and ran as fast as his feet would take him. He'd have to find another place to hide. Now that the big boys knew his spot. They always took his spot.

He had to get far away. He'd have to make it on his own. Could he do it? Yes. He was ten now. Those ruffians couldn't tell him what to do anymore or steal more of his food.

William ran until his legs ached. His stomach felt raw. Smells from a local chop house drew him. Maybe he could work for their scraps.

Looking down at his hands, he tried to wipe off some of the blood and dirt. Would they help him?

He was so tired of feeling alone and unwanted. So tired. . .

"Shhh. . ." Someone soothed William's brow. "You're all right. Just rest."

He shook his head back and forth. Why couldn't he open his eyes? Where was he? He wasn't on the streets of London anymore. Nor was he that lonely, starving boy.

He fought the arms that held him down. Why couldn't he get out of here? He had to get to Virginia. Start over.

Everything burned. Why was it so hot?

"Lie still." That voice. He knew that voice. A vision of a red cloak and soothing brown eyes—an angel?

But exhaustion pulled at him, dragging him back into the depths.

CHAPTER 9

Friday, 6 October 1620

I don't know what to do for him, Dorothy." Hot tears streamed down Mary Elizabeth's cheeks. William's fever had come down but he still slept fitfully and mumbled in his sleep. "Every time I check on him, he's having a nightmare of some sort. He seems so miserable and alone, I can't bear it."

"Have you prayed for him?" Her friend grabbed her hands as they knelt on the floor next to Mr. and Mrs. Raynsford.

With a nod, she bit her lip. "But I don't know what to say. I've prayed over Father and every person on board that I've tried to help. No one seems to be improving."

"Well, the seas don't seem to be improving, so I doubt their sickness will pass until we have some calm days."

"Is God even listening?"

"You know He is, Mary Elizabeth. You're just tired. When was the last time you slept?"

The candle's glow made Dorothy's brown hair appear almost auburn. She was beautiful and smiling. How did she do it? "It's been awhile. I fall asleep, but then either the smell gets to me or I hear someone retching and know they probably need my help. Then I think of William and can't go back to sleep. I hate it that he's suffering so. Father isn't doing well, either. David has been such a big help taking care of him, but I can tell he's wearing out. And I don't want *him* to get sick again. He's too thin as it is."

"Why don't we pray together?" Dorothy squeezed her hands and bowed her head. "Our Father, we come to You now with heavy hearts. We are tired. Many are sick. And we don't know what to do other than come to You. In the prophet Isaiah's book we know that '...But they that wait upon the Lord, shall renew their strength: they shall lift up the wings, as the eagles: they shall run, & not be weary, & they shall walk and not faint.' Help us to wait upon You, Lord. Please renew our strength. In Jesus' name we pray, amen."

Mary Elizabeth felt stronger, but she couldn't think about herself right now. "Lord, my heart is heavy for William Lytton. Please comfort him in his sleep and bring him peace. And Father God, please help my father grow stronger—along with all the other people suffering from illness. In Jesus' name we pray, amen."

"Amen." Dorothy released her hands and sat back on her heels.

"Well, well, well, if it ain't the little saintly women praying again." The twisted voice boomed outside the Raynsfords' quarters.

Dorothy's expression clouded over. "That man!" Standing up as much as she could, she grabbed her candle and swept out of the area to confront him. "You should be ashamed of yourself. Coming down here to taunt the sick like you do," she yelled at her assailant.

Mary Elizabeth followed Dorothy. The filthy young sailor had taken it upon himself to torment the sick passengers as often as he could. As long as Master Jones wasn't around. And since so many were sick, the profane man came down way too often. "You aren't welcome down here. I've a mind to go speak to Master Jones about you and the filthy words you speak."

Dorothy turned to face her, eyebrows raised.

While speaking up in courage wasn't normally something Mary Elizabeth would do, she shrugged. Maybe she was made of sterner stuff than she thought.

"You're not allowed top deck, *miss*." The man sneered, showing off his dirty teeth.

"And I'm certain you're not allowed to harass the passengers of the ship on which you were hired!" Dorothy's voice edged on a shriek.

Mary Elizabeth moved forward and tucked Dorothy behind her.

"You need to leave now. Or I will speak to Mr. Coppin or Master Jones or whomever I need to speak to about your despicable and insidious behavior."

The man growled. "We shouldn't even be taking this trip. It's far too late in the season. Maybe we just need to throw all of ya overboard like Jonah since you seem to love your stories from the Bible so much." Another sneer and then he started laughing. "Let's just see if your God saves you then." He stepped closer.

Mary Elizabeth bristled. "I warned you." Stepping around the man, she held her lantern as high as the ceiling would allow.

The man grabbed her arm. "You'll do no such thing, missy." He flung her down to the floor, spit at her feet, and stomped toward the companionway.

"Foul man." Dorothy leaned over Mary Elizabeth as the man disappeared. "You all right? That was quite brave of you."

Mary Elizabeth shook her head and laughed. "I don't know where that came from. Truly. And I'm fine." She gave Dorothy a look. "I had to do *something*—you looked like you were about to murder him."

"Well. . .maybe not murder. . . But I wish I could clean up the man's mouth. I've never heard anything but profanity and insults exit it."

"There's not enough soap in the world to clean up that young man." Mary Elizabeth stood up and wiped off her skirt.

Dorothy laughed until tears streamed down her face. "I just envisioned you trying to wash the man's mouth out with soap."

Mary Elizabeth hugged her friend and joined in the laughter. "That would be a sight to see, I'm sure. But I think someone is going to have to talk to Master Jones about him."

"You're probably right. But only a few of us aren't sick, and I don't think the ship master or his mate would be too happy if we tried to go on deck while the seas are so tumultuous. Besides, I think he realized you were serious. Maybe he won't be as bad from now on?"

A nod was all she could muster. After their little confrontation, Mary Elizabeth thought she might wilt right there on the spot.

Dorothy took Mary Elizabeth's hands. "Why don't you go take a nap, Mary Elizabeth? I think you'll feel better."

A nap sounded heavenly. "All right. As soon as I check on William."

"William?" A sweet sound broke through the fog of sleep. "William? How are you feeling?" The voice was the most beautiful thing in the world to him.

The sound pulled him out of the dark recesses of his mind. "Hmm?" It came out more of a moan.

"It's me. . .Mary Elizabeth. Mary Elizabeth Chapman. I'm here to check on you and see how you are doing." The soft words washed over him and brought him awake.

As he blinked his eyes several times, the blurry image in front of him transformed. Mary Elizabeth. With a soft halo of light around her linen cap. She was a beautiful sight. "M–Mary Elizabeth." His throat was so dry.

"Here, let me get you something to drink." She left his side and after a few moments reappeared with a small cup. "The only thing we have is beer right now. The fresh water barrels are empty, but this will at least help ease the parch."

He lifted his head with her assistance and took a sip. "Thank you, Mary Elizabeth. It's so kind of you to check on me."

"I've been worried about you. You had a fever for a long while." It was dark, but not enough to cover the flush that crept into her cheeks.

"What day is it?"

"The sixth of October."

Another swell lifted the ship and dropped it again. He never wanted to take another trip like this. Leave the ocean-crossing to others. "I've been sick a long time, then?"

"You don't remember anything?"

"Here and there. . .a little. But not much."

She sighed. "It's probably for the best. You've had a tough time."

"How many others are sick?"

This time she ducked her head. When she lifted it, tears shimmered at the corners of her eyes. "Almost everyone—that is, of the passengers."

He nodded. Their situation was graver than he'd ever imagined. "And you haven't. . . I mean, that is. . . You are well?"

A tiny smile lifted the corners of her lips. "I am well. Thank you for asking."

"Are you taking care of everyone all by yourself?"

Her smile grew. "No. Dorothy and David are helping. A few others aren't ill, but they are weak from lack of sleep taking care of their families and friends."

He lifted his hand from his side and took hold of hers. "Thank you, Mary Elizabeth." A feeling—foreign to him—shot up his arm and into his chest and spread throughout his whole body.

Her cheeks were crimson now, but instead of ducking her head—this time—she stared into his eyes. "You are most welcome. . . William." She gave him another smile. "I best see to the others." Gathering her skirt, she stood up from her kneeling position.

"Will you come back?" What he wouldn't give for her to stay with him all day.

Her face became radiant with a broad smile. "Of course. . . I've been here every day."

He watched her go and felt his heart swell. She'd come to take care of him. Every day. The thought thrilled him.

CHAPTER 10

Tuesday, 10 October 1620

The rocking of the ship increased as another storm hit their ship. Mary Elizabeth looked up to the ceiling over her head. *Lord, we need help.*

Not only was she worried about all the sick, but she'd overheard the shouts from above. Could they survive this journey? It only seemed to be getting worse.

Stumbling through the gun deck, Mary Elizabeth worked to keep her balance. Buckets—used as chamber pots—littered the entire area of the ship. Along with prostrate bodies—they posed great obstacles when it was hard enough to walk in a straight line without falling down. She wiped the sweat from her brow and knelt beside tiny Mary More. The four-year-old hadn't kept anything down for more than a week, and it had begun to worry Mary Elizabeth. The connection she felt to the wee girl wasn't just that they shared a Christian name; it was the child's sweet face—her innocence—that grabbed Mary Elizabeth Chapman's heart. Even though there was gossip about the More children traveling without parents, Father had kept the truth to himself, and Mary Elizabeth couldn't help but feel sorry for the little things.

"How is she doing?" Dorothy knelt beside her.

"She's so small. I don't know if she's going to make it." The sting of tears pricked her eyes. Did anyone care about these precious children? "Dorothy, do you know the story? About the More siblings?"

Her friend ducked her head. "Sadly, yes."

"Father wouldn't tell me when we first set out." She stroked little Mary's head. "Would you?"

Dorothy sighed and sat on her heels. "Samuel More of Shropshire paid for their passage." She fiddled with a string at the cuff of her dress. "The gossip has produced some outlandish stories, but Mr. Brewster told us the truth when he took in Richard—Mary's older brother. Apparently, Katherine—the children's mother—was unfaithful to Samuel, citing their unhappy, arranged marriage. Over time, Mr. More discovered his children's likeness to another man. He divorced Katherine."

Mary Elizabeth gasped. "Divorced? Truly?" These things were simply not done. Didn't God hate divorce?

"Yes. He also retained custody of the four children—who didn't appear to be his."

"Goodness." She laid a hand over her heart. "Now I understand why Father wouldn't speak of it."

"Samuel sent them off with us—'honest and religious' folks—so they wouldn't have the stigma of their illegitimacy following them. But alas, the gossip has made it difficult."

"The poor children." Mary Elizabeth shook her head. "Can you imagine what they've been through?"

"Their family was prominent and quite wealthy. I imagine having nothing and being sent to a new home is quite difficult."

The tears let loose. "Dorothy, don't you understand? These children have no understanding of money yet. The oldest is barely eight years old. That's David's age!" She sucked in her breath. "They've been ripped from their mother's arms. . .and the only father they ever knew. And now they will never see them again. This ordeal will most likely scar them for the rest of their lives."

Dorothy leaned over and covered her hand that was still on top of the child's head. "I'm sorry, Mary Elizabeth. I didn't mean to sound so callous. The life of the wealthy is just beyond my comprehension." She turned her face away. "The gossip has portrayed them as hedonistic and unruly because of their. . .um. . .heritage."

"And the gossip has stained your view?" Mary Elizabeth huffed. "No wonder Father wouldn't allow talk of the children. I can't believe our own people have judged these poor souls so grievously!"

She stood to do—*what* she was uncertain. Never had she been someone to lose her temper over arguments—but the children! Would they be tainted because of their mother's infidelity for the rest of their lives? She loosened the strings to her shift at her neck. What she wouldn't give for some fresh air right now.

Dorothy stood as well and grabbed Mary Elizabeth's shoulders, and they both nearly fell over with the horrendous rocking of the ship. "Mary Elizabeth, I am so sorry. You're right. We've been wrong to look down upon the children. And we've been wrong to listen to the gossip. I know many of the elders are wanting to use it as an example to teach us to remain pure and faithful, but I don't have any right to think less of the Mores."

Mary Elizabeth nodded. Their faith was of utmost importance. The Bible spoke strongly of judging others. But the Separatists wished to remove themselves from worldly behavior—and the attitude of judgment seemed prevalent. This was the first time she'd ever realized it. Was there some way to find a balance? To protect the innocent in all this?

Dorothy knelt back down by the child. Her shoulders slumped. "The poor dear didn't ask for this. . ."

"No, she didn't. They all deserve our love and encouragement. Not our hesitation and scorn. If they are to come to understand almighty God, they need to see us shining His love to all. No matter their background."

Her friend nodded and bit her lip. "Please forgive me, Mary Elizabeth. I will see whatever I can do to help them. The Brewsters have taken in Richard and Mary, the Carvers—Jasper, and the Winslows have the eldest—Ellen. Maybe over time we can help them overcome the difficulty."

Mary Elizabeth felt spent. The realization that so many people looked down on the More children hurt her heart. To think that

Dorothy was one of them made it worse. "I think I will go check on William now. Will you stay with little Mary for a while longer?"

"Of course." Dorothy's words were hushed.

As she staggered her way through the maze, Mary Elizabeth thought through the past few weeks. She'd prayed for courage before this drastic change in her own life, and God had granted it. But not in the way she expected.

She *was* stronger now. Amazing how life had a way of bringing out hidden traits. She shook her head as she thought of her discussion with Dorothy. Never in her life had she stood up for anyone else. In fact, she used to be the quiet and meek one while Dorothy was the bubbly and outspoken one.

Maybe leaving Leyden had changed Mary Elizabeth.

Most extraordinary to her was that while most everyone else was sick and weak, she had been healthy and strong. Without thought, she'd jumped in to take care of first David and then Father. Now she was one of the caregivers of close to one hundred people.

Before Mother's death, she'd thought of herself as frail and insignificant.

Now, months after leaving her home, she realized she was a different person.

As she reached the front of the ship where William shared a small space with Mr. Alden, the boat lifted up on another giant wave. Sea water seeped in through the gun ports as the bow smashed back down. When she sat down beside him, she found William's blankets were wet.

"William?" Mary Elizabeth used her fingers to lift his hair from his forehead. "Can you hear me?"

"Aye." He licked his cracked lips as he blinked his eyes open. "It's good to see you."

His words made her happy—even in the midst of the stench and the storm. "Let me help you drink."

"Thank you." He lifted his head without too much assistance. "I'm feeling a bit better today."

"Thank the Lord! I've been very worried about you, and John has checked on you often, but he looks a bit green himself."

"Is John all right? I haven't seen him in what seems like weeks."

Mary Elizabeth wiped his brow and braced herself as the ship rolled again. "I think so. He looks a bit peaked, but he's had to constantly work on the barrels with all these storms."

William sighed and closed his eyes for a moment.

Mary Elizabeth thought he might be going to sleep.

Then he opened them, and the blue brilliance reached into her heart. "Why don't you tell me about your day so far? I need something to keep my mind off the misery around me."

"Of course. . ." She clasped her hands and laid them in her lap. "Well, the sailor that I told you about?"

"The one who taunts everyone and says he hopes to throw us all overboard?"

A moan erupted from her mouth. "Yes. That's the one." She rolled her eyes. "He came back down here this morning and started in on us all—that it's all our fault these storms are so horrendous—that God must be punishing us for our stupidity."

"He's an insolent fool, isn't he?"

"I heard Mr. Bradford praying for the sailor this morning, and he used those exact same words." She smiled.

"Mr. Bradford is an intelligent man—and a much better man than myself since he's praying for the ruffian." William smiled up at her. "How about the other passengers? Is everyone still sick?"

"For the most part, they have all gotten worse as the storms have tossed us about."

"I was afraid of that. But I'm thankful that I'm beginning to feel slightly better. I just can't move too fast—that brings the sickness back on." He scrunched up his face in displeasure. "How's your father? And David?"

It warmed Mary Elizabeth's heart that even though he'd been seriously ill himself, William asked about her family. "Father is still very ill, but David is doing fine. He's been a big help hauling buckets and anything else we need. He seems to grow stronger every day."

William's hand reached out to cover hers. "Just like you, Mary Elizabeth. You appear stronger in spirit and joy every time I see you." He smiled and paused. "And in beauty too."

She felt the heat rise to her face. Never had she been paid a compliment from a young man. It made her heart flutter. The feelings she felt for William were unlike anything she'd ever known.

She'd always assumed that Father would arrange a marriage for her to someone within their congregation and over time she'd grow to love whomever God had set before her. But now she wasn't sure she could settle for such an arrangement. Not when she'd had a glimpse at what attraction could make her feel. Was that wrong?

"Mary Elizabeth?" William searched her gaze. "I'm sorry. I didn't wish to offend."

She blinked. "You didn't offend me. I thank you for the compliment."

"You deserve it, Mary Elizabeth. And so much more. I. . .I—"

The ship lurched to the right and Mary Elizabeth fell onto her side, her shoulder slamming into the hard, wooden floor.

"Are you all right?"

"I'm fine." The cries of children filled the air. "But I better go check on David and the younger ones." She hated to leave William. Every time she did, she longed for more time with him. And she yearned to share with him about the God who gave her hope. "But I will be back later."

"I look forward to it."

CHAPTER 11

Thursday, 12 October 1620

"One more step." John helped steady William up the companionway to the main deck.

This was the second day of calmer seas, and William couldn't wait to breathe in the fresh air. Weakened by the fever and seasickness that had claimed him the past weeks, he hoped that the worst was past.

On the deck, John released him and walked toward the bulwark. "The wind seems to be at our backs again."

William looked up at the sails—full and taut in the wind. "And the air smells clean." He couldn't help but close his eyes as he inhaled.

His friend laughed and clapped him on the back. "Aye. Which is much better than below. That reminds me, I promised to help Miss Chapman and Miss Raynsford open all the gun ports and hatches. They wanted to air out the living quarters while the weather was nice." John turned and then shot over his shoulder, "You'll be all right for a bit?"

"Yes. I believe I'll be fine."

John's footsteps echoed behind as William looked out to the sea. The great gulf before him stretched as far as the eye could see. Beyond it—somewhere—a new land awaited. Behind them was all civilization as he knew it.

Had he made the right decision? Venturing into the great unknown? In London, he'd had regular work and customers who'd come to respect him.

But there was always the past—lingering around every corner.

And William wanted to forget the past. At least the part before meeting Paul.

Now he was ready for the future. As soon as he thought about building a new life in the new colony, Mary Elizabeth's face appeared in his mind. He didn't know her very well, but his heart hoped his future included her.

The sickness had kept him unaware most of the time, but he remembered hearing her voice, quoting scripture to him as he lay feverish and weak. Something about the Lord being a shepherd.

John had been discussing the Bible with him, but William's opinions had been so long shaped by his unwillingness to see God as a loving Father. Paul—his mentor and only friend—had shown him love and grace for several years. Never pushing for William to see things his way. Just quietly living out his faith. But time and again, William found any excuse he could to keep a wall up between him and God.

On days like today, William wished more than anything that he could sit down with Paul one last time and ask all his questions. But it was too late. By the time he'd been willing to soften his heart and listen, Paul was dead.

William had thought his life might be coming to an end many times in the last few weeks. Was he ready to meet his Maker?

He shook his head. No. He wasn't. But he didn't know how to move forward from here.

God, if You're truly a loving Father and up there listening to me, could You show me how to learn more about You?

Mary Elizabeth's voice floated over to him. He turned and saw her assisting an older gentleman to the bulwark where William stood.

"Good morning, Miss Chapman." He bowed slightly.

"Good morning, Mr. Lytton." She helped the man until his hands were safely on the boards. "Have you met Mr. Brewster? He's the head of our congregation for the new colony."

William smiled. "I believe we've met, yes."

Mr. Brewster looked him over. "Ah, yes. The carpenter. It's good to see someone else up and about."

"I agree, sir."

"Are you feeling strong enough to stand here by yourself while I go help someone else?" Mary Elizabeth laid a hand on the man's arm.

"Yes." Brewster smiled. "I've got Mr. Lytton here to help me if need be."

"Well then, I shall return in a few moments."

"Thank you, Mary Elizabeth." The older gentleman nodded.

William watched the man close his eyes and take in the fresh air just as he had.

How providential that after he'd prayed, this man had appeared. But where did he start?

"I fear many will be too sick to walk up here, but it's divine, is it not?" Brewster looked out at the sea.

"My thoughts are the same, sir." William glanced down at his feet. The time couldn't get better than this. Sucking in a deep breath, he ventured forth. "Mr. Brewster, I was wondering if I could impose on you. . ."

"Of course. Go on."

"I'd like to expand my knowledge of the Bible—and of your faith as well. Might I be able to persuade you to teach me?" There. He'd said it.

The older man's face transformed with his smile. "I'd be honored, young man. Before the seas sought to shake us out of this ship, I was teaching a younger group through the Gospels. Would that interest you?"

"More than I can say, sir. Thank you."

Peter barely had the strength to stand, but he'd made his way to the main deck with Miss Raynsford's help so he could spy on William Lytton.

What didn't make sense was that the man stood talking to one of those Saints. Their leader, too.

What game was he playing?

Was this how he would gain information? By infiltrating their ranks?

As far as Peter knew, the Saints were wary about accepting any of the Strangers. So what was Lytton up to?

The seasickness had been miserable and had slowed down his plan. So far, he hadn't found anything that could help him, but there was still time.

The ship rocked under a swell and it made his stomach lurch. Maybe all this fresh air wasn't so great of an idea.

David watched several sailors climb the masts and rig the sails. What it must be like to be so high in the air! They swung on the great masts and worked with the ropes and sails in a swift manner. Master Jones ordered commands, and the men complied.

The ship's space had begun to feel confining. There were so many people on board and not enough room. All the other children were sick, and it made David feel more grown-up. He'd been able to help take care of people. But what he wouldn't give right now to play a game or run around. Straightening his shoulders, he realized his thoughts were childish. Mary Elizabeth sent him top deck to take care of the animals. He'd best get to it.

As he collected the eggs from the hens, the ship's surgeon—Mr. Giles Heale—passed by him looking quite grim. David followed to the crate closest to the aft castle and listened in as the man reached the ship master.

"Dead?" Jones frowned. "That was quick."

"It was a grievous disease, sir." Mr. Heale said something else under his breath.

Jones looked to the westward sky. "The body will need to be disposed of immediately. More storms are on the horizon." With a nod, the master of the ship retreated up to the poop deck.

Someone died? David wondered who. And what had the surgeon said to Mr. Jones?

Mr. Heale walked toward the forecastle of the ship, where the crew took turns sleeping.

David once again followed. "Mr. Heale?"

The man turned and raised his brows. "Yes?"

"Who died, sir?"

"Ah, so you heard that, did you? It was a member of the crew."

Relief poured through him. Then he felt guilty. What if the man didn't know God? "Will there be a service for him, sir?"

"It's unlikely, son. Master Jones is worried about new storms coming in. But the crew will assemble on deck for the burial."

"Burial, sir?"

"As a seaman, it's only fitting that he be buried at sea." The surgeon turned.

"But sir, if others die, will they be buried at sea as well?"

The man slowly turned back and crouched down in front of him. "Yes, lad. It's the only thing we can do while we are in the middle of the ocean."

David nodded. He didn't like that idea at all.

The surgeon left, and David went back to gathering the eggs.

The thought of dying on the ship made him shiver.

Shuffling behind him caught his attention. Two sailors carried a blanket-wrapped, man-shaped bundle. The rest of the crew followed behind. When they reached the bulwark on the larboard side of the ship, someone said something David couldn't understand, Mr. Jones nodded, and then the two sailors heaved the body over the edge.

The water splashed.

The men dispersed.

David ran over to the side and peered down. Nothing but a large white circle of bubbles as the ship sailed past. He imagined what it must be like in the depths of the sea. Dark, and full of large fish and creatures. Another shiver raced up his spine.

"We all cursed, we be."

David turned at the words and watched two of the crew climb the main mast.

"Lefty shouldn't've cursed and tormented 'em. Their God has done cursed us now."

As the men climbed higher, their words floated in and out. Is that what people thought? That God cursed them if they upset Him in some way? The conversation made David want to speak to Father about it, but he'd been so sick. Maybe Mary Elizabeth could help him understand. But what would she say when she found out the sailor who'd thrown her to the ground had died?

Master Jones stomped down the deck and rushed to the forecastle. "Son, you need to get back down below. Tell them to shut all the gun ports and hatches."

"Yes, sir." David wrapped the eggs in his shirt and ran toward the companionway. The wind whipped at his hair. What had been a beautiful day was now turning dark and gray as they headed farther into the west.

"Storm's a'comin'!" Master Jones's deep voice carried a fearsome undertone.

David hopped down the steps as a drop of rain splattered on his forehead. The people hadn't had enough time to recover from the last bout of seasickness and another storm likely meant days of rolling and crashing on the waves. Would they be able to survive this again? He looked around the dark gun deck and spotted his sister. "Mary Elizabeth! Close the gun ports! Hurry, there's another storm."

CHAPTER 12

Monday, 16 October 1620

Mary Elizabeth knelt beside Elizabeth Hopkins. The squirming baby in her arms let out a squawk. As her heart cinched with longing to have a family of her own, she handed the brand-new baby boy to his mother. "Oceanus is a very fitting name."

The ship continued to roll and quake in the constant storms they seemed to face. The fact that this woman had bravely given birth in the midst of it dumbfounded Mary Elizabeth. Not that the poor woman had much choice in the matter.

"Thank you." Mrs. Hopkins laid back. "I believe I will rest a while longer. Thank you again for all you've done, Mary Elizabeth."

"I'll be back to check on you later." Mary Elizabeth inched her way to the next set of quarters. With so many people packed into such a tiny space, it was amazing they weren't all claustrophobic.

If only the calmer seas had lasted longer. The fresh air had been lovely—what little she'd had of it. But at least they'd had a bit of time to air out the deck and clean up a little.

But the poor passengers. The majority of them were still sick. Only a few of the young men seemed to be recovering. The stormy seas made the rest of them worse.

The *Mayflower* creaked in the torment of the wind, and water sprayed down upon the ill who were already miserable.

Mary Elizabeth had been praying for each person she attended, and the days had all run together. But at least she was busy. William appeared a bit stronger each day and helped the small band of caregivers. But since he wasn't sick anymore, Mary Elizabeth didn't have the opportunity to visit with him as much. She'd only seen him twice the past two days and had only been able to give him a smile.

Besides, although Father was still very ill, he probably wouldn't approve of William. Her new friend wasn't part of their congregation—he wasn't one of the Saints. He was a Stranger.

Thoughts of her father made her feel guilty. Had she neglected him to take care of everyone else? She shook her head. She couldn't allow those thoughts to take root. If she only sat by her father's side all this time, so many other people would have suffered—possibly even died.

As she made her way from person to person, Mary Elizabeth saw Elder Brewster speaking to William. They were huddled under the companionway with what appeared to be a Bible. While the sight encouraged and lifted her heart, she wondered what the outcome could be. Was there hope for her to follow her heart?

She'd never allowed herself to even think such a thing.

"Mary Elizabeth?"

Dorothy's voice jolted her. "Hmm?"

"You were staring at Mr. Lytton and Mr. Brewster. Everything all right?"

"Me? Staring?" Mary Elizabeth looked to the men and then back to Dorothy. "I'm sorry. Yes, I'm fine." She'd better change the subject and fast. "I saw the new baby a little while ago. He's so beautiful."

"You don't fool me for a minute, Mary Elizabeth Chapman." Dorothy grinned. "But yes, the baby is beautiful. Don't you just love his name? Oceanus. It sounds so strong and adventuresome."

"From what I've heard, his father has had quite the adventures already."

"Like father, like son, I suppose." Dorothy shrugged her shoulders. "Well, I need to get David to haul some more buckets for me. You know, when we finally reach dry land, I don't know if my legs will remember how to walk on steady ground."

"Mine either." Mary Elizabeth hugged her friend and headed toward the stern.

When she reached their meager quarters, Mary Elizabeth peeked at Father through the curtain. His complexion was still a pale gray, and he hadn't eaten anything in days. The man who'd always been so strong and capable was now lifeless and weak. She knelt by his side and tried to get a few sips down his throat. "Father?"

No response.

He hadn't spoken to her for several days. She didn't know what to do. Didn't know what to pray anymore. "Lord. . ." Words failed to come.

"When you don't know what to pray, Mary Elizabeth, pray the words Jesus taught us. . .pray scripture." Mother's words floated over her, and a single tear slipped down her cheek. Mary Elizabeth sat beside her father and closed her eyes.

"Our father which art in heaven, hallowed be thy Name. Thy kingdom come. Thy will be done even in earth, as it is in heaven. Give us this day our daily bread. And forgive us our debts, as we also forgive our debtors. And lead us not into tentation, but deliver us from evil: for thine is the kingdom, and the power, and the glory for ever, Amen."

When she opened her eyes, Father was staring at her. "Father?"

"I'm here, child. . . . Th. . .thank you for praying." As his breath washed over her, Mary Elizabeth couldn't help but worry. The putrid smell was what the ship's surgeon, Mr. Heale, called the beginnings of scurvy.

"Father?"

He closed his eyes again, and his deep, steady breathing told her that he was once again asleep.

Mary Elizabeth couldn't be thankful enough for the chance to hear her father's voice. But the concern of scurvy was now firmly implanted in her mind. Her father wasn't the first case. And that was what scared her most. What chance of survival did they have? She tucked the blanket around him tighter and stood up. Oh, to be able to see him walk around again. *Lord, please let it be so.*

"Mary Elizabeth! Come quick!" David called to her.

She slipped through the curtain as fast as she could and found David, Dorothy, and William hunkered down over a sopping wet form near the companionway. "What happened?"

"It's John Howland." William looked at her. "We need a warm blanket."

She ran to John's little area and grabbed the blanket off his make-shift bed. When she brought it back, he was upright and sputtering. Handing the blanket to William, she knelt down with the rest of them. "John, are you all right?"

A huge smile lit his face as he shivered. "Heavens, I'm thankful to be alive! But let's not do that again."

"What happened?" This time it was William who asked the question.

"As we lay at hull, I thought that perchance the storm had calmed. . .and I was desperate for some fresh air."

Dorothy gasped and covered her mouth.

Mary Elizabeth couldn't believe it. "You went out there? On purpose?"

"Aye." John nodded, his teeth chattering. "As soon as I was top deck, I knew the storm was indeed fierce. . .and the captain had rigged the ship just so to keep her upright." He pulled the blanket tighter around him. "Before I knew it, a huge wave blasted me, and I went sailing overboard. The ship almost turned on her side, and I was able to grab hold of the topsail halyards."

William's eyebrows shot up. "Unbelievable, man! Go on."

"I held on as tight as I could, but the sea took me way down into its depths and I was afraid I was done for until the sailors pulled me up by the rope and then grabbed me with a boat hook. After they saved me, Mr. Coppin tossed me down the steps and told me not to go on deck again during a storm." John's laugh turned into a scratchy cough. "I'll say it again—I'm thankful to be alive."

Mary Elizabeth shook her head. "Let's get you to your bed, Mr.

Howland. You've got to get warmed up and dry."

Dorothy smiled. "Why don't you let David and me help him, Mary Elizabeth?" She helped the man to his feet, and David took a spot under John's arm. "I'm sure we will need something for Mr. Howland to drink and eat."

William caught Mary Elizabeth's elbow as she turned. "How can I help?"

"Could you get a ration for John to eat?"

The look on his face showed disappointment.

Just like she felt. If only the circumstances were different and they could spend time together.

"Certainly." His nod made her heart ache.

Reaching out, she grabbed his hand. "Thank you, William."

William worked to keep steady as the ship thrashed about. There was so much to record in his journal. While seasickness had laid most of the passengers ill, the signs of scurvy had begun to set in on some of the sickest passengers. Mr. Heale had warned them all, but what could they do? Everything was rationed daily, even though many complaints were heard. A lot of people feared they would die anyway, so why couldn't they have more food?

William knew what it felt like to retch after each tiny meal and then feel half-starved to death. With no land in sight and no end to the tumultuous seas, he feared people would start to revolt. If they found the energy to move.

The Saints made it clear at the beginning of the voyage that they wanted the rest of the ship to follow their rules and religious practices. The Strangers didn't want much to do with the Separatists and their strict rules, so the trip hadn't started off in a congenial manner. Then came that awful sailor and his insults. When the seas turned on them all, as well, the storms came one after another. Then came the sickness. Between that and the stench, they'd all just about gone mad.

He stopped writing and held the quill above the page. What could he report truthfully? How could he honor this job for Mr. Crawford and the other investors? Right now, the outcome of the *Mayflower's* voyage appeared grim. But William had come to care for their small band of travelers—these colonists who all shared a common goal. There had to be a way to gain a positive result.

The more he thought about the quandary, the more his heart felt heavy. It wasn't just the storms, the horrendous seas, or even their great delay—a greater problem existed.

The rift between the people on board. Saints and Strangers.

The thing was, William was a Stranger. Yet he found himself drawn increasingly to the ways and beliefs of the Separatists. His time with Elder Brewster had made him question his thoughts of God and examine his previous doubts. The valiant sacrifice each of these people made to stay true to their beliefs was beyond question.

To sum it all up? At the root of it all was the faithfulness to scripture.

That's how Paul had believed. For years, he'd tried to convey the same thing to William.

The chance to meet with Mr. Brewster had been enlightening, but how could he ease the misery of the fellow passengers when they didn't even trust one another?

The problem seemed too difficult to solve by himself.

Crack!

The sound was of wood splintering. And not just any wood. It had to be some large beam. The ship shifted hard to the right and William lost his balance. Righting himself, he grabbed the journal and tucked it back into the trunk and locked it.

As he ran up to the main deck, William spotted Master Jones at the main mast. A giant crack ran down the post into the deck of the ship.

"Get me the carpenter!" Jones yelled into the wind. Sailors ran in every direction.

Rain splattered William's face and dripped down his chin. "Sir! Might I be of assistance? I'm a carpenter."

"Aye. I remember you, Lytton. We will need every hand and mind that can help." The master waved his hand. "Follow me."

William walked with several of the crew into the steerage room that housed the whipstaff. The tiny room couldn't hold many, but at least they were out of the rain and wind and would be able to hear each other.

Master Jones cleared his throat and held a hand up in the air. "Men, we need to determine the extent of the damage down into the ship from the crack that is in the main mast, and then we need to know how to fix it. We're already too far into the voyage to turn back, if we could even make it. We are low on supplies and rations and too many are sick."

"Sir." John Clarke—the ship's pilot—spoke up. "The crack goes down into the gun deck, but not into the cargo hold. It's created a good-sized leak."

"Can we stop the leak?" Jones stood with his hands behind his back.

"If we can fix the crack." Clarke nodded.

"How is she under water?" The master looked to Coppin.

"She's holding firm, sir."

"Good."

The faces around William showed fear, uncertainty, and questions. Even the master of the ship seemed concerned with their great problem. But what were they to do? Then it hit him. "Master Jones?"

"Yes, Mr. Lytton."

"I recall seeing a great house jack being loaded onto the ship."

"House jack?"

"Yes, sir. It's like a great iron screw to help raise up beams and such when building houses."

The master's eyebrows raised. "Go on."

"If we were to use it to raise the beam into place, we could secure the mast with another post." William could see it in his mind but wasn't sure the captain of their ship would understand. After all, he was a skilled carpenter on land. Not at sea.

The ship's carpenter and John Alden joined them in the steerage room. "What needs to be done?" John's voice was always one of action.

Jones nodded to his carpenter. "Mr. Lytton here thinks that if we use the machinery he called a house jack, we could hoist the beam into position and brace it. Do you think it can be done?"

The smaller man nodded and drops of water splashed around him. "Aye, sir."

"Then you two get to work on the plan. The rest of the men will do whatever needs to be done to help. Once the mast is repaired, I'll need the carpenters to caulk everything they can and stop the leaking."

William followed the ship's carpenter out of the room. "Do you think it will work?"

"We better pray for a miracle, because if it *doesn't* work, we'll all be on the bottom of the sea by morning."

The *Mayflower* groaned and creaked with each plunge into the swells. William had lost count of how many times he'd been thrown to the deck by the crashing waves. But they had to fix the main mast, or all their hopes were lost.

John Alden worked next to him as they cranked the house jack to lift the beam back into position.

Master Jones yelled above the raging storm, "We need more hands on those supports!"

It didn't help that with every wave another man fell down. If they could keep everyone upright at the same time, they might make some progress.

"Lord, we could use some divine assistance." John's voice as he prayed and worked next to William had lost its usual confidence.

Dripping wet and weary from their efforts, the men stayed at it. No one wanted to go down with a ship.

"Heave!" Coppin yelled. "Just a few more inches."

Grunts and moans echoed around him as they worked to correct the beam. The house jack was working. Now if they could just get it back together and secure the supports in place.

Thunk! The beam snapped back into place.

"Secure the supports!" Master Jones eyed the men from his perch atop the poop deck.

Water sprayed over William's shoulder as another large wave shook the boat and rolled it larboard.

William held his support in place as John secured it.

"Get those women below deck *now*!" Jones sounded angry.

Women? What women? Looking over his shoulder while he held the support, William spotted Dorothy's and Mary Elizabeth's heads peeking out the opening of the companionway. Worry etched their faces as rain pelted them from above. He shook his head. Why weren't they going below?

The *Mayflower* rocked hard to steerboard, and William's feet flew out from under him. Water rushed over his head and body as he was washed to the bulwark.

Grasping for anything he could get his hands on, William felt panic rise up in his throat. It couldn't end this way. He wasn't ready.

"Help!" The cry was drowned by water filling his mouth.

But the waves were too strong and too tall, the ship was almost on its side as it heaved up onto another swell. When it came down, he'd be tossed overboard.

Lord, please save the ship and her passengers. . .

William closed his eyes as the seconds stretched, and he tried to grab for a hold. When he opened them, he was tossed upside down and then bounced off the bulwark and over the side.

"*William!*" Mary's scream was filled with anguish, and he could do nothing to comfort her.

This was the end.

Chapter 13

"N o!" Mary Elizabeth choked on the word. Tears blurred her already watery vision. Turning into Dorothy's arms, she wanted to jump into the water and save him. Why William? *Why, Lord?*

This couldn't be happening.

Thunder rumbled above their heads.

She sobbed into her friend's shoulder.

Dorothy gasped. "Mary Elizabeth. Look." Her friend grabbed her shoulders and made her turn.

As the ship shifted and rolled to lean to the other side, John Alden hung over the bulwark at his waist, his legs kicking in the air. Mr. Coppin jumped to grab John's legs and then sat on the deck and pulled.

Could it be?

"I've got him!" John's shout could be heard from the other side of the bulwark.

Mary Elizabeth let out the breath she'd been holding. Was it true?

Several other men went to assist in the efforts, and John was pulled up so only his arms hung over the ship.

He grimaced as they all strained to pull until a booted leg appeared grasped in John's hand. Within seconds, a sputtering William Lytton lay on the deck of the ship. He reached up for John's hand and nodded.

Mary Elizabeth couldn't wait any longer. She climbed up the rest of the steps and half ran, half slipped her way to William. "Are you hurt?"

The smile that stretched across his face melted her heart. He reached up a finger to touch her cheek. "I couldn't be better."

His brilliant blue eyes bore into hers. She wanted to relish his touch on her face for all her days.

"Get below deck. Now!" Master Jones's command was not to be disobeyed.

Nodding, she raced back to the companionway and looked back at William. Oh, how she loved that smile. . .

Mary Elizabeth woke with a start. The stench below deck reminded her that she was no longer watching William be rescued. But he was alive, and she would be forever grateful.

She sat up and scooted next to her father. When she touched his brow, it felt warm. But as she was still chilled from her adventure top deck, Mary Elizabeth couldn't gauge if he was *too* warm. One thing was certain—he'd gotten weaker and slept almost around the clock. What could she do for him?

As the waves continued to toss the *Mayflower* about and thunder cracked and sounded like cannons above them, Mary Elizabeth prayed. For Father's health. For the men working on the main mast. Were they done? For William and John. For the seas to calm and for the leaks to be stopped. And most fervently—that their journey would be over soon.

They all desperately needed to see land. To smell fresh air, and to be dry and warm. No water seeping in through the gun ports. No dark and smelly confined quarters.

After this journey, she would never complain about her circumstances ever again. She would be joyful and praise the Lord.

Father's favorite song from the psalter they used in church back home came to mind. As she sang softly to her father, the words ministered to her own burdened heart:

All people that on earth do dwell,
Sing to the Lord with cheerful voice.
Him serve with fear, His praise forth tell;

Come ye before Him and rejoice.

The Lord, ye know, is God indeed;
Without our aid He did us make,
We are His flock, He doth us feed,
And for His sheep He doth us take.

O enter then His gates with praise;
Approach with joy His courts unto;
Praise, laud, and bless His Name always,
For it is seemly so to do.

For why? The Lord our God is good;
His mercy is forever sure;
His truth at all times firmly stood,
And shall from age to age endure.

To Father, Son, and Holy Ghost,
The God whom Heaven and earth adore,
From men and from the angel host
Be praise and glory evermore.

The drippy, leaky ship couldn't take away that God's mercy was forever sure. The winds and the rain couldn't deny that His truth would endure. No matter if the mast was fixed or not. Nor if the ship even sank.

God's truth would endure.

The words that the apostle Paul wrote to the church in Philippi came to her, and she said the words aloud. "I speak not because of want: for I have learned in whatsoever state I am, therewith to be content. And I can be abased, & I can abund: every where in all things I am instructed both to be full, & to be hungry, & to abund, & to have want. I am able to *do* all things through the help of Christ, which strengtheneth me."

The depth of the words struck her heart. She could be content in whatever circumstances she faced. . .because she had the help of Christ. What a powerful thought.

Bolstered by the words of scripture and the song, Mary Elizabeth leaned over her father and kissed his forehead. She looked at little David and smiled. Everything would be all right because God was good, and she would rejoice. No matter what happened.

As she stood to go check on the others, Mary Elizabeth realized how much she'd changed over the past few weeks. The tragedy of losing Mother had almost broken her. Or so she thought. But she'd needed to learn how to give it over to God the Father. She needed to know that His strength and peace were always with her. For so long, she'd thought of herself as timid and afraid. Never courageous. But now, somehow, her thinking had changed.

Reaching the companionway, Mary Elizabeth had to slosh through an inch or so of water. As she looked up through the opening to the deck above, rain poured down on her and on the men working so hard on the ship.

William was one.

She crept back up the steps. Just to see his face again. Watching the men, well—if she were honest—watching William, made Mary Elizabeth all too aware of his masculinity. Moving away from the opening, she knew her mind needed guarding above all else. What would Father say if he knew she'd been watching William not out of curiosity or worry, but with appreciation and attraction?

Yet after his harrowing fall and rescue, Mary Elizabeth's heart knew the truth. She cared for him. Far more than she'd admitted to herself.

She shook her head and went to check on Mrs. Hopkins and the new baby. Best to keep her mind on other things. If only Mother were still alive, she could talk to her about the struggle.

Dorothy was holding the baby when Mary Elizabeth reached the Hopkinses' quarters. "Oh, Mary Elizabeth. Isn't he just the most gorgeous baby?"

She nodded. "He is." Kneeling down beside her friend, Mary Elizabeth watched the little fingers move. They were so tiny. What a miracle.

"Would you like to hold him?" Mrs. Hopkins tilted her head and smiled.

Mary Elizabeth loved babies and ached to hold the little guy again. "I'd love to."

Dorothy leaned toward her in slow, gentle movements. As she placed the tiny bundle in Mary Elizabeth's arms, Oceanus opened his eyes and looked up.

"Oh my. . ." Mary Elizabeth breathed.

Little Oceanus studied her face for a moment and then closed his eyes again.

"Mary Elizabeth, you have the touch." Mrs. Hopkins shifted on her bed. The woman grimaced as she moved.

Swaying back and forth with the baby, Mary Elizabeth let the rolling of the ship guide her rhythm. "Are you feeling all right, Mrs. Hopkins?"

"A bit sorer than the last one, but that's to be expected when giving birth in the middle of a storm."

Dorothy stood. "Perhaps some food sounds good?"

The woman sighed. "That sounds lovely, thank you."

"You'll need to build up your strength. Especially after the seasickness." Mary Elizabeth stared down at the wee one as she spoke to his mother. "This little one will need his strength too. He has lots of growing to do." The soft fuzz on top of his head reminded her of velvet.

"Here we are." Dorothy's singsong voice made the baby squirm. "I've got some dried meat and cheese."

"Thank you." Elizabeth Hopkins sighed. "Won't it be nice to cook something different once we reach the new land?"

Mary Elizabeth stifled a laugh. "Yes. I don't even care what we have, as long as it is something different."

"When we first set out"—Dorothy sat back down—"I didn't

know if I could handle any more fish after weeks of it. But now I would love to eat it again."

Mary Elizabeth laughed at her friend's dramatic expression. "I agree. The men haven't been able to fish in these storms, but I'll take fresh fish over dried meat every day."

Mrs. Hopkins nodded as she chewed the dried food.

A new thought struck Mary Elizabeth. "We sound a lot like the Israelites, don't we? The Lord provided manna for them, yet they asked for something else."

The ladies laughed together. And Oceanus woke up with a cry.

"I believe someone is hungry as well." Mrs. Hopkins reached for her son.

"We'll be back to check on you later." Rising up, Mary Elizabeth smiled down. "Dorothy or I will make sure the children are fed."

"Thank you."

As she and Dorothy made their way toward another family, William and another man came down the steps.

"Good day, Mr. Lytton." Dorothy tugged on Mary Elizabeth's arm.

"Good day, ladies." He smiled at Mary Elizabeth.

"I'm so thankful you're safe." Mary Elizabeth couldn't keep the words inside. "I was so worried when I saw you go over."

"Well, I'm a bit bruised from the tumble and soaked through to my bones, but God spared me, and for that, I am grateful." He stared into her eyes.

She stared back, unwilling to break the connection.

Dorothy cleared her throat.

"Yes, well. We have the mast secured, and now we must caulk as much as we can to seal off the leaks." William looked at Dorothy.

"That sounds like a big job." Her friend continued the conversation and poked her elbow into Mary Elizabeth's side.

She stopped staring and looked to her feet. What could she do with these feelings? When William went over the side, she thought her heart would wrench in two. This was all so new, and she didn't understand it. "It is a large task, and we must get to it." The other man with William ducked and headed toward the bow.

William nodded to them. "I'd better get to work, as well." He turned toward the stern.

The thought of the strong, tarry scent of the oakum cords they would need to stuff into the cracks didn't sound appealing. But then again, that smell would be better than the stench of sickness. Dorothy pinched Mary Elizabeth's arm.

"Ow. What was that for?" Mary Elizabeth watched William work his way to the back of the gun deck.

"You were staring. What's going on?" Hands on her hips, Dorothy squinted her eyes.

Mary Elizabeth wasn't sure what to say. "I...well..."

"I noticed the way he smiled at you. Mary Elizabeth, you can talk to me."

"Hush your words, Dorothy. I don't need everyone listening in." Mary Elizabeth grabbed her friend's elbow and walked over to the companionway. They'd get wet, but at least there weren't as many listening ears. She took a deep breath. "I've been thinking about William a lot."

"Aye. And...?"

"I realized a little bit ago that I've been...well..."

"Go on...."

"Appreciative of his looks." There she said it.

Dorothy put a hand to her mouth. When she uncovered it again, a small smile at the corner of her mouth appeared. "Mary Elizabeth, I already guessed that you liked the man. I think it's a bit more than an appreciation for his looks. You nearly clawed your way across the deck when he went over. I think you need to be honest."

Heat rose to her cheeks. Her friend was correct. "It's difficult for me. I don't...well, I haven't felt this way before." What was she trying to say? And what would Dorothy think?

"It's plain to see that you care for him, Mary Elizabeth." Dorothy touched her arm. "And I'm happy for you."

"But don't you understand?" She lowered her voice to the barest of whispers. "I can't be unequally yoked. He's a Stranger. And it's not pure to have such thoughts."

"What kind of thoughts are we talking about?" Dorothy's smile turned into a frown.

"Just that. He's very handsome. And masculine. . .and strong. He's also smart and caring. He appears to be a very good carpenter and a hard worker."

Dorothy released her breath in a big sigh. She put a hand to her chest. "For a moment you scared me. Little, innocent Mary Elizabeth—my mother told me it was fine to find a young man attractive, but we can't allow our minds to"—her voice lowered and she looked around—"*lust* after them."

Mary Elizabeth's heart beat a little faster. While she hadn't allowed her thoughts to go past her admiration of William, she wished her mother were still alive. These were the kinds of things she should be talking of with her. Mary Elizabeth sat on one of the wet steps. "Did your parents speak to you about marriage?"

"Why yes, of course."

"Did they talk to you about arranging a marriage?"

Dorothy nodded.

"But have they ever spoken of love?"

"No." Her friend shook her head. "My parents' marriage was arranged, and they seem very happy."

How could she explain what she was pondering? She sighed. Dorothy had been her dearest friend and confidante. Maybe she'd have some sort of advice. "Before my mother died, she told me that things have been a certain way with marriage for a long time. Marriages were arranged for good matches and for procreation—the continuation of family lines. The world has tainted that by so many husbands and wives being unfaithful—all in the name of love." She bit her lip. "The way mother explained it is that marriage became a duty, and they sought their affection. . .elsewhere."

Dorothy raised her brows.

"I know. I was a little shocked too. But my mother and father were different. She told me that even though their marriage was arranged, she'd asked her parents to arrange it because she was in love with Father. She told me she wanted the same for me, but that I was to seek God first. Marriage was His design in the first place."

"And so, you wish for love in a marriage from the very beginning." A smile lifted Dorothy's lips. She reached over and grabbed Mary Elizabeth's hand. "I've had the same desire. Perhaps every young woman seeks that deep down in her heart."

"I know. But that is why I'm conflicted."

"I'm not sure I understand."

"I find William fascinating. Not to mention, *very* appealing." She sucked in a breath. "But to honor God in marriage, I need to honor my father and our faith and what we stand for. . ." She let the words drop off. What was she trying to say? Her thoughts were like a tangled ball of yarn.

"It sounds to me like you're afraid."

Once again, her friend was right. But she hadn't wanted to admit it. "Yes, I'm afraid. The future is so uncertain. And I want to be a Godly young woman."

"I understand, Mary Elizabeth, I do. You spent a lot of time caring for him while he was sick. Your heart is already attached to him, and you're worried. But have you seen William lately? He's been studying with Elder Brewster. Isn't that encouraging?" She tilted her head. "Don't run away from this because you're frightened. You need to give him a chance."

Chapter 14

Tuesday, 24 October 1620

The seas hadn't given up their fight, and William wondered if they would ever see land again. It seemed each day a new storm appeared to torment them. The crew was worn out. The passengers were worn out.

Their ship was worn out.

While the posts they'd installed against the main mast beam held, the ship had hardly been able to use its sails for days on end.

People sat or lay in misery in the damp, rocking vessel.

The only bright spots to his day were seeing Mary Elizabeth and studying with Mr. Brewster. Mary Elizabeth had been busy taking care of people and feeding them, so he'd only seen her a few times a day in passing. They'd exchange a brief word or a smile—and once he'd been able to hold her hand and assist her down the stairs to the cargo hold below. The warmth that spread up his arm and into his chest again confirmed that what he felt for Mary Elizabeth Chapman was true. But how could he ever deserve her? And would her father ever approve?

Before meeting her, he'd thought all his dreams were to start a new life in Virginia Colony. To be a successful carpenter—a well-respected member of society.

But now it had all changed. He'd begun to seek God.

And he hoped for love.

As he found his way to the Brewsters' quarters, William wondered what it would be like to have a wife and family.

"Ah, William. . . I'm glad you could join us again." The Elder's kind smile welcomed him.

"Thank you, Mr. Brewster."

The older man opened his Bible and looked to the two other men who were strong enough to sit up and join them. "We've been studying in the book of Matthew, chapter five. I'd like to start where we left off, verse eleven."

William moved closer so he could read over the man's shoulder.

"'Blessed shall ye be when men revile you, & persecute you, & say all manner of evil against you for my sake, falsely. Rejoice and be glad, for great is your reward in heaven: for so persecuted they the Prophets which were before you.'" Brewster read and then looked up at the men. "We've had to deal with some of this on the voyage, haven't we? Being reviled and persecuted for our faith."

The others nodded.

William thought of the nasty sailor who had said such awful things to the group of Saints. "Elder Brewster, might I ask a question before you continue?"

"Of course."

"When it says, 'revile you, & persecute you,' did you find it hard to *rejoice* when the sailor came down here and harassed everyone?"

Brewster's brow furrowed. "That's a good question, young man. It's difficult to be persecuted for our faith—especially when people say horrible things, like he looked forward to throwing us all overboard—but Jesus is saying here that yes, we need to rejoice in that. Because we are storing up treasure in heaven, not on earth."

William nodded as another man asked a question. The words hit the depths of his heart. He'd spent the majority of his life being reviled by others. Taunted and teased and ridiculed for being an orphan. This passage of scripture confused him.

"Mr. Lytton." Elder Brewster's voice brought him back to the moment. "If we go back to the beginning of the passage, we see Jesus say, 'Blessed *are* the poore in spirit, for theirs is the kingdom of heaven.'" William looked down to the page where Brewster pointed.

He nodded. He'd always been poor until recent years. That was something he understood all too well. But what did it mean to be poor in spirit?

"I can see you are puzzled." The man didn't mock him or make him feel uncomfortable. He reminded William of Paul. "Let me try to explain. To be 'poor in spirit' means to know the depth of our lacking—to know we are broken and unusable as we are. That we are sinners in need of a Savior and can't possibly attain anything on our own. When we come to that place of understanding and are truly 'poor in spirit,' then we acknowledge Jesus as our Savior—that it is only through His sacrifice that we can be saved—and then we can be cleansed and transformed. Then—oh what a beautiful thought—then the kingdom of heaven is ours. To live eternally with our heavenly Father."

William looked down to his hands. He understood the depth of lacking that Brewster spoke about. His whole life he'd felt empty—like something important was missing. When Paul took him in, that was the first time he'd ever felt any kind of love or belonging. It took a long time for that frightened and hurt boy to love back, but he had. Did Paul know before he died how much William cared? How thankful he was?

His eyes burned with the thoughts. Prayerfully, his friend and mentor knew.

The fact remained that William knew he needed God. The undeniable truth was in front of him, but the process seemed illusive. Was it really so simple as faith?

Monday, 30 October 1620

The small space was getting tiresome. David had done everything he could to help take care of people, but they were all tired of being stuck in a storm on a ship.

Father was sick.

Mary Elizabeth was busy.

She'd been short with him that morning when he asked her to play bowls with him. He'd kept his toys packed up in the trunk all this time. After he'd begged her to play, she scolded him about how she didn't have time and the balls rolling around could make someone trip and hurt themselves. He would never want someone to get hurt.

But he was bored.

It was hard growing up. Trying to be a man. Think like a man. Act like a man. Some days he just wanted to be able to play and be a child.

There was nowhere to run and play on a ship. Not when they had a hundred people crammed into a space smaller than their house in Leyden.

Guilt began to fill his gut. These thoughts weren't fitting for a God-fearing young man. He shouldn't be complaining. Father said that lots of children would love to have the chance that he had. He wasn't old enough to have a share in the Adventurers' and Planters' agreement, but Father said the children under ten years of age would have fifty acres in their name once the debts were paid and the company liquidated.

Land was worth more than anything else in David's mind. He needed to be grateful.

Especially that he wasn't sick like the majority of the people. Although, every time he had to empty a chamber pot, he thought he might get sick.

David decided to go check on each of the other children. There were about thirty of them aboard, but most of them were really sick.

As he made his way through the gun deck, he visited each family and said hello, asked if they needed anything. Not knowing what else to do, he wandered around the deck and looked for things he could help with.

Mary Elizabeth stopped him under the companionway. "I'm sorry, David. I shouldn't have responded to you this morning in such a harsh manner."

Peering down at his shoes, David shrugged. "It's all right, Mary Elizabeth. I knew you were busy."

She took his shoulders in her hands. "I know. But even though the journey has taken its toll on all of us, I shouldn't have spoken to you that way. Papa is still very ill, and this morning I was feeling guilty for leaving him. . .failing him."

"You haven't failed him, Mary Elizabeth. Almost everyone is sick, and you've been needed. Papa sleeps all the time anyway. I know he appreciates all you've done." He reached up and kissed her cheek.

A small smile lifted her lips. She laid a hand on his shoulder. "You've grown into such a sweet young man, David. I'm very proud of you. Would you like to help me bring food to people?"

"Yes, very much." Finally, another job. Something to keep his mind off the confining quarters.

Handing him a small cloth, she tucked some dried meat and dried vegetables inside. "This is for Mr. Fuller and his servant—young William Butten. Will you be able to help them sit up?"

"Yes, Mary Elizabeth. I can do it." He took off to see Mr. Fuller. The man had been a doctor back in Leyden but hadn't been able to help anyone on the ship because he'd suffered from seasickness since they set out to sea.

"Mr. Fuller?" David found the man sitting on his bed, his face pale.

"Aye."

"I've brought you some food. For young William too."

"Thank you, son." He leaned forward. "But I'm worried about the youth. He hasn't moved much the past couple days."

David looked down at the young man. Several years his senior, the boy appeared very ill. "Is there anything else I can do for you, sir?"

"No, thank you." The man sighed. "I wish there was something I could do to help all these people." He wiped a hand down his face.

"I'm sure we will be very appreciative of your assistance once we're in the new settlement, sir."

"If we make it there alive. . ." Mr. Fuller's face fell. "I'm sorry, son." Lying back on his bed, he closed his eyes.

All David's earlier thoughts rushed to his mind. Now he was

ashamed. So many of the people were fighting to stay alive, and he'd been complaining that there was nowhere to play. He could change that.

He'd just have to find a way to put his plan into action.

Chapter 15

Monday, 6 November 1620

Mary Elizabeth's heart thundered in her ears. She couldn't wake Father. For hours he'd been motionless, and she couldn't rouse him.

"Mary Elizabeth, why isn't he waking?" David's voice sounded so small. The poor dear had found Father this way earlier.

She closed her eyes and sent a quick prayer heavenward for wisdom. "I don't know, David. But I need for you to see if Mr. Heale can come down and see him, all right?"

Her little brother flung the curtain aside and took off at a run, leaping over obstacles and buckets.

Lord, please help me to know what to do.

"Father, please, I need you to wake up."

Several moments passed, and then she heard footsteps. Mary Elizabeth turned just in time to see Mr. Heale approach. "Thank you for coming." Pulling back from Father, she gave the surgeon some space. "He's not responding to me."

Giles Heale put his head to Father's chest. "His heart is very slow. How long has he been sick?"

She swallowed the tears building in her throat. "Weeks."

He nodded. "That's what I thought. I brought some smelling salts with me. We can only hope the intense ammonia will make him take a deep breath. Maybe then we can bring him out of this deep sleep."

"Please. Let's try."

The surgeon nodded to her and put the potent concoction under

Father's nose. It took a couple seconds, but then Father inhaled sharply. His eyelids fluttered. "Talk to him, Mary Elizabeth." He stepped back.

"Father, please, wake up."

Her father moaned.

"Please, we need you to wake up."

Mr. Heale stepped forward and tried again.

With a jolt, Father's eyes opened as he took a deep breath. He blinked several times and then locked eyes with her. "Mary Elizabeth?"

Tears streamed down her face. "Oh, Father. I was so worried."

"Miss Chapman?" Mr. Heale summoned her with a finger. "Might I speak with you for a moment?"

"Of course." She grabbed David's hand and pulled him close. "You talk with Father for a bit, all right? See if you can keep him awake."

Her little brother knelt beside their father and Mary Elizabeth exited the curtained off area.

"Thank you, Mr. Heale." She swiped at her face to dry the tears.

He shook his head. "I'm sorry, Mary Elizabeth, but I'm afraid your father is still very ill. Try to keep him awake as long as you can, but his heart is weak, and I'm certain he will fall back into that deep sleep."

"Isn't there anything we can do?"

"Whatever it is that has taken hold has weakened him. Unless we can get him to eat and move about, he won't be able to gain strength—he'll only lose it." The surgeon nodded and bowed slightly. "I'm sorry."

As the man walked away, Mary Elizabeth didn't know what to think of his words. What did it mean? Was he implying that Father would die? She shook her head. No. She was worrying too much.

She stepped back into the curtained off area and saw Father give David a tiny smile. "It's good to see you smile, Father."

"Aye. It's good to see your faces." He lifted his hand a few inches. "Would you get me something to drink, David?"

"Yes, Father." He dashed off.

"Mary Elizabeth, there's something I need to speak with you

about." His voice was raspy and light.

"Yes, Father?"

"I may not make it through this. And I'm at peace with God about it."

"Please, don't talk like that." A tear slipped down her cheek.

"No, child. I need you to listen. I'm tired already, and it takes too much energy to speak."

Mary Elizabeth nodded.

"If something happens to me, promise me that you will look after your brother." A horrible cough wracked her father's frame. "You have a share in the venture...since you are over sixteen, and you will inherit my share. . . . David is too young to receive a share, but he will receive acreage. Mr. Bradford. . .and Mr. Brewster have copies of all the contracts, and I have papers in the trunk." The cough returned, and he closed his eyes.

"No, Father. Please don't go back to sleep. You need something to drink, remember?"

He nodded. "I know I haven't been myself since your Mother died—God rest her soul—but if it's my time, I will gladly go. I just regret not taking the time to. . ." His voice sounded so weak.

"Father, there's nothing to regret." She held his hands.

"No, I neglected you and David in my grief. This trip to the New World gave me something new to think about, but I didn't realize what it did to you. For that, I am sorry."

"Oh, Father. . ."

"More than anything, I hope you know how much I love you."

She nodded as more tears collected at the corners of her eyes. "I love you too." She needed to be strong. David would return at any moment, and she didn't want him to see her falling apart.

"Did I tell you that young Mr. Lytton has come to see me?"

A gasp took her breath away. She leaned back. "Mr. Lytton? When?"

Her father nodded. "A day or so ago, I guess. I don't know. It appears he is quite fascinated with you, my dear. He's come to check on me several times while you were taking care of the others."

She didn't know what to say. What did her father think of the handsome Stranger?

"He's been sharing with me what he's learned in the scriptures. Most of the time, I'm not very good company... I tend to drift in and out..." Father's head bobbed to the right and his eyes shut.

David entered with a cup in his hand.

Mary Elizabeth took it and lifted her father's head. "I need you to drink, so don't go to sleep on me yet."

He moaned but took a few sips.

"Is he all right?" The squeak in David's voice made her want to hug him tight.

She laid her father's head back down. "He wore himself out talking, David. That's all." She didn't have the heart to share what the surgeon had spoken.

"Will he get better?"

"We'll just have to pray and keep helping him, aye?"

David nodded and ducked his head. Standing, he wrapped his small arms around Mary Elizabeth's neck as she knelt beside their father.

Someone cleared their throat.

Mary Elizabeth peered out the curtain and saw William hunched outside. "Oh, William, please come in."

He shook his head. "I'm sorry, Mary Elizabeth, but I think you need to come. It's Dorothy. She's taken ill."

All sound around her diminished as Mary Elizabeth went to see the Raynsfords. They'd swapped places with another family before everyone got sick. Around the gun deck lay the sick, the weak. Very few sat or stood or walked. Taking in the faces, she felt like time had slowed. What would become of them?

She felt William's presence as he walked right behind her, and she wished she had some of his strength.

The entire Raynsford family rested on their makeshift beds. Still. Pale. Silent.

"What has happened? Why are they all sick?" She sobbed into the blanket covering her dearest friend in all the world.

"We don't know. The surgeon was here, but he's just as confused as the rest of us. The seasickness has made many people weak, and now scurvy has set in. But just like that young sailor, there seems to be something else afflicting people."

"No...no...no..." Mary Elizabeth shook her head. Dorothy had been her lifeline. Her steady encourager.

The thoughts made her stop.

That wasn't true. She sniffed and sat up a little. Gazing down at her beloved friend, she realized that through all the loss of Mother, Leyden, and her church family, she'd grown up and learned a lot. It wasn't Mother, or Father, Dorothy, or David who had been her strength—had kept her going. It had been God working in her life through those people.

The words from the eighteenth Psalm flowed over her and exited her lips. " 'The Lord *is* my rock, & my fortress...' " As she spoke, her voice grew stronger... her heart grew stronger. "...& He that delivereth me, my God & my strength: in him will I trust, my shield, the horn also of my salvation, & my refuge.' " God was indeed her strength. She would trust in Him.

New determination filled her heart. She would rejoice in this time of trial because trials made a person stronger. Didn't James say something about that? What was the verse? The words came out in a rushed whisper. " '...Count it exceeding joy, when ye fall into divers tentations, Knowing that the trying of your faith bringeth forth patience. And let patience have her perfect work, that ye may be perfect and entire, lacking nothing.' "

All her life she'd been timid. A worrier. A doubter. Yet now she knew she was made to be strong in the Lord. Her mother had always exuded such joy and confidence. Mary Elizabeth understood now.

"Mary Elizabeth?" Dorothy's voice was just a whisper.

She looked back down to her friend. "I'm here."

"I'm sorry I am. . .sick."

"Me too."

"I know this creates more work for you." Dorothy closed her eyes. "Please take care of Mother and Father." Her head lolled to the side.

"I will." Mary Elizabeth put a hand on her friend's forehead. It was way too hot. "Dorothy? Dorothy?"

"Hmm?" Her eyes stayed closed.

"Can you stay awake?"

"No. . .so tired."

William laid a hand on Mary Elizabeth's shoulder. "It's all right. Let her rest. She's been working so hard and probably not getting enough rest."

She nodded and blinked back tears. William helped her to her feet, and she just stood there, shoulders hunched, staring at the floor. The Lord was her strength. She could do this.

"Is there any way we can go up for some air?"

William took a deep breath and let it out. "I don't know, Mary Elizabeth. The waves don't feel as treacherous right now, but we don't know what we might face up top."

She nodded and walked to the companionway. The steps were wet, but the skies weren't as dark as they had been in previous days. Sitting on one of the steps, she put her face in her hands.

A creak next to her made her think that William had sat as well. "I'm just going to sit here with you for a while, if that's acceptable to you."

"Yes." The words sounded muffled against her skin. There wasn't anything else to say.

And so they sat in silence.

Above them the sounds of the crew shouting back and forth to one another blended with the creaks and groans of the *Mayflower* as she cut through the water for yet another day. Two months had passed since they'd left Southampton. More than three months since they'd departed Leyden.

Her back ached from sleeping on the floor and not being able to stand up straight for all this time. Her hands were dirty, her clothes stank, and her shoes were wearing thin.

"You know, Mary Elizabeth, Mr. Brewster has been allowing me to read his Bible." William's voice soothed the frayed edges of her heart. "Lately, I've enjoyed the Psalms, and today I read through several. My favorite was the seventy-first. I memorized one of the verses. It says, 'But I will wait continually, & will praise thee more and more.'"

She lifted her head and looked into his beautiful blue eyes. He was so close she could feel his warmth and see the light reflected in his eyes.

"I just wanted to share that with you. In case it could help."

"It does help. Very much." She sucked in a breath. "Thank you."

Boots appeared in front of them. "I'm sorry, Miss Chapman. But I'm afraid I have some bad news."

Mary Elizabeth looked up into the surgeon's face and held her breath.

"Samuel Fuller's young servant has died."

"William Butten?" William grabbed her hand. "But he was just a child!"

She closed her eyes and slowly exhaled.

"Aye. A mere youth. But he's gone. I have a man wrapping and weighting the body. We'll have to get him overboard as soon as we can."

Mary Elizabeth didn't know what to think. There wouldn't be any prayer service or funeral procession. The boy would be tossed into the sea. And that made her ache even more.

The surgeon walked away, and William pulled on her hand. "Come, let's go up before they bring up the body."

The tiny thread that kept her emotions in place felt like it was frayed to the very last strand. But there was nowhere to run.

William kept hold of her hand as he led her to the bulwark on the larboard side. "I'm so sorry, Mary Elizabeth. There are no words."

Elder Brewster made his way up the steps, followed by the men with the body of William Butten. The crew joined their little group as Mr. Brewster prayed.

Two of the crew heaved the bundle overboard, and Master Jones barked his commands as soon as it was over.

Mere seconds had passed, and it was done.

The crew went back to work.

Mary Elizabeth took a deep breath of the salty and damp air as the wind whipped her hair from beneath her cornet. " 'But I will hope continually, & will praise thee more and more.' " The words came out on a great sob, and she threw herself into William's arms.

CHAPTER 16

The arms around his waist and the head against his chest were unlike anything William had ever felt before. Mary Elizabeth sobbed into him, and he wrapped his arms around her.

Never had he held a woman. Or anyone else, for that matter.

Never had anyone held him.

Words couldn't express the emotions that ran through him. He wanted to relish this moment forever. He longed to protect this woman he held, ease her pain and her fears.

She shook in his arms, and he remembered the grief and agony she must be feeling. The utter exhaustion. The overwhelming pain.

William understood loss.

The last thing he wanted was to lose this. This woman. This new faith and group of people he was beginning to trust.

But as he held Mary Elizabeth, he thought of all the bickering he'd heard between the Saints and the Strangers. The Saints wanted the others to follow their rules. The Strangers thought the Saints were sanctimonious and self-righteous.

The only reason the bickering had stopped was because the storms made everyone sick. God had essentially shut them up.

William banished the thought. That's not what God wanted for them. Nor was it the way He worked. If he'd learned anything from Elder Brewster, it was that God loved them more than anything else. So much that He sent His only Son as the sacrifice for all.

But there had to be a way to bring these two groups of people together—especially if they were going to survive as a new colony.

Mary Elizabeth sniffed, and his thoughts returned to how wonderful it felt to hold her in his arms.

"I'm so sorry, Mary Elizabeth."

She pulled back and wiped the tears from her face. A deep flush filled her cheeks, and she ducked her head. "No. It should be me who is apologizing. That was totally inappropriate for me to. . .well. . .to. . ."

"You were grieving." William looked around the deck to see if the crew was still watching them. "Besides, it was nice." When all else failed, it was best to be honest.

She lifted her chin, and he got a look into those deep brown eyes. They twinkled in the daylight. "Yes, it was." Lowering her head again, she gave him a curtsy. "And now I must go back down below."

He smiled as he watched her walk away. He needed to talk to her father again. And soon.

Thursday, 9 November 1620

"Just a few sips. You can do it." William lifted Mr. Chapman's head.

The older man struggled to swallow and held up a hand to stop. "That's enough."

William nodded and laid the man back down. "Is there anything else I can do for you?"

"No. Thank you." He grabbed William's hand—the grip was weak and clammy. "It has been good to get to know you."

"And I, you." William gave the man a smile.

"Mr. Bradford is a man of keen perceptions and delicate sensibilities. He will be a good adviser."

"Thank you, sir."

Mr. Chapman closed his eyes, and his breathing deepened. Again. The man didn't stay awake very long, and he appeared so very weak.

William stayed with him until he was certain the older man was asleep. Since the ship didn't seem to be rolling quite as much, he hoped to get top deck and take in some fresh air.

As he made his way to the companionway in the early morning hours, a ray of sunshine broke through the clouds and cast a beautiful glow on the steps. William couldn't pass up the chance. He climbed the steep ladder and stood at the top with his chin lifted to the sky.

How glorious to feel the sun on his face!

"Land, ho!" The shout from above his head shocked him. Had he heard correctly?

"Land, ho!" With the second shout, confirmation was made.

Master Jones strode purposefully across the deck to the forecastle. He leapt up the steps and pulled out his spyglass. "Indeed! Land, ho, Mates!"

William ran to the steerboard side and peered over. Squinting toward the horizon, he saw it. They'd made it! The New World was before them.

Making his way back down the companionway, William couldn't wait to tell Mary Elizabeth. And John Alden. And Elder Brewster! They'd seen land.

He found Mary Elizabeth sitting with Dorothy. "Mary Elizabeth, they've spotted land."

She jumped to her feet and hit her head on the ceiling. Rubbing the offended spot, she smiled up at him. "Truly?"

"Yes." He grinned back. "I need to tell the others."

He found John asleep on his bed, the poor man had been repairing barrels throughout the night. "John." He shook his friend. "Wake up, man. Land!"

Without waiting for an answer, William went to find Mr. Brewster. But he found several of the men already congratulating each other. They all headed toward the steps.

While the seas weren't anywhere near calm yet, they had slowed to a deep roll. So many people couldn't join them on deck for this historic moment, but William would tell them all about it as soon as he could.

Back on the main deck, William marveled at the sight of seagulls and the tiny edge of land on the horizon that grew in size as they inched closer. Several other people chattered on in excitement while Miles Standish spoke with Master Jones. It was good to see people standing, even though most appeared exceedingly weak as they leaned on one another for support. The rest of the passengers were still abed, and William prayed for them to recover. They would need everyone healthy and strong if they were going to build a settlement and survive.

He watched in fascination as Master Jones held up a cross-staff—a calibrated stick with a sliding transom—and spoke to Standish. They studied it, and Standish nodded. Leaving the ship master's side, he approached Mr. Brewster and Bradford. The men talked for a moment, and Standish called the remaining people on deck to come closer.

Standish wasn't a tall man, so he stood on a crate. "It appears, folks, that we are well north of our intended destination of the Hudson River, which as you know is in the northern corner of the Virginia territory. Where our patent lies."

Murmurs echoed through the small group as the reality of the situation settled upon them with Standish's last statement.

Standish held up both his hands. "Master Jones believes he has calculated our latitude to that of Cape Cod."

"Where is Cape Cod?" John Carver voiced the question most everyone probably thought.

Standish sighed. "It's in New England. North. Too far north."

Gasps were heard, and then several people shouted questions.

William listened to the discussion and watched the faces around him. Land was before them. But it wasn't where they were supposed to be. This could present a huge problem.

Elder Brewster quieted the people. "Let's not panic. When we reach the shore, if it is indeed Cape Cod, then a decision will be made about what to do."

"What's going on?" Mary Elizabeth's voice beside him drew William's attention.

"I'm so glad you made it up." He led her over to the bulwark and pointed. "Look."

She clasped her hands under her chin. "Oh my. Isn't it a beautiful sight?"

"Indeed." He watched her face light with excitement.

"What is all the commotion about?" She nodded toward the group of people speaking with Mr. Standish.

"We're not in Virginia. Apparently the storms blew us far north. We're somewhere in what Mr. Standish called New England."

"Oh." Her brow furrowed. "I saw that map when we headed out. Are they certain?"

"We'll know more when we reach the shore, but I believe they are pretty sure." He turned to fully face her. "How is your father?"

She sighed. "Very weak. But now that we are close to land, he must get better, right?"

"We can hope and pray." The wind held a sharp chill. "How is Dorothy?"

"Worse, I'm afraid." Mary Elizabeth shivered. "Her parents have been battling whatever illness it is for a long while now. It makes me worry."

John Alden joined them at the bulwark. "I just heard that we are too far north."

"Yes." William nodded at his friend.

"Well, I guess we will have to wait and see what they decide to do." John bowed to Mary Elizabeth. "It's good to see you again, Miss Chapman."

"Thank you, Mr. Alden."

"How's our little David doing?"

"Quite well, thank you." She looked around. "I'm surprised he's not up here."

William watched her face turn from joyous expectation to a worried frown. "Would you like me to go look for him? You look like you could use some more fresh air."

A small smile lit her face. "I should be the one to search for him."

"Nonsense. You stay up here for a bit and enjoy the view. I'm sure John won't mind keeping you company—you deserve it after all you've done to take care of everyone." William backed away a few steps. "I'll be back in a jiffy."

"All right." Mary Elizabeth's laugh was exactly what his heart needed. To see her truly happy was a wonderful sight, and William hoped he could be the one to keep her happy for the rest of their lives.

"Father?" David knelt beside Father and reached out to touch his pale face.

"Da. . .vid?" The voice was soft and scratchy. Not at all like the normal, strong voice of his parent. "My boy. . .it's so good to see you."

"It's good to see you too. I wanted to tell you that they've spotted land."

"Praise. . .God."

"Today we'll be at the New World. We'll find fresh food and start to build a house." Even if David had to build it by himself, he would do it. He was almost a man now. And it had to be done. For Father and Mary Elizabeth.

A smile started, but Father's face went lax again. His eyes closed.

Fear and uncertainty flooded his mind. *Why couldn't Father stay awake?* He began to cry. *What could he do?* "Once we're ashore, we'll find a way to get you better." Tears dripped down his nose. David laid his hand on top of his father's. David's seemed so small in comparison. But there wasn't any warmth to Father's hand. It just lay there. He sucked in a breath. He couldn't be childish anymore. "You'll see. We're at the New World, and it will be everything you hoped for." He bent over and laid his head on Papa's chest. What he wouldn't give to hear the booming voice and feel strong arms around him again.

"David?" A voice outside their quarters made David sniff and wipe his eyes.

"I'm in here."

William came through the curtain. "Your sister was worried about you."

"I just wanted to visit my father and give him the news."

"That was a wonderful idea. Did you get to tell him?"

David nodded and took a deep breath. "He was awake for a few moments."

"That's good." William turned his body toward the curtain. "Have you been up to see it yet?"

He shook his head. Looking down at his father, he knew the man was in a deep sleep. David stood. "Is Mary Elizabeth up there?"

"She is. And she's excited to share it with you." Mr. Lytton placed a hand on his shoulder and led him out of the quarters.

"Mr. Lytton, could I ask a favor of you?"

"Of course."

David clasped his hands behind his back like he'd seen so many of the men do as they discussed important topics. "Would you help me build a house for my family?"

CHAPTER 17

As the *Mayflower* drew nearer to the shore, a new sense of delight made Mary Elizabeth smile. After so many days at sea, they were finally here. No matter what they faced next, it couldn't be near as horrifying as what they'd been through already. She was sure of it.

With David at her side, she watched the approaching land.

"Look at the birds, Mary Elizabeth!" David pointed up. "There's a lot more of them now."

"Aye. There are." She looked down at her little brother and wrapped an arm around his shoulder. "It's exciting, isn't it?"

He beamed a smile up to her.

"Mary Elizabeth—I've got some news." William walked up beside them. "They've determined that it is indeed Cape Cod before us, and so we will begin to head south."

"We can't stay here?" Her brother chimed in.

William tilted his head. "Well, you see, we don't have the documents that we need to stay here. Our patent is for Virginia territory—near the Hudson River."

"Ugh." David slouched and smacked his forehead with his hand. Then he looked up to her. "Does this mean we have to stay on this boat for a lot longer?"

Laughter started in her stomach and bubbled up as she watched David's dramatic disgust with this new information. "Hopefully not a great deal longer. Just enough time for us to reach Virginia."

"And Master Jones will no doubt keep us close to shore as we travel, so we'll get to see lots of new sights." William nodded to David.

Her little brother furrowed his brow. "How will he know where it's safe to sail?"

Mary Elizabeth grimaced. "I don't know." She looked to William—hopefully he knew more about sailing than she did.

William took David by the shoulder and pointed. "See that man standing on the forecastle?"

"Aye."

"That man's job is to let the ship master know the depth."

"How does he know?"

Mary Elizabeth was just as curious as David, and she stepped forward too.

William chuckled. "He's got two different lead lines. So he's called the leadsman. One is a shorter line called a hand lead, and the other is called a dipsy lead or deep-sea lead. There's a large weight on the end of a long line that the leadsman heaves overboard. He measures the depth by how much line goes out."

"Oh. That makes sense." David nodded.

William pointed behind them to Master Jones standing high up on the aft castle poop deck. "From up there, Jones can see everything that's ahead. The leadsman shouts the depth, and then Master Jones can direct the helmsman who's in the small steerage room below him."

"Do you think we'll get there today?"

"Probably not."

"Well, that's no fun. I was hoping to run on shore today." David turned to Mary Elizabeth. "Don't forget about our race. You promised."

"I won't." The little imp. Of course he'd have to bring that up now.

William raised an eyebrow and smirked at her. "What's this?"

David rolled his eyes and sighed. "Mary Elizabeth says she's gonna race me when we get to the new land. She made a deal with me when I was sick. But you know girls. They're not very fast. Especially when they're old like she is."

William's laughter echoed over the whole deck.

It made Mary Elizabeth smile. "That's quite enough, David. You never know, I just might beat you in that race."

"I don't know." William gave her a wink. "You're awfully *old.*"

Peter watched Lytton talking to those Saint people. Well at least he was occupied for the time being.

He looked around the deck. John Alden was on the other side, talking to some of the other passengers. Enough people were top deck that maybe Peter wouldn't be noticed if he snuck down below.

Making his way down the steps, the dim interior of the gun deck was in stark contrast to the sunlight from above. No one had thought to open up the gun ports yet today. Probably because they were all too worried about seeing land and how they would get to the right place.

It offered him the perfect opportunity to snoop.

As he came to Lytton's bed and trunk, he noticed the lock. Now why would a man lock his trunk unless he was hiding something? He'd have to make note of that to anyone who would listen when he brought all this to light. Another reason why Mr. William Lytton couldn't be trusted.

Peter dug around in the bed and came up with nothing.

The book he'd seen Lytton so diligently write in must be in the trunk.

Well, he wouldn't be able to keep it hidden forever.

The disagreements between the Saints and the Strangers would play right into Peter's hand. If he could keep them from working together, then he could accuse William of sabotage for his own gain, and the man would lose the trust of everyone.

Once word got back to the Merchant Adventurers, Peter could ask for the job.

Then all would be as it should.

The sunshine, the cold, crisp air, and the shore on the steerboard side of the *Mayflower* made William smile. They were here.

Soon they'd find a place for the settlement and begin to build. This first winter might be hard since they'd arrived so late, but the days of being stuck on a ship with no land in sight were finally over.

Mary Elizabeth had gone down below with David to help feed people too sick to move. But as the day progressed, many more of the weakened passengers made their way to the main deck. The calmer seas along with the knowledge that land was in sight was enough to rouse many from their beds.

William watched several people lean on the larboard bulwark. With all the excitement of the morning behind him, he had to admit there was gravity in their situation. This wouldn't be easy. The sixty-plus day journey had taken its toll on all of them. Most were weakened and on the verge of scurvy and who knew what else. Still many were bedridden with disease. Rations were low, and the beer barrels were almost empty.

"Avast! *Yaw, Yaw, Yaw!*"

William jerked his head toward the leadsman on the forecastle and then back to Jones on the aft castle. The leadsman pointed ahead.

Jones looked through his spyglass and barked commands to the crew.

Men climbed the masts like monkeys and began to work the five square sails. One man climbed out on the bowsprit to tame the sprit-sail. The *Mayflower* shifted its bow larboard, and William got a look at what lay ahead.

Roaring breakers and white-capped seas tumbled over one another. This was what the ship master had been worried about. The uncharted seas between Virginia and Cape Cod held dangers they knew nothing about.

Apparently, they were about to find out how dangerous.

Footsteps sounded behind William.

"What is it? What's going on?" Mary Elizabeth tugged on his arm.

"There seas ahead of us appear to be quite tumultuous." William pointed.

Mary Elizabeth gasped and put a hand over her mouth. "What should I do?"

"Make sure everyone is secure below and make sure all the gun ports and hatches are closed. . .just in case." William gave her hand a swift squeeze. He didn't have the right, but they'd been through so much together already and he wanted her to know his comfort. "And we really should pray."

Brewster stood on deck, directing his parishioners back below. His calm voice was reassuring and gentle. But William wondered what the man was thinking.

He looked heavenward. *Lord, You've brought Your people this far. They sure could use Your help.*

William wasn't sure about how to pray, but Mr. Brewster had told him just to talk to God. For now, that would have to do.

The wind was from the north pushing them south—which had been lovely and aimed them in the correct direction until they'd hit the breakers. Now they didn't have a way to turn around or break free from the dangerous water ahead.

Master Jones yelled commands that William didn't understand. How would he be able to get them through? The ship sat sideways dangerously close to getting swept into the current and tide that seemed to go every which direction.

As they were sucked into the waves, William got a closer look. These weren't just treacherous tides and breakers, there were shoals just below the surface that could cause them to shipwreck.

Lord, help us.

CHAPTER 18

After hours of fighting the seas and much prayer below decks, the *Mayflower* freed herself from the peril. Mary Elizabeth sat with her father and told him all about what had happened. She wasn't sure if he could hear her or not, but it soothed her heart to be able to share it with him.

The only problem now was that Master Jones had made a decision and turned them back toward Cape Cod.

"Father, I don't know what is going to happen. We don't have permission to settle there, but Mr. Jones fears it is too dangerous for us to venture on. We don't have enough food nor drink." She sighed and looked down at the frayed handkerchief in her lap. "While most of us are eager to have the sea journey over and be on dry land, there's still the problem with our patent. And so the bickering is back. Elder Brewster and Mr. Bradford are doing their best to calm everyone, but I am afraid it will be a mess."

"Miss Chapman?" The sound of William's deep voice made her stomach do a flip.

"I'm in here with Father."

He entered through the curtain and knelt beside her. "How is he doing?"

"He hasn't been awake for some time, but I was just telling him all about the adventures of the day." Mary Elizabeth smiled. She felt such a strong pull—a connection—to the man beside her. Even though she knew little about his past—and so many other things.

William covered her hand with his own. "I try to visit him often."

She ducked her head and felt the heat rush to her cheeks. "I know. Father told me."

"I don't wish to make you uncomfortable." He touched her cheek with his knuckle.

Mary Elizabeth shook her head. "Not at all. I'm glad you're here."

"I saw David a few minutes ago. He was entertaining the younger More children."

"He's been such a big help." She looked back down at the handkerchief. Awkward silence spread between them. Why couldn't they just share their hearts?

"Well, I thought maybe you'd like me to sit with your father while you go see Dorothy." William rescued her from saying something silly.

"Thank you. I know Father would like that." She hurried out through the curtain and put her hands to her cheeks. This was exactly why she'd never spent time with a young man before.

She had no idea what she was doing. William probably thought she was an ignorant and naive little girl.

Shaking her head, she went to see Dorothy. Her friend had gotten worse, and the Raynsfords weren't improving either. If only she could have a heart-to-heart chat with her friend right now. She needed guidance.

Dorothy opened her eyes a hair's breadth when Mary Elizabeth sat next to her. "Hi."

"Oh, my friend. How are you feeling?" Mary Elizabeth took Dorothy's chilled hand into her own.

"Not very good." Her lips were chapped, and was that blood between her teeth?

Mary Elizabeth worked to keep the tears at bay, but her eyes stung. "We'll have you better in no time. We should be in a safe harbor soon."

"They've spotted land?" Dorothy's voice cracked.

"Yes. And it's a glorious sight."

"God is good, isn't He, Mary Elizabeth?" She closed her eyes.

"Yes, He is, my friend."

"How's William?" Dorothy's lips stretched into a slight smile. "Are you betrothed yet?"

"Dorothy Raynsford, hush your mouth." Mary Elizabeth looked around to make sure no one was listening.

A half groan, half laugh escaped her friend's lips. "I have to tease you. You're my dearest friend."

"And you're mine. So I need you to fight whatever this is so you can tease me some more and keep me on my toes."

Dorothy gave a slight nod. "Give my little King David a hug."

"I will." Mary Elizabeth leaned down to kiss her friend's forehead. It was still so very hot, but Dorothy's hands were like ice in contrast. "I love you." Her whispered words floated in the air.

Dorothy was already asleep again.

Standing up, Mary Elizabeth left her friend's side and checked on a few of the sickest. Little Jasper More hadn't spoken in days, even though his siblings seemed to be improving. Then there was the beautiful Priscilla Mullins who'd been the first person to get seasick. As Mary Elizabeth went to check on her, she found the lady sitting up.

"Miss Mullins." Mary Elizabeth was shocked. "It's so good to see you up."

"Thank you, Miss Chapman. I hear you are the one I need to thank."

"For what?" Mary Elizabeth sat down next to her.

"For taking care of all of us." The young woman had to be around Mary Elizabeth's own age. But her cheeks were pale and thin.

"It was the Christian thing to do." Mary Elizabeth had never been good at taking compliments. She ducked her head.

"I hope that we can be friends." Priscilla's hand touched Mary Elizabeth's.

She nodded. "I'd like that very much. Is there anything I can do for you?"

"No. That is not unless you want to take me up the steps for some fresh air." Priscilla laughed. "I don't think I can walk yet, but I sure would love to see the sky."

"I don't think I could manage it on my own, but let me recruit some help."

"That would be lovely." Priscilla's smile lit up the dim area.

"I'll be back." Mary Elizabeth left with a lift to her spirits. Even surrounded by all these people for months on end, she'd felt alone in so many ways. And now God had seen fit to give her new friends. William, John, Priscilla. . . The future seemed very bright.

When she made it back to her quarters, William was still beside her father. "William, could you find John Alden for me?"

"Of course." He stood. "Can I be of assistance in any way?"

"Well, I was hoping John could carry Priscilla Mullins top deck, and then the four of us could see the stars together."

His smile filled his face.

"That sounds like a wonderful idea."

The brilliance of the night sky couldn't compare to the woman beside him. William watched Mary Elizabeth's face as she gazed at the canopy of stars above them.

"Do you know many of the constellations?" She looked at him, a sweet smile parting her red lips.

"Sadly, no." He pointed to the one he knew. "That's the Big Dipper. And that's the extent of my knowledge in the area." How could he tell her that he lived on the streets of London as a child and didn't have much schooling? Paul had helped him learn the basics. How to read and write quite well, and to work with sums. But there hadn't been time for anything else as he'd apprenticed as a carpenter. Would she think he was uneducated?

"That's all right. I don't remember many of them either. I guess I would make a paltry sailor." Her light laughter sounded like chimes in the air.

"What are the things you love most, Mary Elizabeth?" William leaned on the bulwark and stared at her profile as she looked into the sky. She was beautiful.

She turned her face to him and blinked several times. "Well. . .I'm not sure. No one's ever asked me that before."

"What do you love to do? What are your hopes and dreams?"

More blinking. But she didn't look away. "Love to do? Hmmm. . ." She bit her lip. "I enjoy cooking. And sewing. . . Is that what you mean?"

He smiled. "I just want to know more about you. Is that all you love to do? You also didn't answer about your hopes and dreams. . ."

"Well, I guess, I don't know what I love to do. I enjoy many things, but I've always been pretty. . .occupied with chores and work. As to your other question, I want what I presume every young woman wants. . .to marry and have a family." Her cheeks turned pink.

"Anything else?"

"To raise my children so that they love the Lord." She looked back to the sky. "What about you?"

William's heart pounded in his chest. "I always thought I wanted to do something important and be somebody influential. But now, my dreams have changed."

"In what way?" She turned back to him.

"I want to find love. Real love. Get married and raise a family." He gazed deep into her eyes. "And I want to help orphan children. Not just take them in and work them as servants, but show them that they are important too. That they are. . .loved."

"Oh, William." She took a step closer to him.

"Good evening," John called from the top step of the companionway. William took a deep breath and glanced at his friend.

"Would it be all right if we join you?" His friend carried a lovely young woman over to the steerboard bulwark.

Mary Elizabeth waved her arm. "Of course, that was the whole plan." She moved a crate closer to her. "Here's a place for Miss Mullins to sit in case she can't stand for very long."

"Oh, thank you, Mary Elizabeth." The other woman nodded.

John set her down on the crate. Then Mary Elizabeth wrapped

her in another blanket.

"Thank you, Mr. Alden."

John bowed. "It was my privilege, miss." He clapped his hands together and rubbed his arms. "It's a might chilly."

"I hadn't noticed." William gave Mary Elizabeth a smile.

"So. . ." John looked between William and Mary Elizabeth. "What are we talking about?"

CHAPTER 19

Saturday, 11 November 1620

As the sun rose in the east, the *Mayflower* rounded the top of the hook-shaped land that they'd all come to know was Cape Cod. William gathered with the other men to finalize the document that they all hoped would allow them to go ashore legally and with combined purpose.

The past day hadn't been a fun one.

Once the bickering started when Master Jones turned back to New England, they all knew some order would have to be made. Without the patent for their location, they wouldn't have land distributed to them once their obligations to the company were fulfilled. And without that same patent, the company had no right to govern. They either had to join together for the good of the settlement, or they would perish in disharmony. Everyone's livelihood depended upon them coming together.

Finally, a decision had been made and a document created. The men would all sign the document to create a government together. They would choose a leader together, work together, and get word back for their fellows in England to obtain the patent for the land they chose.

As the ship readied to lay anchor, each able-bodied man came forward to sign:

In the name of God, Amen. We whose names are underwritten, the loyal subjects of our dread Sovereign Lord King James, by the Grace of God of

Great Britain, France, and Ireland King, Defender of the Faith, etc.

Having undertaken for the Glory of God and advancement of the Christian Faith and Honour of our King and Country, a voyage to plant the First Colony in the Northern Parts of Virginia, do by these presents solemnly and mutually in the presence of God and one of another, covenant, and combine ourselves together in a civil body politic, for our better ordering and preservation and furtherance of the ends aforesaid; and by virtue hereof to enact, constitute and frame such just and equal laws, ordinances, acts, constitutions and offices from time to time, as shall be thought most meet and convenient for the general good of the Colony, unto which we promise all due submission and obedience. In witness whereof we have hereunder subscribed our names at Cape Cod, the 11th of November, in the year of the reign of our Sovereign Lord King James, of England, France and Ireland the eighteenth, and of Scotland the fifty-fourth. Anno Domini 1620.

Signed...

John Carver, William Bradford, Edward Winslow, William Brewster, Isaac Allerton, Myles Standish, John Alden, Samuel Fuller, Christopher Martin, William Mullins, William White, Richard Warren, John Howland, Stephen Hopkins, Edward Tilley, John Tilley, Francis Cooke, Thomas Rogers, Thomas Tinker, John Rigsdale, Edward Fuller, John Turner, Francis Eaton, James Chilton, John Crackstone, John Billington, Moses Fletcher, John Goodman, Degory Priest, Thomas Williams, Gilbert Winslow, Edmund Margesson, Peter Browne, Richard Britteridge, George Soule, Richard Clarke, Richard Gardiner, John Allerton, Thomas English, Edward Doty, Edward Leister

William watched as the men shook hands with John Carver, who'd been chosen as their first governor.

Now they could finally go ashore.

Master Jones had the *Mayflower* secured in the harbor just within the hook of Cape Cod, and the crew took care of the sails and rigging.

Governor Carver called the group together.

"Our first objective should be to get the shallop put back together. Master Jones has offered to use their longboat to take people back and forth to the shore, and the ship's carpenter will begin work on reconstructing the shallop."

William lifted his hand. "I'd be glad to assist with that, sir."

"Aye, and me." John Alden raised his hand.

"Good, good." Carver chose several other men who were able to stand more readily. Since most everyone had been sick, there weren't many who had strength to chop wood. "We will need you to go ashore and secure firewood." He turned to a couple other men. "I'll need you to search for a source of fresh water. Tomorrow is the Sabbath, so we must accomplish everything we can today."

The men nodded and set to work. Instead of being cooped up on a ship, they finally had a purpose. William followed John down to the gun deck, where the shallop was stored in pieces. Several people had been living within the pieces, and it had all taken a bruising during some of the fiercest storms.

Once the ship pieces were top deck, they were lowered into the long boat. "Go get your tools, men," Carver shouted.

William raced down the steps one more time. At the bottom, he ran into Mary Elizabeth. "I'm so glad to see you. I have been assigned to go ashore and work on the shallop. As soon as we can get it back together, we'll be able to explore the whole shoreline and find the spot for the settlement."

Her eyes twinkled as she gave him a small smile. "That's wonderful news, William. I'll be praying for you."

"Thank you. Now, I need to go fetch my tools." He turned to go to his quarters and then spun back around. He couldn't leave without saying one more thing. "Mary Elizabeth?"

"Yes?"

"I'll be thinking of you. . ."

"Aye." She ducked her head. "And I you."

Sunday, 12 November 1620

The Sunday morning dawned bright and cheerful. Their first day ashore had brought them plenty of wood to burn, and many thankful prayers had been offered heavenward. The passengers who were strong enough stood gathered together on the main deck for their day of worship.

Even the Strangers who had been most against the Saints' rules and regulations gladly stood alongside and joined in on the praise to God and study of scripture. William was amazed.

God *had* been good to them. And now they were working together.

The only knot in the workings was the shallop. It would take days—possibly even weeks—to repair all the broken pieces and reassemble the small sailing vessel. While they had the longboat, it could only carry so many, and Master Jones was encouraging them to find a settlement as quickly as possible so he, his crew, and his ship could return to England. That meant the longboat would go with them.

Myles Standish decided to organize some groups to explore what they could on foot. But all that would have to wait. Because Sunday was their holy day.

Elder Brewster stood up on a crate and led them all in prayer. As William bowed his head, he felt a hand in his. After the *amen*, he looked beside him to find Mary Elizabeth. The beautiful red cloak was wrapped around her shoulders, and her eyes shone.

She released his hand and smiled. "Good morning."

"Good morning," he whispered, and his heart soared. She'd sought him out and held his hand. Before she appeared, William wondered how he would stay warm during the whole service, but now the cold couldn't touch him.

The people all sat down around the deck as their leader read from Psalm sixty-seven. For the first time in his life, William discovered a church service that wasn't boring. The words came alive and ministered to his heart.

" '…Let the people praise Thee, O God: let all the people praise thee. *Then* shall the earth bring forth her increase, & God, *even* our God shall bless us. God shall bless us, & all the ends of the earth shall fear him.' " Elder Brewster lowered his head for a moment in silence. When he raised it back up, his eyes held the sheen of tears. "My brothers and sisters, our God has indeed blessed us. And we will pray for the Lord to anoint the earth to yield her increase to us as we work in His name."

Several amens sounded around the deck.

"Let's look at Psalm seventy-one now. 'In thee, O Lord, I trust: let me never be ashamed. Rescue me and deliver me in thy righteousness: incline thine ear unto me, and save me. Be thou my strong rock.' "

The same psalm that Brewster had taken William through awhile back. It washed over him like a cleansing stream. *Yes, Lord, in You I put my trust.*

As he sat next to Mary Elizabeth, the meaning became even clearer. If he was going to be an honorable man worthy of her love and affection, he'd have to continually put his trust in the Lord. For the first time in his life, all the pain and despair of his past melted away. He didn't have to carry it around anymore, for the Lord was his refuge. The Lord was his strength. The Lord had given him hope.

Last night as he'd recorded all the day's happenings in the journal, he'd thought of Mary Elizabeth. Maybe it was time to tell her everything about his past. Maybe it was time to tell her how he cared for her.

He looked at the beautiful lady next to him. Could he deserve such a love?

Taking her hand in his, he gave it a squeeze. She may not understand now, but he would explain it to her one day.

Hopefully soon.

CHAPTER 20

Wednesday, 15 November 1620

Mary Elizabeth stretched her back and stood at the bulwark, watching the men go ashore. For two days, she'd done nothing but help the women with their laundry. Lots and lots of laundry. Two months' worth. While most of them wore the same clothes the entirety of the voyage, they now had a newborn aboard in addition to the younger children who needed changes of clothes more often than the adults. But her heart ached a bit watching the men leave. Even though the work of laundry had been grueling, it gave her the chance to go ashore and stand on solid ground again for the first time in weeks. And it didn't hurt that she'd been able to see William as he worked on the shallop.

Shaking her head, she tried to focus on something else. Thoughts of William seemed to invade her mind a lot these days.

And she wouldn't be seeing him at all today since they were separated, so there was no use wallowing in that. Mary Elizabeth turned her gaze back to the ship's deck. Looking around, she placed her hands on her hips. What could she be thankful for?

They made it across the ocean and didn't shipwreck.

There was access to land and prayerfully they'd find fresh water.

But so many were still sick. Her heart sank.

Shaking her head, Mary Elizabeth closed her eyes. She wouldn't allow her thoughts to go there. Father and Dorothy would get better now that they were anchored and safe.

And at least the horrific stench was finally going away on the gun deck. Since they'd been at anchor for several days and the weather was relatively calm, the seasickness had finally stopped. Many still suffered from disease which she could only assume was scurvy. That's what she should concentrate on. Helping the sick.

She'd been doing it for weeks, and it was a useful occupation of her mind. Turning back to the bulwark, she determined to see the men reach shore and then get back to work. It was the least she could do to help the surgeon.

Poor Mr. Heale. Mary Elizabeth found out that he'd hired on as the ship's surgeon and it had been his first contract on a ship since he'd only finished his apprenticeship the August prior. With so much sickness and two already dead, it had to be difficult for the poor man. Several of the sailors had been injured during one of the storms, and now he had this scurvy problem.

They'd relied on him a lot. But he was just as anxious to get back to England as the rest of the crew because he'd filed his intent to marry Mary Jarrett back in London. New resolve flooded through her. She would do whatever she could to help.

If only Mr. Fuller could fully recover. The man was a doctor but had also been too sick to help anyone else. They'd definitely need him if they were to survive the winter.

The men reached the shore and waved back to the *Mayflower*. The longboat would come back for another group of men to scavenge for food and water.

She turned from the bulwark and headed for the steps. Every muscle in her body ached from all that scrubbing, but at least it had kept her busy and her mind off William.

She would miss seeing his face.

She shook her head. Time to get her mind off of her handsome carpenter. Dorothy needed her and so did Father, along with the many others who still suffered.

When she reached the gun deck, the gun ports and hatches were all open and a nice, crisp breeze helped to air out the tight space. David sat in the middle of the floor spinning his top for several of the younger children.

The voyage across the ocean had changed him. He'd not only grown in stature but also in maturity. Helping with everything from emptying chamber pots to feeding those too weak to feed themselves, David was a bright spot on the ship. It made her heart swell to think of her little brother bringing joy to others around them.

She worked her way back to their little, curtained-off area that had been home for so long. While it had been safe and secure on the ship, she couldn't help but look forward to the day when they had a home again.

"Mary Elizabeth, is that you?"

She raced to Father's side and knelt down. "It's me. I'm so sorry I wasn't here when you awoke."

"Don't worry, child. I just opened my eyes when I heard your footsteps."

"It's good to hear your voice." She couldn't help it; the tears sprang to her eyes unbidden.

He reached up to touch her cheek. "Don't cry on my behalf."

She pasted on a smile. "Would you like me to open the curtain so you can see some of the light coming in?"

Father nodded.

Pulling the curtain aside at his feet, she hoped the light shining toward his face would be pleasant.

"That's nice, Mary Elizabeth. Thank you for thinking of that." He patted the spot beside him. "Come, sit." His breaths came in short gasps when he spoke.

Taking her place, she placed a hand on his forehead. "Is there anything you need or that I could get for you?"

"No. I just need to speak to my daughter." His eyes turned sad. "I miss your mother."

"I do too."

He laid a hand on hers. "What I'm trying to say is that I think it's time for the Lord to. . .take me home." A single tear slipped down his cheek. He swallowed and took a shaky breath.

Mary Elizabeth shook her head. "No, Father, don't say—"

"Hush, child. Let me speak. I will want to speak to David while I still have the energy, but I need you to know...that I trust you to raise him up in the Lord."

Emotion swelled into her throat. No. He couldn't be dying, could he?

"The papers in the trunk are in order." He paused for a moment. "Elder Brewster saw to that yesterday. . . . You will inherit my share...along with yours and the property allotted to...David." He closed his eyes for a moment and took several long but shallow breaths. "The seven-year contract should go by fast and...you will be well set for your future."

"But Father. . ." Great sobs shook her shoulders as the tears streaked down her face.

"No, Mary Elizabeth. It's time... I know it is. I only asked the Lord for enough energy to speak to you one last time." He took another shaky breath. "That young Mr. Lytton is a good man. Elder Brewster speaks highly...of him."

She nodded.

"Do you love him, Mary Elizabeth?"

"I...I don't know...but I think I might."

Father lifted his lips in a slight smile. "Your mother and I always wished that...you would marry for love as we did. . . . We were ready to arrange a marriage for you...if that was what you wanted." He patted her hand and then put his arm back across his chest. His breaths were rapid and short. "If William joins the congregation, you have my full blessing, my child."

"But Father, I want. . .no I *need* you to be there for my wedding. Can't you please fight this disease?"

"You have no need but that of a relationship with your Savior, my child." He closed his eyes again. It seemed to take all his strength just to speak.

"Father, please, don't waste all your energy on me."

He shook his head. "It's not a waste. . . . I would want nothing more than to see my daughter wed, if. . .I wasn't called home to the Lord. . . . You have to let me go, Mary Elizabeth. You have to be strong. . . . For David. For William. . . For the colony."

She sucked in a breath and nodded her head.

"I love you, my beautiful, precious daughter."

"I love you too, Papa."

"Go get David, I don't have much left in me."

Mary Elizabeth stood and kissed her father on the forehead, then called down the deck for David.

"Mary Elizabeth?"

"Yes, Father?"

"Would you ask one of the elders to come pray with me?"

"Of course." She stepped out of their quarters.

David ran toward her and stopped short when he saw her face. "Is everything all right?"

She hugged him tight and crouched down in front of him. "I need you to be very brave. Father wants to speak to you, and he doesn't think he'll be with us for much longer. Can you be strong for him?"

"Yes, Mary Elizabeth. I'm a man now." He strode purposefully toward Father's bed.

Her heart squeezed with emotion for her little brother. So much heartache at such a young age.

With a deep breath, she swallowed her tears and went to fulfill her father's request.

William climbed aboard the *Mayflower*, exhausted and sore. Night had fallen, and they expected the crew of explorers would stay ashore as they'd journeyed a great distance down the cape. The shallop was in such sad shape that it would take them weeks to put it back together again. If they had the right materials, they could construct it faster, but they had to work with what they had. No matter the time involved, he was willing to do whatever was necessary to help their group accomplish its goal. The barren wilderness surrounded them in this unoccupied territory. It would probably take a long time to explore it all and find a decent spot to settle. Winter was already upon them.

He longed for his bed and something to eat. But more than that, he hoped he could see Mary Elizabeth. It would be a lift to his spirits.

A good fire was going in the firebox as William stepped onto the main deck with the other men who'd been working on the smaller ship. He moved closer to it and warmed his hands from the damp ride over.

"William?" Mary Elizabeth appeared around the mast in her red cloak.

"Aye." He moved toward her. The firelight shone on her face. It was streaked with tears. "What's happened?"

"It's Father. He spoke to me earlier." She swiped at a cheek. "Told me that he didn't think he would be here much longer and asked to speak to David."

"Is he. . . ?"

"He fell back to sleep but hasn't moved since."

"May I go see him?"

She nodded.

When they reached the top of the steps, William took her in his arms. "I'm so sorry, Mary Elizabeth. I'm so sorry I wasn't here."

She pulled back and with a nod headed down the steps.

William knelt next to Mr. Chapman's bed with Mary Elizabeth beside him. David sat on the other side holding his Father's right hand. The man was so still. So peaceful looking. If it wasn't for the slight rise and fall of his chest, William would've thought that he was already gone.

After they'd been by the man's side for about an hour, William was at a loss for what to say or do. *Lord, I don't know what to do. But please comfort Mary Elizabeth and David.*

Mr. Chapman gasped and opened his eyes.

"Father?" Mary Elizabeth leaned forward.

He blinked several times and looked over to William. "Mr. Lytton."

"Aye, I'm here. Please call me William."

"I'd like to call you. . .son."

"Sir, I'm honored."

Mr. Chapman gasped again. "Take. . .care of them. . .for me."

"Yes, sir. I will."

Mr. Chapman closed his eyes. A long, last tremor of air left his body.

Mary Elizabeth put a hand to her father's chest. She shook her head. "No. He can't be gone." Sobs shook her body.

David sniffed, and a single tear slid down his cheek.

Reaching out a hand to David, William wrapped his other arm around Mary Elizabeth's shoulders. The road before them just became tougher than he could have ever imagined.

CHAPTER 21

David watched the men carry his Father's bundled body up the companionway. It wasn't supposed to be this way. They were supposed to all come to the New World together and start a new life.

Wasn't it bad enough that Mother had died?

He swiped a hand under his nose and sniffed. He wouldn't cry. He had to completely be a man now. He was the only Chapman male left.

The sun wasn't up yet and probably wouldn't be for a good hour. But Mary Elizabeth stood straight and tall next to him. She'd cried a lot during the night, and now she just stood there.

Mr. Brewster came up to them. "We are here for you two if you need anything. The colony is your family. Trust in the Lord for His strength to carry you through."

Mary Elizabeth nodded.

David sniffed.

The men came to the side, and David sucked in a deep breath.

Mr. Brewster prayed.

They dropped Father into the sea.

Mary Elizabeth shook beside him and grabbed his hand.

More than anything, David wanted to run. But there wasn't anywhere to go. Nowhere to hide. And there were people everywhere.

This wasn't how it was supposed to be.

"Mary Elizabeth, I. . ." William stood in front of them, his hat in his hands. "I don't know what to say."

"There's nothing to say, William, but thank you."

David looked up to the man who had tears in his eyes. "It's not fair, William. It's not *fair*." He threw himself into the older man's arms.

"Oh, David." Mary Elizabeth put a hand on his head.

William held him for a few minutes and let him cry. "There's nothing wrong with a man shedding tears, David."

He nodded against William's coat. He wanted to curl up in a ball and cry in his bed, but he couldn't do that to Mary Elizabeth. She needed him.

William pulled back and crouched down in front of him. "Why don't we sit down for a minute and talk. There's something I want to talk to you both about."

David sat on the deck while William pulled up a crate for Mary Elizabeth. His heart felt ripped apart.

"My parents died when I was a baby." William paced for a moment and then sat next to David.

Mary Elizabeth started to cry.

He reached out and took her hand. "I was given to family members to raise me. And I'm sad to say they weren't very nice. When I was nine years old, they threw me out into the streets of London to fend for myself."

David leaned forward. *He* was almost nine. "What did you do?"

William shrugged. "I scrounged for food, worked every job I could find, and slept under people's porches, bridges, in abandoned buildings—you get the idea."

"How long did you do that?" Mary Elizabeth chimed in as she wiped tears from her cheeks.

"About four years. Until a really nice man named Paul Brookshire found me in an alley one day digging in the garbage for food. He took me home, cleaned me up, bought me new clothes, and told me I could stay for as long as I wanted.

"I wasn't very nice to Paul at first, because I had been treated badly by adults and teased by other kids. But Paul wore me down with his kindness. Over time, he taught me everything I'd missed in school, and he began to train me as a carpenter."

"What happened next?" David couldn't believe that tall, strong William had gone through all that.

"Well, I apprenticed for him and worked in his shop until Paul had this grand idea for me to go to the New World. You see, I was still miserable. Didn't think that anyone would ever think anything of me except I was an orphan, and orphans were looked down upon. But Paul had been talking to me about God. He'd taken me to church. Told me how valuable I was to God and to him. I couldn't understand a loving heavenly Father because I'd never had an earthly father who loved me.

"At the time, I couldn't see that Paul had loved me like a son for all those years. That he had been trying to share with me the love of God through how he cared for me."

"Why isn't Paul with you?" David furrowed his brow. The Paul fellow sounded like a good man.

"Well, I was just getting to that. You see, Paul was sick, and the doctor told him he was dying. So he bought me passage on the *Mayflower* and purchased shares for me in the venture. Before he died, he made me promise to make the most of my life, throw off the baggage of the past, and seek God."

"Paul died too?" It didn't seem fair. William had never had anyone in his life who cared, and then when that man came along, he died. David didn't know what to think about that.

"Yes, he did." William took a deep breath. "But that's not the end of the story. I came on this voyage to do what I'd promised, 'make the most of my life,' but what I didn't know at the time is that I couldn't do that without seeking God first. I've faced a lot of loss, David. I've had people treat me poorly. But it wasn't until I found salvation through Jesus Christ and my new faith that I was able to let go of the past. Paul knew I'd been carrying it around like heavy baggage. He loved me enough to set my feet on the path, but he knew I had to find this out for myself."

"Is that why you've been talking to Elder Brewster?"

"Yes, David." William chuckled. "I've asked him to teach me. And then I went to your father."

"You did?"

"Aye. And soon I will spend time with Mr. Bradford, because your father arranged for him to be an adviser to me, and I have a lot to learn still. But the point I'm trying to make is that for twenty years, I've thought I was alone. But I'm not. God's always been right there."

David looked at Mary Elizabeth and the way she looked at William. Then he looked down at their hands. They were intertwined.

"God is right here with you too, David. You're not alone. And your sister and I will be here for you, and the whole congregation. . ."

Hot tears streamed down David's face. No, he wasn't alone.

William opened his arms, and David ran into them.

He missed Father, and he didn't understand why God had to take him to heaven, but William was right.

He wasn't alone. If only it didn't hurt so much.

The sight of her little brother clinging to William made Mary Elizabeth's heart melt. She'd had no idea of what William had been through. All this time, she'd thought of him as a strong and capable man. She'd never known that inside he'd been so hurt and alone.

Although she should have guessed.

The nightmares he had during his fever had made her heart ache. Now she understood.

David pulled back from William and then hugged Mary Elizabeth. He whispered in her ear. "I love you."

"I love you too."

"Do you think Elder Brewster would have time to talk to me, Mary Elizabeth?"

She lowered her brows. "Well, of course, he would. Do you need me to go with you?"

"No. I want to do it alone."

"All right."

Her little brother walked off, a deep sag to his shoulders. The normal spring in his step was gone, but he'd just said goodbye to his father. Could she blame him?

William stood and held out a hand to her. "We will be getting ready to go ashore soon so we can work on the shallop."

"Aye." She looked down at the deck.

"I wish I could stay with you, Mary Elizabeth."

Tears pricked her eyes again. "I wish you could too. But they need your help, and I can't be selfish."

"Mary Elizabeth." He took both of her hands in his and pulled her closer. The deep blue of his eyes seemed darker in the early morning hours. "I know I don't have any right to be saying this—especially on today of all days—but I can't let another minute go by without sharing what's on my heart."

She held her breath.

"I care for you a great deal, Mary Elizabeth Chapman. And I intend to court you and seek you as my wife."

"Truly?" The words left on an exhale.

"Your father and I spoke of it often toward the end. And I want to honor him. . .and David too."

The love in his eyes overwhelmed her, and she had to look down at their hands.

Releasing one hand, he lifted her chin back up. "I need you to look in my eyes, Mary Elizabeth. Tell me the truth. Do you care for me too?"

"I do."

He crushed her against him in a great hug and whispered, "You've made me the happiest man alive." He released her once again and stepped back. "Forgive me." He smirked.

"There's nothing to forgive, William."

He took another step back. "I should be off. I need to gather my tools and such for the day."

"All right." She gave him a smile.

"May I see you tonight?"

"Of course. We can look at the stars together."

"I'd like that." With a wink, he turned on his heel and headed down the companionway.

Mary Elizabeth turned back toward the bulwark and looked at the sea below. Somewhere in the depths, the earthly shell of her father was laid to rest. But she knew he wasn't there. The scripture from 2 Corinthians, chapter five, she'd heard Pastor Robinson speak over her mother's grave came back to mind. *'Nevertheless, we are bold, & love rather to remove out of the body, and to dwell in the Lord.'*

Father dwelt with the Lord and would see Mother again. The thought gave her a little joy. The coming days would be difficult, and she had no idea how it would all work out. But she would rest in the Lord, as well. Because He was her rock and her strength.

Two tears dripped into the sea, and she lifted her face toward the sky. "Goodbye, Father. We'll be all right."

CHAPTER 22

Monday, 20 November 1620

The weather was bitter and dreary. Since Father's passing, Mary Elizabeth hadn't seen William much, and David had gone ashore to help stack wood while the men chopped. He'd insisted that he do his part, and Mary Elizabeth couldn't deny him wanting to work for their survival. While he was still small for his age, he'd begun to grow and build strength.

The weight of finding a settlement rested on every man, woman, and child's mind. It needed to happen fast. But circumstances weren't cooperating.

As she stirred the fire in the fire box, she worked to keep the grief and doubt from overwhelming her. What could she be thankful for?

Wood. She was very thankful for wood. They'd gone so long without it on the voyage over that she never wanted to take it for granted again. She'd be able to cook fish for everyone today, and that would be a treat.

David. Another bright spot in her life. It may have been the Lord's will for Mother and Father to leave this earth, but at least she wasn't alone.

Oh, and William. She was very thankful for him. She'd never been in love, but she assumed this was what it felt like. New understanding of the emotion helped her to understand the fervent love between first, Christ and His church, and second, a husband and wife—ideas that were shared in scripture. Although she'd never want to admit to the elders that she had spent some time studying Song of Solomon.

Thoughts of love made her cheeks heat. She missed William. He spent his days on the shore working with several others to rebuild the shallop that they desperately needed if they were to explore farther. It was difficult not getting to see him—especially after his declaration—but she knew it was for the best.

The first group of explorers came back with a tale of seeing six men and a dog that ran for the woods. The stories had been circulating for days that it must have been Indians and the *Mayflower* voyagers weren't here alone. Everyone thought of it as good news. They would need help farming in this new land, and it would be very advantageous to trade with native people. A few naysayers, though, kept churning up worry about the dangers the Indians could present.

But explorers also came back with dried corn they found buried in mounds in the ground. Mary Elizabeth wasn't too sure why they did what they did—other than the thoughts of their own survival—but she didn't say anything when the group returned. Unsure of what she thought about them "stealing" from other people, she prayed that their leaders would make good choices. The men insisted they were borrowing it for the good of the colony and they would pay the owners for it. Mary Elizabeth could only hope that it would be true and the owners wouldn't hunt them down in retaliation.

The men had gotten lost in vast thickets and woods and had trouble finding drinkable water until they finally found some freshwater ponds.

Something else to be thankful for—they finally had access to fresh water.

Overall, the expedition didn't seem to result in much. No. She couldn't resort to negative thinking again. She needed to stay positive.

After everyone had listened to the men relay their experiences, the stories took on new life as they were shared from group to group. One version even stated that the corn seed that was dug up was found in graves and the natives would certainly come in the night and kill them all for such desecration.

Mary Elizabeth shook her head. The men said they had found

a grave, yes, but they'd put it back to rights when they knew what it was. They really needed to settle somewhere soon and get off this ship. Maybe that would help keep the gossip at bay.

Cleaning the cod a couple of men had caught that morning, Mary Elizabeth took a moment to look around her. While so many were finally up and about again and recovered from their seasickness, just as many had become sicker. Samuel Fuller was on his feet again and tried to help the people with his doctoring skills as much as possible, but disease had taken hold.

And this worried her. Winter was upon them. They had no shelter other than the ship they'd been living on for months already.

Without Father, she wondered what would happen to her and David. Would they need to live with the Raynsfords until they could build their own home?

The smell from the fish in her hand brought her back to the task at hand. It didn't do any good to worry about the future. Right now she had mouths to feed.

After their luncheon of fish, Mary Elizabeth went to check on each person who was still bedridden. Maybe she could do laundry for those who couldn't do it themselves. Clean clothes might help them feel better. Armed with a new plan, she went to Dorothy's bedside to check on her friend.

"Mary Elizabeth." Her friend's voice was weak in the greeting.

"How are you feeling today?"

Dorothy shook her head, and tears came loose at the corners of her eyes.

"I am so sorry." Mary Elizabeth sat and took Dorothy's hands in hers.

"I'm scared."

Closing her eyes, she searched her mind for the words to say. *Lord, guide me.* She thought of Psalm fifty-six. " 'When I was afraid, I trusted in thee. I will rejoice in God *because* of his word, I trust in

God, & will not fear what flesh can do unto me.'"

Dorothy relaxed a bit. "Thank you, I needed to hear those words. 'When I was afraid, I trusted in thee.'"

"I wish I could do more for you, my friend."

"You've been taking care of me for so long. You're doing everything you can."

"I still wish it was more."

"You've changed, Mary Elizabeth." Dorothy's voice crackled. "You're so much stronger and braver now. I'm proud of you."

"I owe much to you. Because you believed in me."

A faint smile lifted Dorothy's lips. "And I always will." Her eyes closed. " 'I will not fear what flesh can do unto me. . .'" She squeezed Mary Elizabeth's hand. "Keep praying for me, Mary Elizabeth."

"I will."

"So. . .what can you talk about while I rest? I know. . . . Tell me about William."

"He's doing well. He's working on the shallop, so I don't get to see him very often. But it's for the best of the settlement. We all have to do what we can." She looked down. It appeared Dorothy was asleep, but she'd keep talking just in case. "It gets tedious, taking care of people and feeding people. I have to say, because of the change of scenery, it's nice to go ashore and do laundry. But I'm really looking forward to the day when we have houses built and can start to live off this new land.

"William is a wonderful carpenter. He's talked about building furniture and houses, and I can't wait to see the beautiful work he'll do in the colony. He spoke to my father, you know. And he declared his intentions to court me. I can't tell you how much that thrilled me to hear those words. But this is all so new. I don't know what I'm doing."

"It's all right, because I don't know what I'm doing either." William's voice startled her.

She put a hand to her throat and once again felt the fiery heat fill her cheeks. "You surprised me."

"I had to come see you. They were bringing a load of wood back to the ship, and I needed a few more tools."

Pulling herself together, she looked down. Goodness, what had he overheard? "I'm glad you did."

He knelt beside her. "I didn't mean to intrude on your private conversation. That's why I made my presence known." Lifting her chin with his finger, he ducked his head and looked into her eyes. "Will you forgive me?"

"Of course." His eyes drew her in and whisked the world away.

"Mary Elizabeth. . .I. . ."

"Yes?"

"I love you." Leaning in, William kissed her softly.

Peter followed William to his quarters. Lytton opened his trunk and pulled out the journal and several other things and set them aside. He dug around and pulled out a couple of tools.

He placed the other items back in and shut the lid.

"Mr. Lytton?"

"Yes?" William turned, his brow furrowed.

"I'd like to speak to you about training as a carpenter."

The man relaxed. "Go ahead. But I need to get back to the longboat."

"Let me walk with you then." Peter headed for the steps to the upper deck. "Have you ever considered taking on an apprentice?"

"Hmmm. . ." He raised his eyebrows. "Can't say that I have."

"Do you think—after the settlement is established, obviously—you might think of taking me on?"

William walked over to the longboat. "It's definitely something I'll need to pray about."

Peter offered his hand to shake. "I appreciate that."

"Good day." William nodded and went back to the other boat.

Pasting a smile on his face until the boat was lowered out of sight, Peter congratulated himself. If his eyes hadn't deceived him, he'd interrupted Mr. Lytton before he had a chance to place the lock back on his trunk.

He took the steps back down to the gun deck and snuck over to where William kept his trunk.

Indeed. The lock wasn't in place.

Peter glanced around and then opened the lid and pulled out the journal. Flipping through the pages, he saw just what he needed.

And it fit with his plan.

Perfectly.

William shivered in the cold as he climbed onto the deck of the *Mayflower* and gazed back out to the shore. The shallop had been finished, and they'd taken it out on another exploration with Master Jones accompanying the group. Other than finding more corn and beans—along with several other graves—they'd only come to the conclusion that the whole area they'd surveyed wouldn't work for their settlement. They needed good land and a safe harbor and plenty of fresh water.

Discouragement had taken over several of the men. It hadn't helped that half a foot of snow had fallen one night and made it that much harder to trudge through the thick terrain. A few men developed bad coughs and deep colds. That fact didn't boost matters or morale, either.

God, I don't understand what You are doing. I don't want to complain, but we sure could use Your assistance.

Before he left a few days ago, he'd noticed the decline in the Raynsfords as well as a few others. Mary Elizabeth rarely left Dorothy's side as her friend suffered with an illness that Mr. Heale could only describe as a bad case of pneumonia compounded with scurvy. And William didn't want to pull her away from the Raynsfords. They were the closest thing to family—other than David—that Mary Elizabeth had left.

Once again, the feeling of loneliness took up residence in his heart. He didn't have any good reason for it, and when he took the time to examine it, he knew it wasn't true. But they all were desperate for some good news—something encouraging and uplifting. And he was tired.

Young David Chapman ran across the deck and greeted him. "William!"

"It's good to see you, David." He hugged the boy and crouched down in front of him.

"Did you find where we can build?"

"Not yet, I'm afraid." William let out a sigh.

"Well, we've got some exciting news." The boy bounced up and down. "Susanna White had her baby. It's a boy, and they named him Peregrine."

"Now that *is* good news." William stood and lifted his face to the sky. Guess the good Lord was listening after all. Maybe he needed to work on his attitude. "How are the Raynsfords doing?"

David shook his head. "Not very good, I'm afraid."

Movement and shuffling behind him reminded William that he needed to help. "How about you catch me up on the news later this evening after I help unload the shallop?"

"We can sit by the fire and look up at the stars?"

"Absolutely, as long as you stay warm enough. Please tell your sister I'm back and I will come see her as soon as I'm done."

"All right, I can do that."

"Thanks, David."

"I'm glad you're back."

"Me too."

William went over to where the men were working and hefted his tools and an armload of wood. Funny how a simple conversation could change his outlook. He needed to fight the discouragement and loneliness. The Lord had blessed him, and he would be thankful.

Now all he needed was to see Mary Elizabeth.

Monday, 4 December 1620

"Dorothy. . .please. . .no. . ." Great sobs wracked Mary Elizabeth's body. Her face was wet with tears, and she didn't think she could breathe as her throat clogged with grief. She shook her friend's shoulders again, but Dorothy didn't respond.

Mr. and Mrs. Raynsford had passed sometime in the night. Their bodies were white and stiff. Now Dorothy's breathing had slowed, and Mary Elizabeth knew deep in her heart that her friend was leaving.

This couldn't be happening. Not after all they'd been through. Dorothy had never even stepped foot in the New World, and she'd been the one so excited about this new adventure. *God, why?*

"You've been the best friend I could have ever asked for." Mary Elizabeth sucked in a deep breath. "This was *your* adventure. I was just along to be by your side. You can't leave me now. . . ." Sobs overtook her, and she cried out her anguish over Dorothy's still form.

"Mary Elizabeth. . ." A warm arm wrapped around her shoulders.

She sat up and found William kneeling beside her. "Oh, William. . ." Her grief washed over in great waves of pain. She went into his arms. How was this possible? Vibrant and joyous Dorothy? No. It couldn't be happening. No.

Pulling back, she looked into William's face. "Thank you for coming down here. I just can't bear it. First Mother, then Father. . .and now. . ." She buried her face back in his shoulder.

"I want to be here for you, Mary Elizabeth."

All she could manage was a nod as she pulled back again. Wiping the tears from her face, she looked back to her friend. "She's been my best friend. . .all my life. I was always the hesitant one, she the adventurer."

"Her spirit will live on though. You can keep her memory alive and honor her through how you live your life."

"I know that it's selfish of me to want her to stay here when she has heaven waiting for her, but I wish she could be *here*. . . ." Tears poured from her eyes as she leaned over her friend and kissed her forehead. "Go with God, Dorothy."

Her friend took a short breath, and Mary Elizabeth felt the air brush her face.

Dorothy didn't breathe again.

The morning sun shimmered on the water, and the wind had ceased. Across the harbor from the *Mayflower*, ice and snow on the shore appeared like crystals sparkling in the light.

Dorothy had always loved the snow. She'd loved winter. It was a pity she hadn't seen the beauty in the winter here. She'd never even been top deck to see the land.

And now men carried the bodies of the entire Raynsford family and young Edward Thompson, who'd also died in the night, out into the glorious sunlit top deck. All to see them buried at sea. Mary Elizabeth's heart broke a little at the thought.

William's steady presence at her side gave her the strength to stand. But there were no words. Her heart felt like it had been broken into a million pieces. How was she ever to put it back together again?

Elder Brewster spoke a brief prayer, and several people cried. No grave would be dug. No marker. Nothing to commemorate these people's lives.

Only the memories that the Leyden congregation would carry with them.

The little group of Saints and Strangers had banded together in hopes to build a thriving colony across the ocean away from everyone and everything they'd known. Now those numbers had decreased, along with their supplies and so much of their strength.

The men lifted a body.

Mary Elizabeth looked down. She couldn't watch.

Splashes of water told her when it was over. The mood on deck was quiet, somber. Sickness seemed to have hold of too many, and it created an unspoken fear among the passengers.

Would *any* of them survive the winter?

Wednesday, 6 December 1620

As the shallop left the *Mayflower* again, William hoped it would be the last expedition needed. This one had to prove profitable or they'd have no hope of getting anything built before spring. Already the weather had turned worse with rain, sleet, and snow a constant companion. Master Jones also voiced his displeasure and encouraged the passengers to search daily for a place so he and his crew could return to England.

William had great hopes that he'd be able to speak to Elder Brewster about what he needed to do to become betrothed to Mary Elizabeth on this trip. He'd already asked to join the Saints' congregation but would have to wait to be baptized until the water warmed. His new faith had given him so much joy, and he looked forward to the future with great anticipation. Mr. Bradford had been a wealth of wisdom and knowledge, and William found that studying the scriptures daily was his favorite part of the day.

But with the deaths of the Raynsfords so fresh, he didn't want to intrude on Mary Elizabeth's grief. He wanted to give her time. It didn't stop him from longing for the day when he could plan for building their own house in the settlement. He wanted her to know that he loved her and David and would do everything he could to give them the best life he could offer.

Waiting was not his favorite occupation. He'd already waited so long to get this far, and now he was ready for his new life to begin. Tension filled the air around him. It must be heavy on everyone's minds. The need to move forward with life. To locate a settlement and start building.

The *Mayflower*'s pilot—John Clarke—and master's mate—Robert Coppin—led their expedition, along with the master gunner and three other sailors. Sickness and the freezing temperatures kept many of the other men aboard the main ship, so they only had half the men they took on the last expedition. But William was hopeful.

They would find a good place for the settlement. He was sure of it.

They hadn't journeyed far when the salty spray began to freeze on the men's clothes. But they pushed forward with their sail and watched the coastline for people, another good anchorage, or a good river. When the evening came with nothing to show for it, they anchored and went ashore to build a barricade and sleep.

The next morning, they were certain they had seen people, and a few men set out on foot to explore while some went in the shallop. But the natives weren't to be found.

William and the others found several more graves but no sign of anyone alive. Were they truly alone in this vast wilderness? He understood that it would be good to connect with others, but it distracted them from their purpose. Besides, William wasn't too sure the natives would like to find out that some of their corn had been taken.

The men trudged on in icy conditions, and again no suitable site was found. After a good deal of discussion on the shallop, they finally went ashore again to call it a day. William helped build a fire, while Mr. Coppin talked with some of the leaders. He talked of a harbor around the bay and north up the coast that he called Thievish Harbor. Since he had sailed to this area before, they all agreed it would be good to head in that direction the next morning. Maybe they would have better luck, or Providence would guide them to a suitable location. The weary men once again barricaded themselves and slept ashore.

The cold and lack of progress wearied William. He was a man of action, and here it was December and they hadn't even decided where to build. Sleep was hard to come by, but he finally drifted off with thoughts of Mary Elizabeth.

Horrible screams brought him out of his sleep. Were they being attacked?

The screams sounded again. This time closer.

Having no experience with a musket, William watched as the other men scrambled for their weapons. The fog of sleep still hung over his head, and he wasn't sure if this was a dream. But as he crawled behind a rock, an arrow hit the sand beside him.

Indians!

Fascination drove him to peek around the rock, but he couldn't see a thing. He swiped a hand down his face. What could he do?

Arrows flew and musket fire sounded in the air. Several of their company took off after the native warriors, chasing them into the thick growth.

William's heart pounded. It definitely hadn't been a warm welcome. Did the Indians know that their group had taken corn and beans from their stores?

He wasn't a leader or anyone important, yet he felt the need to make peace. If these were going to be their only neighbors, shouldn't they try to befriend them rather than shoot them? Maybe the Indians were just afraid of an attack and they shot arrows as a warning. Or maybe other travelers from afar had been unkind to them. Hadn't Coppin told them all that he'd been here before? Perhaps other ships had too.

William and another man waited back at their barricade. But without anything to defend themselves, they would be easy targets if the Indians came back before the other men.

A shiver raced up his spine. He couldn't think that way. Peace had been his previous thoughts, and no matter the fear in his mind, he needed to focus on that.

The minutes dragged by. William sat close to the fire, attempting to stay warm. When the other men ran back into their little barricade, a sigh of relief rushed out of him upon learning none were hurt. But what of the Indians?

Too many things were unknown. Many of the men were uncertain about what even happened. Roused out of their sleep by the screams, no one could remember who struck first.

William shook his head. One thing was sure: they hadn't made a friendly impression on the Indians, and hopes of building trade with them dwindled.

CHAPTER 24

Friday, 8 December 1620

The icy wind did nothing to help Mary Elizabeth's mood as she stood at the bulwark and stared out at the water. *Why* had they left Holland? Why were they here? The burdens had been too much for her to bear. Seven-year-old Jasper More died of sickness the day the expedition team had left; William Bradford's wife, Dorothy, fell off the ship and drowned in the icy waters with no one to help her; and then James Chilton, the oldest man among the passengers, passed away.

In three days' time, they'd lost three more people.

Added to those dismal facts, they'd all heard the musket fire the other night. As it echoed across the water, they had no way to determine where the men had gone, much less discover if the men were injured or even alive.

Sickness and disease affected more than half of the people remaining on the *Mayflower*. Fear reached into her mind and tried to spread its icy fingers throughout her soul. Closing her eyes, she shook her head. Fear was not of the Lord. It didn't do anyone any good for her to sink into despair.

Lord, help me. I'm not strong enough for this trial, and I'm afraid. Please keep the men safe—keep William safe. Help them to locate a safe place for us to settle. We need food and water. We need for people to get well. Her thoughts drifted to all she'd lost. Holland, Mother, Father, Dorothy, the Raynsfords—the list seemed endless. Tears streamed down her cheeks.

This wasn't at all what anyone had expected.

"Mary Elizabeth?"

She turned and wiped tears off her cheeks. Tears she hadn't even realized she'd shed. "Hello, Priscilla. It's so good to see you up and about."

Her new friend strode over and reached for her hands. "You've been crying. What can I do to help?"

Mary Elizabeth ducked her head. "I'm ashamed of it, really. Discouragement attacks me every day—and I know that we have so much to be thankful for." She took a deep breath and looked back up at her friend. "But I believe God sent you at just this moment so I wouldn't be overcome with loss. I really should stop this nonsense and get back to work."

Priscilla's beautiful face lit up with a smile. "Well, I'm glad to be of use. Please. . .you always have someone to talk to if you need me."

"I appreciate that. It's all a bit overwhelming. Especially with Father gone. And little Jasper. . ." She choked on a sob. "He was so young." Shaking her head, she closed her eyes to pull herself together. "I'm not sure what the future holds. Or what I'm supposed to do. My parents are both gone now, and there's David to think about."

Priscilla squeezed her hands. "It seems Mr. Lytton has taken quite a fancy to you. Do you feel the same for him?"

Mary Elizabeth felt the heat rise up into her cheeks and couldn't help but smile. "I do. He's talked of the future, but I don't wish to be a burden to anyone."

That made Priscilla laugh. "I don't think *you* can be a burden to a man who's so clearly in love with you."

She felt her jaw drop. Truly? Was it clear that William was. . .in love with her?

"My apologies. I've embarrassed you." Priscilla leaned close and giggled. "If you need an alternative to life with Mr. Lytton, I could talk to my father for you. He's a shoemaker, and he brought over 250 shoes plus thirteen pairs of boots." She sat up straight and wiggled her eyebrows. "I'm sure he'll need help polishing them."

Laughter bubbled up from Mary Elizabeth's throat. "I'll be sure to remember that. But let's not speak to your father just yet."

Priscilla winked. "I thought you might say that. So why don't we get some food for everyone?"

Even though her heart was heavy, Mary Elizabeth had new strength and encouragement to face her grief. All through a precious new friend. *Thank You, Lord.* "I think that's a marvelous idea."

The weary men spent the day traveling up the coast on the west side of the bay, looking for the harbor that Mr. Coppin told them about. But so far they hadn't found it.

William looked to the sky. The sun was setting and soon they would lose all their light. He sent a prayer heavenward that the men would be wise in their decisions and get to safety, but the leaders pressed on, determined to find Coppin's harbor.

As darkness settled upon them, the winds picked up, and Coppin was unsure of their location. It had been many years since he'd sailed these waters.

William watched the men's discussion turn into an argument. He couldn't let it escalate anymore. He stood to his feet. "Gentlemen!" He raised his voice above the wind. "This bickering will get us nowhere. Right now, our main concern should be getting to safety, not who is right and who is wrong."

John Alden was at the other end of the ship and nodded. Several of the others followed suit.

Coppin lowered his head. "William is correct. We can continue searching for the harbor in the morning. My apologies."

A few grumbles echoed through the men, but they all nodded.

"Which way do we head?" one of the men at the sail shouted.

"To the west, we need to get to shore." Coppin nodded in that direction, but as soon as the words were out of his mouth, a large gust of wind pushed them in the opposite direction.

Water began to slosh into the small ship as the waves threatened to overtake them.

It took every man on the shallop to work the small sail and keep it upright.

William was at the stern of the boat when he heard an awful *thunking* sound. He peered over the edge and his heart sank.

"What is it, William?" Coppin shouted.

He closed his eyes. "It's not good. I think the rudder has come unhinged."

Wind blew them sideways, and William spotted the oars in the bottom of the boat. "We're going to have to steer her manually."

"Aye." Coppin grabbed an oar. "It'll take all our strength, men!"

Oars were passed out and directions were given. They'd have to attempt to keep the boat upright as they worked against the wind. William didn't want to voice his fear—that the wind could push them straight out to sea. That thought was a bit too much to swallow. He looked at John and saw the tinge of fear in his friend's eyes. But he knew what he had to do. Best to bring his concerns to the Lord.

God, I don't know how we will manage this. The wind is getting too strong, and the waves are big enough to take this small ship over. We need Your help. Please give us the strength to push against the wind, and guide us to safety. In Your holy name I pray, amen.

Coppin yelled commands above the roar of the wind, and the men took turns battling the waves with the oars. When one man would get tired, another would take his place.

Time passed in the oblivion of battling the elements. A deep darkness descended upon them as exhaustion took its toll. Hours must have passed, but William couldn't tell the time other than by his own weariness. As the wind picked up again, his heart sank. *Lord, help!*

Another large blast hit them and sent them all falling to the larboard side of the shallop.

Crack!

In an instant, the mast of the small ship snapped into two pieces. Despair descended on the men like a thick blanket. William looked from one drenched face to another.

Bradford stood up against the wind and rain. "Gentlemen, this is no time to fear. Our trust remains in the Lord—He will take care of us."

Coppin nodded and yelled for every man to row as hard as they could.

Another gust of wind blew and the shallop plowed forward. It shook as it struck something hard. They all jolted forward.

"Land! I believe we've hit land!" Coppin turned back to the men, and they cheered.

William woke up in the middle of night and shivered. His mind spun with the hardships they faced. True, they'd hit land, but the damage to the boat could be devastating in the daylight. They knew the rudder wasn't functioning, and the mast had clearly snapped into several pieces. On top of that, they didn't even know where they were.

Elder Brewster's words came back to him: *"It's in the toughest of times that we are challenged to trust Him. Because He is almighty God."*

Trust.

It wasn't an easy thing for William to do. Never had been. People had let him down all his life. But deep down, he knew he could trust God. Putting it into practice was the hard part, but he had to try.

Lord, the men have told me that I can come to You with anything. Well, I need to know how to trust You, and so I'm asking for You to teach me, show me. . .whatever it takes. I want to trust You.

As he gazed up into the sky, stars twinkled between the clouds. God had put all of them into place. He had put William in London and had led Paul to him. Without God, he wouldn't be here in the New World. He wouldn't have met Mary Elizabeth.

Yes, he could trust God. He closed his eyes and thanked the Lord one more time for saving him.

Saturday, 9 December 1620

The sun peeked in and out of the clouds as the men worked to put the shallop to rights. It was a good thing William had brought all his tools with him. John worked by his side as the other men waited for orders on what they needed to fetch to help with repairs.

William checked the new mast in the shallop to make sure it was ready to go out on the water again.

His arms ached. It took an entire day to fix the boat, but tomorrow was Sunday and they would be able to rest, worship, and study the scriptures together. And he desperately needed the encouragement. After all, they were shipwrecked on an island and needed to find the harbor and a good place to settle.

William was tired of mishaps and horrible situations. It was almost mid-December. Since he'd left England, it seemed like he'd faced one catastrophe after another. Everything except Mary Elizabeth.

When Monday dawned bright and beautiful, William was refreshed by the rest from the day before.

Today was a new day.

As the men assembled at the shallop, Mr. Bradford led them all in a prayer. "Father God, we ask for You to grant us Your mercy today as we seek to find a settlement. . . ."

William prayed it would be true. Even though they were on an island, they now knew that they were within a good-sized inlet—a bay—and they would explore it to find what they were looking for.

The men loaded into the shallop and, with renewed energy, started sounding the bay with the lead lines. They discovered the harbor could handle a ship the size of the *Mayflower* and were encouraged.

Myles Standish pulled out Captain Smith's map of New England and figured out that the island they'd run into was within the sheltered harbor. As he showed the men where they were, he shook his head. "Look. Smith named this area over here Plimouth."

The men scoured the shore and decided that Plimouth would be a good place to investigate. In the dead of night and the midst of those terrible winds, God had blown them directly into the place they had been trying to find. A safe harbor.

When the shallop reached shore, William was pleased with the area. Affirmations rang through the group of men. Maybe this was it.

They split up into several groups and spent the morning exploring. William was grateful to be with Mr. Bradford. Mr. Chapman had been correct—the man was full of wisdom and was sensible and level-headed.

He took a deep breath. This was the moment he'd been waiting for. "Sir, might I ask you a question?"

"Of course, William. Why don't we rest over here on these rocks for a while?" The older man sat. "Now what is it you'd like to discuss?"

"I'd like to inquire about Miss Chapman." But where did he begin?

"Ah, yes. The elders have discussed your interest in the lovely Mary Elizabeth."

"Prayerfully, sir, you know my heart now. When I boarded the *Mayflower*, I was indeed a Stranger. Not only to your congregation but to God. It's been a difficult journey, but I feel firm in my faith now, and you've already heard my request to join your congregation."

"Indeed. You are most welcome to join us." He held up a hand so William didn't say anything else. "And we all know that you wish to court Miss Chapman."

"I do." He took a deep breath. "But I'd like to go a step further and know what your church's rules are on betrothal?"

Bradford laughed. "Son, we don't have set rules on the subject. Even though I appreciate you asking and your sincerity in the matter. I will say this: since Mary Elizabeth's father approved and gave his blessing, we are most eager to follow his lead and will not stand in the way."

William let out his long breath. "Truly?"

"Aye, son."

"So what do I do next?"

"Well, you should start by telling her your intentions. Then ask her if she is willing."

That sounded straightforward. And Mary Elizabeth already knew his intentions. He sure hoped she was willing, but the only way to find out was to go ahead and ask her. He couldn't wait.

William dipped his quill in the ink and sat on his bed to fill in all the details of the last few days. While his mind spun with all the happenings, words couldn't express the utter despair that hit the explorers when they returned to the *Mayflower*. Learning of the deaths of little Jasper, Bradford's wife, and Mr. Chilton had shaken them all to their cores.

Even the news that they had found a suitable harbor and place for a settlement couldn't break the grip of grief that had descended.

The sick were expanding in number, and the weather wasn't pleasant. It was winter in New England in the New World.

As the *Mayflower* cut through the water toward her new anchorage, William thought back. A month ago, hopes had buoyed. They'd reached land so the worst was behind them. Certainly there wouldn't be more loss.

But now he wondered how many more would die. How did the settlement have any chance of surviving—much less paying back the debts owed?

If they didn't have enough people to labor, they wouldn't be able to produce what was needed.

At this point, the outlook was dim. William hated to record his thoughts in such a foreboding manner, but he'd promised to be faithful in his job. And he didn't see any other truth.

The investors would have to understand what a difficult journey they'd had so far.

He looked up from the journal and waited for the ink to dry. It had begun to press on his heart that maybe he needed to share with Mr. Brewster and Bradford what he'd been asked to do for the company. Crawford hadn't wanted to alarm the people when they didn't know and trust one another, but William didn't believe it was supposed to be kept a complete secret. The whole point had been to build trust and be good stewards. He also wanted to tell Mary Elizabeth.

There was no reason he shouldn't since he'd hoped to ask her to be his wife.

Mary Elizabeth.

What he'd hoped to be a joyful reunion had been a time of sorrow as the news was shared. She still grieved her father and the Raynsfords, and each death took its toll. The only remedy William could see? Time.

William needed advice, but Elder Brewster had spent the days praying over each sick person, and Mr. Bradford had hidden himself away for a time after the news of his wife was shared. He couldn't blame the man.

He longed to spend some time with Mary Elizabeth and share his heart, but the circumstances seemed to dictate patience. So he'd waited. She looked worn out from caring for all the sick, and he knew how much she had come to care for the More children. Another blow like this could devastate her heart for some time, and William was unsure how to proceed.

Lord, I need help. Everyone on this ship needs help. Please give us Your wisdom and discernment as to how to proceed.

William tucked the blotter, journal, and quill back into his trunk. Perhaps he could be of some service to Master Jones on deck.

As he climbed the steps, he forced his mind to look forward. Past all the grief, past the building and settling. He could see himself thriving here for the rest of his days. God willing.

With Mary Elizabeth by his side, he felt he could do anything. He would cling to that—dreams of the future—and pray they would survive.

Saturday, 16 December 1620

The ship sat in its new harbor, and David watched the shallop and longboat take all the able-bodied men to shore. They were going to scout and find a place to build. Soon he'd get to run on dry land, and he couldn't wait.

Once they'd reached the New World, it hadn't been anything like he'd expected. He'd seen a lot of sandy shores and woods, and they'd had to stay on the *Mayflower* for all these weeks. Other than getting to go and help stack the firewood, there hadn't been much excitement for him.

Mother and Father were gone, and now Mary Elizabeth was needed again to help with the sick around the clock. She fell into bed for short naps each day but hardly had anything to say.

David felt like he'd lost everyone.

The boats reached the shore, and he wished he was with them.

"There you are, David. I've been looking for you." His sister's voice made him turn around. "Do you think you could try and catch some fish for us today?"

He nodded.

"What's wrong?"

"Nothing."

She stepped closer. "It doesn't look like it's 'nothing.'"

With a sigh, he looked into her eyes. "You haven't been yourself lately."

"There's been a lot to take care of, David." Her words sounded weak. . .defeated, as she looked off into the distance.

He couldn't take it anymore. "But don't you understand? You barely eat. You barely sleep. And you never talk to me anymore. . .or even William."

Tears filled his sister's eyes. She ducked her head.

He didn't mean to make her sadder.

"It's been very hard losing Father and then Dorothy"—she sniffed—"and all the others."

"I know, Mary Elizabeth." He didn't want to cry, but hot tears burned at the corners of his eyes. He threw himself into her arms. "That's why I'm scared. I don't want to lose you too."

CHAPTER 25

I *don't want to lose you too.*" David's words had pierced Mary Elizabeth's heart. As she leaned over Solomon Prower, she realized that she had allowed her grief to cover her in a fog. She wasn't the only one to face great loss. Everyone on board the ship had felt tragedy in one way or another. They'd all left behind family and friends and everything they knew.

"Take a sip, Solomon." Mary Elizabeth encouraged the man to drink. She needed some fresh air, time away from caring for the sick in the belly of the ship. Time to lift her eyes toward heaven and pour her heart out to God.

It'd been too many days since she'd allowed herself to feel anything. David was right to be concerned, and Mary Elizabeth should've seen this coming. She should've been strong enough to fight off the melancholy and sorrow. They couldn't afford to wallow in their anguish.

"Mary Elizabeth, how is Mr. Prower doing?"

She turned to see Mr. Bradford kneeling beside her with his Bible clutched to his chest. "He's just had some sips of water."

The man nodded. "I guess that's the best we can hope for now."

She bit her lip. Dare she speak to the man about his loss? "How are you doing?"

He took a deep breath and let it out. "I keep thinking of Job and his words, 'Naked came I out of my mother's womb, & naked shall I return thither: the Lord hath given, & the Lord hath taken it: blessed be the Name of the Lord.' " His eyes appeared teary as he gave her a sad smile. "While it doesn't take away the pain, it encourages me to praise the Lord even in this time of sorrow."

Mary Elizabeth blinked at him. The man had lost his wife, whom he seemed to love dearly, yet he was able to cling to God and his faith so beautifully.

"You look like you are struggling, my dear."

She nodded. "It has been pretty trying the last couple of weeks." Mary Elizabeth ducked her head. The only happy moments she could remember were with Priscilla and seeing William again, but then they'd had to share about the losses, and she'd tumbled back into her own grief.

While Mr. Bradford wasn't quite as old as her father had been, she still looked up to him as a father figure and one of the elders for their church. "I understand that, Mary Elizabeth. I do. And I wish I could take away the heartache you've had to endure. That everyone has had to endure on this voyage. I don't think any of us imagined it to be this way." He sighed and shook his head. "In the book of First Peter, we are reminded to 'rejoice, though now for a season (if need require) ye are in heaviness,' and indeed the times have been heavy with trials and loss. I keep asking the Lord for wisdom in how to rejoice through this, and even though I don't know the answer fully, I am encouraged to keep living one moment at a time. To keep serving Him. That's what this whole journey was about, my dear. To free ourselves from other restraints and be able to worship Him wholly. If we lose sight of that and dwell on our grief, we will tarnish the memories of those who've given up their lives on this venture."

The words sank deep into her mind and heart. "Thank you, Mr. Bradford. I haven't had enough rest, I know that, and I've allowed the sadness to drag me down. Had David not told me his heart earlier—his fear of losing me too—I might have gone further into the depths of despair. And I know that's not of the Lord."

"No, my child, it's not. Neither is fear. And I know many are fearful of the future right now. We must do our best to encourage them." He stood up and patted her shoulder. "How is Mr. Lytton doing? I thought you fancied him."

Mary Elizabeth felt yet another blush rise to her face. "I do. He's a good man."

"Aye. He is."

"But I'm afraid I haven't had much time with him, either, of late."

"Maybe you can change that."

She smiled. "Yes, maybe I can."

As she watched the man walk away, she resolved to do just that.

She stood up and went to their quarters. The lid of the trunk opened with ease, and she pulled out Father's Bible. It was hers now. And she would treasure it.

Making her way to the main deck, Mary Elizabeth hummed one of the psalms they sang from the psalter. If she wanted to lift the fog, she'd have to fight it. That meant getting enough rest to have the strength to fight it too. Something she'd neglected for far too long. It took David's scolding to help her to see it.

On deck, she positioned herself at the bulwark where she could see the boats on the shore. "Lord, I commit to You my heart and mind. Please help me to release this darkness that I've allowed to take me captive. David needs me, and I haven't been much of an encouragement and light to him lately. Please guide the men ashore as they seek to do Your will and find a suitable settlement for us all. I ask all these things in the holy name of Jesus, amen."

Her prayer left on the wind, and she closed her eyes and let the winter sun shine on her face. Letting go was hard to do. Losing people you loved, even harder. But she needed to keep her focus on the source of true joy—the Lord.

What could she praise Him for today?

Opening her eyes, she looked at the shore. William was her biggest source of praise. He gave her a hope for a future that she'd dreamed of since she was a little girl—to be married and have a family. Then there was David. Her precious brother. There was still so much growing for him to do, and she needed to help guide him in the right path.

This new land was another thing worthy of praise. And the fact that the long sea journey was over. Then there were new friends.

As she counted up the things to praise God for, she felt the heaviness begin to lift. She went over to a crate and sat down. Opening up the Bible, she went to the very first Psalm and began to read:

'Blessed is the man that doeth not walk in the counsel of the wicked, nor stand in the way of sinners, nor sit in the seat of the scornful: but his delight is in the Law of the Lord, & in his Law doeth he meditate day and night.'

'For he shall be like a tree planted by the rivers of waters, that will bring forth her fruit in due season: whose leaf shall not fade: so whatsoever he shall do shall prosper.'

She wanted to find her delight in the law of the Lord again. Not wander around in this blackness. The people needed her, David needed her. . .and William did too. Closing her eyes again, the weariness from lack of sleep hit her. She'd neglected her own health to care for the others.

Maybe the best idea she had right now was to get some rest, and then she could look forward to seeing William tonight.

The day of exploring had gone well, and William was exhausted. His bed sounded exceedingly welcoming, but more than anything, he wished he could see Mary Elizabeth. To look into her eyes and see her smile.

That hadn't occurred much of late. And he knew he shouldn't expect it, but he could still hope.

When they reached the deck of the *Mayflower*, Master Jones was waiting for them. "Any news?"

William nodded. "It appears we are close to making a decision."

"Good, good." The man's stern expression with his hands clasped behind his back seemed to be his normal posture.

"William!" That was Mary Elizabeth's voice, and it lifted his spirits, just hearing it.

He turned toward the sound. "Mary Elizabeth."

She came to him with a smile and took his hands in hers. "I'm so glad you're back."

"It's good to see you as well." Better than he even imagined. Especially with her bright smile. "To what do I owe this wonderful pleasure?"

Ducking her head, she squeezed his hands. "I didn't realize how much I had. . .neglected you."

With the crook of his finger, he lifted her chin. Something he'd had to do often. "Look at me, Mary Elizabeth. There's no reason for you to feel guilt or shame—or hide your face from me. Do you remember what I told you?"

Her cheeks turned pink. "Aye." The smile grew.

"I meant it, Mary Elizabeth. I love you. I want to know everything about you. I want to spend every moment the Good Lord gives me with you."

The look on her face did funny things to his heart.

"I know you've had your hands full taking care of all the sick—and that makes me love you even more. You have a beautiful, tender heart. But I have missed you a great deal."

"And I you." Her brown eyes shimmered. "There's something else. I'm very sorry for my distance. I didn't realize how much hurt I had caused until David spoke with me this morning."

"It's understandable, my love. I had resolved to give you time in your grief."

"I didn't do it intentionally. I guess I just didn't realize how weary I had become."

He ran a finger down her cheek. "But you look quite rested and happy now. It's good to see color in your cheeks again."

She lowered her eyes to his chest and smiled. "I slept a good part of the morning after I spent some time in prayer and in the scriptures. The happiness you see is because of you, William."

He put her hand to his chest. "You make my heart overflow, Miss Chapman."

"You do the same for mine." She smiled, and then her brow furrowed. "Mr. Bradford spoke to me after David did, and I was very convicted by his words. It's amazing to me that he's resting in God's will and yet just suffered so much. He mentioned Job this morning, and I think I might like to study that book."

"His faith astounds me every day."

"Aye. And his wife has only been gone a few days. It breaks my heart for him." She looked toward the water.

"Maybe we could study Job together?"

"I'd like that." The light was back in her eyes. "We could ask Mr. Bradford for help if there's something we don't understand."

William dared to step closer and lifted their joined hands to his chest. "Bradford has been my mentor and adviser at your father's suggestion. I think that's a wonderful idea." Was this the right time? He had no experience in this area, but he forged on ahead. "I know I don't have much to offer you, Mary Elizabeth, and there's no place or time to court you properly. But the elders have approved my request anyway." He took a deep breath. "What I'm trying to say is that. . .I'd like to ask you to be my wife."

She took a slight step back and smiled. "Aye. William Lytton, I'd be honored to be your wife."

"Hoo, hoo!" William threw his hat in the air.

Everyone on deck turned toward them and stared.

"She said *yes!*"

CHAPTER 26

Thursday, 28 December 1620

William climbed the hill where they planned to build a platform for the cannon. It would serve well as a lookout and help protect their settlement. His job was to get the structure started with John Alden's help while the others worked on the common house.

They'd hit one problem after another. First, the decision couldn't be made about where to settle. Several of the men said the island on which they'd almost shipwrecked would be a good place because it would keep them safe from the Indians. But even the pilot John Clarke—who'd had the island named after him since he'd been the first to step on it—argued that being on the mainland would be more beneficial in the long run. So a vote had been cast, and they'd settled upon what Captain John Smith had dubbed on his map, "Plimouth." And they decided to spell it Plimouth.

The last port they'd left in England was Plymouth, so it seemed providential.

Then the weather had turned stormy and they'd lost three more lives—one a stillborn baby. By Sunday, December 24, many members had lost hope of having anything accomplished by January.

William had shared his hopes and dreams for a house with Mary Elizabeth but had to wait on the rest of the men to decide how they would approach the planning of their town. If he'd ever prayed for patience, he knew now not to do it again. Learning how to be patient was proving to be his greatest enemy.

But on Christmas Day, they'd finally erected the first frame of their buildings. It was to be the common house and would measure twenty feet square.

Today they were supposed to plan out their town and get this platform built.

As he stood at the top of the hill, William looked out on the area around him. A good deal of land had been cleared by presumably some native people. And at one point, corn had been planted. The remains still stood in the fields. But when they'd scouted, they'd only found abandoned hut-like structures. William hated to say it out loud, but it did appear that something catastrophic had happened to whoever had lived there.

A beautiful brook ran by the hillside and provided them with plenty of fresh water. They had affectionately named it Town Brook. And at the mouth of the brook was a great place to harbor the shallop and other small boats.

From the top of the hill where he stood, he could see the tip of Cape Cod—where they'd first anchored—across the bay. As he turned, he saw plenty of trees in the distance to provide wood for them.

They had chosen well. This land should provide for them for years to come.

William pulled out his satchel of tools and set to work. Hopefully he'd hear soon about the plan for the town and he'd be able to work on that as well.

Anxious to get started and get the people situated on the land, William worked fast with his hatchet.

After he'd trimmed about ten logs, he heard rustling in the grass.

"Hello!" John Alden called from the side of the hill.

"Good day to you, John!" William took the opportunity to catch his breath and drink some water he'd brought up from the stream.

"And to you." John crested the hill and walked up to him. "Looks like you've made a lot of progress."

"Aye. When you have good motivation, it tends to keep you going."

"That is true." His friend patted him on the back. "Where would you like me to start?"

William pointed to the pile of trees he'd felled. "The rest of those need to be trimmed and sized."

John took his hatchet and went to work. "I have some good news."

William nodded and kept working.

"They've laid out where the houses will be built."

"Aye. That is indeed good news." He split another log.

"There will be a street down the middle with nineteen plots—one for each family unit—on either side. Fifty feet will be their depth and eight feet per person will be the width determining each for their house and garden." The repetitive *thunk* of John's hatchet accentuated his words. "Once we get the common house completed, each family will be responsible for building their own house."

It sounded great to William. At least it was a good start.

They worked in silence for a good while, the hard work keeping them warm in the frigid temperatures.

John let out a groan and stretched. "I think I got soft being on the ship for so long."

"It feels good though, doesn't it? To get back to work?"

"Aye. It does." John moved around a bit more. "Although tomorrow, I'm sure my body will protest."

William chuckled at the thought.

"So. . ." John raised his eyebrows. "Have you and Mary Elizabeth decided when you will have the wedding?"

"We've been discussing it with Elder Brewster. I think we will wait until we have a house built and most of the sickness is past. That way, the whole community can celebrate with us."

"When do you think that will be?"

"Hopefully by the end of January. That gives us plenty of time to plan and build."

Monday, 15 January 1620/1

"We'll be praying for you every day, William." Mary Elizabeth held David's hand on the top deck. How she hated goodbyes. He'd only be on the mainland, but she'd hardly seen him as it was. When the weather was decent enough, the men had worked long and hard to fell trees and build the common house.

"Thank you, Mary Elizabeth." He touched her cheek, his blue eyes almost gray today. "It won't be long." He leaned forward and whispered in her ear. "I love you."

Heat filled her face as he pulled back, and she gave him a smile.

With a nod, he walked away and joined the few other men who were to go ashore and live in the common house and work on the fort and the houses.

The original plan had been a good one, but no one had counted on the storms growing worse and the sick growing in number by the day. Some had gotten better and then succumbed again—this time much worse.

They needed men to hunt and fish so they would have food, and then thatch had to be gathered for roofs, timber needed to be chopped and hauled. It wouldn't be so bad if everyone were well and strong.

A tickle in her throat made Mary Elizabeth pull her cape up to her nose. She didn't want to cough in this cold, damp air. Last time she did, her lungs felt like they were on fire.

"Mary Elizabeth, I don't feel so good." David shivered and tugged on her hand.

"Let's get you closer to the fire, all right?" Weariness rested on her shoulders once again. No. She couldn't allow it to take over again. She would delight in the Lord. He would be her strength. They'd made it this far; He would see them through. She sat David down on a crate by the fire box. "How's that?"

"Much better. But my throat hurts, and I can't breathe through my nose."

She nodded and crouched down beside him. "Let me see if I can find anything to help you with that." Taking off her cape, she wrapped it around her brother's shoulders. "I'll be back."

She went down the steps to find Samuel Fuller. He had been taking care of the ones who were the worst that morning.

"Mary Elizabeth, I'm so glad you're down here." Mr. Fuller waved her over. "We need some extra hands—is David with you?"

"That's why I was looking for you, as well. David is complaining of a sore throat and that he can't breathe through his nose."

"It sounds like his humours are out of balance."

"So what should I do?" Mary Elizabeth followed the man to the next bed.

"I believe there is a little dried mint left in my satchel. Boil it in some water and have him breathe it in and then have him drink it. That's the best I have to offer. Everything else has been depleted." He squeezed her arm. "When you're done, could you come assist me?"

"Of course. I'll be quick."

Gathering what she needed for David, she sent another prayer heavenward. She hoped it wouldn't turn into another case of pneumonia for her poor brother. It had started the same way.

Climbing the steps to the main deck, she tripped over her skirt. There wasn't need for reckless behavior. Now would not be a good time to injure herself. She found David asleep by the fire. "Wake up. We need to get you to bed."

"I don't feel good, Mary Elizabeth." David's head lolled back as she lifted him up.

"I know. That's why I'm going to take good care of you. But I need you to walk; you're too big for me to carry."

She barely managed to get him down the steps when the tickle came back to her throat. A horrible cough wracked her chest as she led David to bed.

Mr. Fuller appeared at their curtain. "Was that you coughing, Mary Elizabeth?"

She nodded as another coughing spell came over her. "I don't know what's come over me."

The man shook his head. "It looks like it's not going to be just David going to bed. You are too."

CHAPTER 27

Thursday, 8 February 1620/1

The snow, sleet, and wind hammered the men in the common house. William stayed close to the fire to watch for embers flying—they didn't need any more fires to burn thatch roofs—and prayed for divine help. The storms had been so bad the past few days that there was a good amount of damage done to the structures they'd been working on. They were already behind, and now this would set them back even further.

Word had come from the *Mayflower* that Mary Elizabeth and David had both gotten sick but were finally on the mend. That news was better than most. The little Plimouth colony was already beginning to disappear, and they hadn't even truly settled. The few that were strong and healthy enough lived on shore and helped build, while the rest were cared for on the ship.

William didn't even want to think about the number who'd died.

If truth be told, the only thing that kept him going was his newfound faith. If he hadn't found the Lord on the journey over, William would've wanted to quit and head back with the crew to England.

But Master Jones wasn't even sure when he could leave. There weren't enough places to house the people who would be staying, and a good portion of his crew had fallen sick.

The times continued to oppress them.

Was this what it was like for the early believers? The past few days had given William lots of time to read God's Word, and he found that there were so many different passages that spoke on suffering for the sake of Christ and how to rejoice in the midst of suffering. Since it was addressed so much, he could only assume that there was a good reason.

There'd obviously been a lot of persecution—William knew of it from the bits of history that Paul had taught him—and he'd been learning of the persecution so many had suffered from the Church of England. From Bloody Mary to King James, differing beliefs could put lives on the line.

Last night while the winds howled around them, Elder Brewster talked about when their congregation had first fled England. It took years and several tries to get everyone together. They'd been betrayed, robbed, and imprisoned.

All for their faith.

While William had joined the journey to the New World for a fresh start and what he hoped would be a grand adventure, it had turned into so much more than that. He'd found life. And he'd found Mary Elizabeth.

But the price had been high. For everyone.

The thought of losing Mary Elizabeth and David struck his heart. It was a good thing he hadn't learned of their sickness until they were on the mend. Who knew what he would have done to get back to them and help. The doubts of his past plagued him on a daily basis, and he felt battle weary from the attacks.

But prayer was a beautiful thing. As soon as he laid his burdens down at the heavenly Father's feet, he knew he'd done the right thing.

His thoughts returned to the colony. And his journal. Would they be able to recover from such hardship? At this point, it would be a miracle if they survived, and they hadn't even thought about how to repay the company. The *Mayflower* would need to return to England, and even after all this time, the colonists had nothing to send back to put into the company's coffers. In fact, they needed more help— which would put them into greater debt.

John Carver had a heavy burden to bear—to be sure. As elected governor of their group, he was the leader and the one ultimately responsible for the decisions made.

The Compact they'd signed would ensure that the people would have their say. That's why votes had been cast about the settlement location and also about the layout of the town. But they still needed a strong leader.

In the glow of the firelight, William flipped through the pages of the Bible Elder Brewster let him borrow. The book of Acts fascinated him. Reading about the early church and how they cared for one another. Whether rich or poor, station or no station, they pulled all their monies together to clothe each other and feed everyone.

No wonder the Saints wanted to be separate from the Church of England. It had gotten away from what scripture demonstrated a church should do.

It was full of rituals and readings and ceremonies. While people's hearts might be in the right place, they were following man-made rules and mandates rather than scripture.

Paul had taken him to church the whole seven years he'd lived in the older man's care. But Paul seemed to believe very much like the Separatists—that scripture was the final authority. But they'd gone to the church in London, anyway. When William was younger, he'd asked a lot about the rituals they seemed to go through because he'd been bored. Paul's response was that it wasn't right to forsake the fellowship of the brethren. There would never be a perfect church because it was filled with imperfect people.

William never understood that until he read Hebrews, chapter ten: *"And let us consider one another, to provoke unto love, & to good works, Not forsaking the fellowship that we have among our selves, as the manner of some is: but let us exhort one another, & that so much the more because ye see that the day draweth near."*

Paul had been raised in the church of England, and even though later in life he disagreed with some of the practices, he still found the fellowship he needed there. It might not have been what he wanted in a church, but he had remained faithful.

The difference between Paul's faith and the Saints' wasn't great—if there was any at all. But now William began to understand why Paul had urged him to go with the Separatists.

"He wanted to go himself but couldn't." As he said the words aloud, a moment of comprehension struck him.

William remembered a conversation he'd had with Paul before he died. At the time, he hadn't understood it at all. . .

"If only I'd had the courage to do it long ago, things would be different. Maybe I could help you more. But I stayed in my comfortable place—even though the Lord prodded me on."

"You've helped me more than you will ever know. There's nothing for you to regret."

"Oh, but there is, my boy. I can't let you make the same mistake. It's time for you to make the most of your life. Throw off the past and follow God. The Separatists have done it right."

A rush of emotion filled his chest as he remembered the dear man's words. At the time, William was still too hardened and bitter to understand. But now he did.

The man had loved him like a son and wanted him to serve the Lord.

As all the events of the past few months filled his memories, William knew one thing to be true.

God was in control. He had directed their steps thus far. William would trust Him the rest of the way. No matter the cost.

Hunting for fowl was not Peter's choice of labor, but it was better than chopping and trimming logs or gathering thatch.

And they all needed food. He felt like he could eat an entire goose himself.

Today had not been a productive day, though. He missed every bird he'd shot at. If he could just kill one, he'd build a fire and roast it up. Forget about sharing with the rest of the men.

Several deer passed by his hiding spot. Venison had never been popular in England, and he had no idea what to do with it, but the thought of a big steak sure made his mouth water. None of the men had experience hunting the game, but maybe he could show them all by snagging one.

Crouching down into the grass, Peter took aim. A twig snapped under his elbow, and the deer skittered off into the trees.

This whole trip had been a waste of time. It was miserable, they were almost out of beer, and he'd been sick twice. More people died each week, and he determined he wasn't going to be one of them. He had no desire to work his fingers to the bone and live in some tiny thatched hut. That might be good enough for the others, but not for him.

No way was he going to stay here unless the company paid him a lot of money. And right now the job belonged to someone else.

Something he needed to change. And soon.

Wednesday, 28 February 1620/1

Twenty-five people were dead. Just in the past two months. William thrust his pick into the ground on the small hill they were using as their burial ground. He'd almost spent as much time burying people as he had building the small buildings the rest would soon live in. The thought made him shake his head.

As he'd spent more time with the elders and men of the Separatist congregation, he'd come to find that memorizing scripture was a vital part of faith. That way he could keep it on his mind and heart just like Psalm 119:11 read.

The verse he'd memorized this morning was from 2 Corinthians. Chapter four, verse nine. He said the words aloud to banish the discouraging thoughts as he dug another grave. " 'We are persecuted, but not forsaken; cast downe, but we perish not.' "

Many of the men had shared the same verse with him—they probably all needed the encouragement and reminder.

Their flesh might perish. They might all die and the little colony return to dust. But their souls wouldn't. Eternity in heaven looked better each day.

The physical labor kept his mind focused on the work ahead. They needed to get everyone off the ship and living in suitable housing. The cramped quarters for all these months had to breed the disease in some way that had infected all the people. It was the only thing that made sense to him.

He was just thankful that Mary was again healthy and recovered. All the time she'd spent with the sick made him worry.

Had it really only been two days since he'd seen her last? Ever since they'd anchored off Cape Cod, laundry had been done on Mondays, since that was their first opportunity. The tradition continued all these weeks, and now he wished that Monday was closer. Or maybe there was another reason he could give for going to see her.

The thought made him smile. Several of the other men teased him about the upcoming wedding. It was good to have the camaraderie and a topic that brought smiles and laughter rather than tears and sadness.

But would he make a good husband? A good father? He'd never had any real example other than Paul. And the Leyden men had been good to him, but he realized that he didn't know the first thing about being a husband or a father.

Maybe that was the next subject he should broach with Mr. Bradford and the elders. Before he said his vows, he should probably study what a Godly husband looked like and if there was any way he could be one.

CHAPTER 28

Monday, 12 March 1620/1

Spring was just around the corner. The thought brought a smile to Mary Elizabeth's face. They all needed a smile after the past few months. Even though she didn't have a house finished yet, she was anxious to be able to start the garden. The lettuce and peas could go in, and that thought thrilled her. Something fresh instead of hard tack, dried meat, and dried vegetables. They enjoyed the occasional fish and fowl if the men had time to hunt or fish, but with so few healthy, the majority of them worked on the construction of the town.

Because Master Jones had made it clear that the *Mayflower* would leave. And soon.

If half of the crew weren't sick, he would've left already.

Everyone who was able had come to shore this morning. The ladies had to do mounds of laundry, and the men were working on the houses.

She'd had a brief moment with William when they'd first made it to shore. He had prayed with her, which made her heart soar. Her dreams of a Godly husband to be the head of their household were coming true.

Perhaps she'd get the opportunity to see him again when they broke for the meal. That was enough encouragement to see her through the grueling hours of scrubbing clothes.

David ran up to her side. "Mr. Carver said I can help stack wood again. Is that all right with you, Mary Elizabeth?"

Anything was better to a young boy than helping with laundry. "As long as you aren't the one wielding the ax, you have my permission."

He took off running down the beach. The cold temperature didn't seem to bother him one bit. Mary Elizabeth laughed and went back to her scrubbing.

A couple of the other ladies chattered about what they planned to plant in their gardens. A few children played on the beach. But what caught Mary Elizabeth's eye was the sight of two girls sitting on a rock together. They didn't seem to be talking. They just sat.

Setting down the skirt she'd been scrubbing, Mary Elizabeth headed over to the two and realized it was Elizabeth Tilley and Mary Chilton. No wonder they were sitting together in silence. They'd both been orphaned this winter.

"Good day, Elizabeth, Mary." She nodded at them.

"Good day, Miss Chapman." Miss Tilley threw a small shell into the water.

The other girl didn't speak.

Maybe she should try another tactic. "Would either of you know how to fish?"

The girls shook their heads.

"What about hunt?"

Elizabeth giggled. "Girls don't hunt; only the boys do that."

"Oh, I guess you're right." Mary Elizabeth tapped her chin. "What about a game of bowls? Do you know how to play that?"

The quiet Mary shrugged. But Miss Tilley nodded. And there— that was a spark in the girl's eye. Progress!

"Well, I happen to know where a set of bowls are. And if we get the washing done, I think we should all play."

"Oh, could we, Miss Chapman? It's been ages since we've done anything fun." Elizabeth jumped off the rock.

"I'll say we have a plan. But I need to get the laundry done first, agreed?"

Mary followed her friend and nodded. At least that was something.

The little group went to work on the clothes, and Mary Elizabeth realized the girls were only a few years younger than herself. If she remembered correctly, they were both thirteen. On the cusp of womanhood but still longing for the happiness of childhood. She couldn't blame them—especially with their futures unknown. Prayerfully, the girls could stay together with one of the families. They were going to need each other's friendship.

Like hers with Dorothy.

The thought of her dear friend made her heart clinch. It didn't hurt as much as it had, but she had a feeling the ache would never truly go away.

When they'd finished the wash, Mary Elizabeth went to the common house and pulled the bowls out of their trunk. They'd gradually moved a lot of the cargo to the shelter in hopes that they'd all be living in Plimouth soon.

She walked back to the beach and began to play with the girls. It took her a while to find her footing—it had been far too long since she'd played. But the hour of laughter was well worth it.

Making her way back to the common house, she looked forward to standing by a fire. Her toes had gotten quite cold.

Then she'd have to check the laundry and see if there was any chance it was drying. Several times she'd had to bring frozen pieces of clothing back to the ship to warm them up so they could dry.

A commotion by one of the new houses drew her attention.

William stood with his hands on his hips. "That doesn't belong to you, Peter."

Mary Elizabeth wasn't sure what he was talking about, so she moved in closer.

Most of the elders and men were now gathered around the two.

Peter held a book up in the air and shouted. "This book proves that William Lytton is a spy."

Everyone started talking at once.

Mr. Carver held up his hands. "Calm down, Peter. Exactly what are you trying to accuse Mr. Lytton of? Who would he be a spy for?"

"The company." Peter held up a little pouch and shook it. "And here's the proof. He was paid to keep records on all of us."

William shook his head.

Their governor spoke again. "Exactly why would they need a spy?"

Peter glared at the crowd. "To ensure that we failed."

Gasps and murmurs filled the air.

"That is not true." William took a step forward.

Peter opened the book and read. "The explorers stumbled upon mounds on their first trip and, after digging, discovered baskets of corn. Although it didn't belong to them, the men took the corn for themselves."

This time Mr. Carver stepped closer to William. "Why would you write that, William?"

William stood tall and lifted his chin. "Because it was true, sir. But that's not the whole part. Of course it sounds negative when read in this manner."

Peter turned to another page and read, "The death toll rises. At this rate, there is nothing to show for the settlement except graves and debt. I fear the investors will be disappointed with our efforts."

"That's enough, Peter." Mr. Carver held out his hand. "Kindly hand me the book."

The young man stood there for a moment and looked at the faces around him. "We can't let him get away with this." Handing the book to the governor, he crossed his arms over his chest and frowned. "Surely you all can see that he's been working against us—so that we'll owe the precious investors more money."

Several others murmured their agreement.

Mr. Carver went to the front of the group and held both his hands in the air. "I think we all understand why Peter is so upset, but we haven't given William the chance to explain himself. Now please, quiet down so we can get to the truth of the matter." He turned back to William. "Did the company hire you to spy on us?"

"No, sir. But the company *did* hire me to keep accurate records."

Mary Elizabeth took a deep breath. *What?*

"Exactly what kind of records?"

"Everything. The work we did, the land we chose, the house we built, the timber we cut, fish we caught, everything for the settlement. Since the investors didn't have a representative here, they asked me to be it."

Mr. Carver sighed. "When did they ask you to do this job?"

"The day I was loading my things on the *Mayflower*, sir."

"So you had already planned to journey with us."

"Yes, sir." William held out his hands in front of him. "It was a good job for me, a good opportunity—and it seemed like an honorable thing to do to make sure we were all good stewards of the investors' money."

"I understand that, Mr. Lytton." Mr. Carver took off his hat and ran a hand through his hair. "But what I don't understand is why you didn't tell any of us."

It was at that moment that William noticed her at the edge of the crowd.

Oh, William. Her heart sank. Why hadn't he said anything?

William held her gaze as he spoke to the crowd. "I was one of the Strangers at the beginning. I didn't know any of you, and you didn't know me. I wanted to build trust so that you would know I was an honorable man in my dealings."

"So why didn't you tell us after we'd gotten to know you?" Mr. Bradford put the question forth.

William's shoulders sagged. "I'd thought about it many times, but the timing never seemed to be right. Especially with all the loss."

Mr. Carver nodded, even though several negative comments were made in the crowd. He paced back and forth for several minutes.

Mary Elizabeth couldn't handle it any longer. She walked to the center where her betrothed stood. "William hasn't done anything wrong. It's understandable that the Adventurers would have wanted to know what was going on here—it was their money, after all."

David walked through the crowd and stood by William. "I caught Peter snooping in William's things awhile back. I thought he was stealing, but he tried to convince me that he had loaned William something. Did anyone think about how he had to sneak around to find that book and the money? Isn't *that* stealing and spying?"

Mr. Carver continued to pace. Mr. Brewster and Mr. Bradford went over and spoke with the governor.

Whispers went through the crowd.

But Mary Elizabeth couldn't listen. She didn't care what the people were saying or what they thought. William was a good and honorable man. The elders would see that, and this foolishness could be put behind them.

The men turned back toward William, but Mr. Bradford looked at Mary Elizabeth.

"We need to ask you a question, Miss Chapman."

She straightened her shoulders. "Of course."

"Did William—your future husband—tell you anything about his job for the company?"

The air left her lungs in a great sigh. She looked at William.

He nodded to her and put his hands on David's shoulders.

The truth was her only answer. "No. He did not."

CHAPTER 29

Friday, 16 March 1620/1

The past few days had been torture. Other than Mary Elizabeth and David, everyone in the settlement treated William differently. The elders and Governor Carver stated they needed to pray about their decision, and he respected that. He just wasn't expecting for everything to change. For the men he'd come to admire to doubt him.

He worked on his house alone, hoping that soon this would all be a distant memory. He would give the money back in a heartbeat if it ensured the people's trust.

As William shoved clay between the logs of the west wall, John Alden joined him. "Are you going to the ceremony today for Standish?"

William shook his head. "I don't think the people want me there." As much as he wanted his friend's trust and missed the camaraderie, he didn't think John could do anything to make things better.

"That's just your pride talking." John grabbed a clump of clay and started working it into another crack.

"No. It's the truth."

"William, why didn't you tell me about the job? I noticed you scribbling in the journal often enough." His friend's tone wasn't accusatory. It sounded more hurt.

"I've asked myself that a million times since Monday."

John continued to work. "I'm sure you have. I trust you, William, and I don't believe you've done anything untoward."

"Thank you, John."

"But these people—the Saints especially—have been hurt by so many people in the past. They've been completely betrayed and lost everything."

William had forgotten about that. No wonder they wouldn't take him at his word. And he couldn't blame them.

"Give it time. They'll come around."

"My only thoughts were to do the right and honorable thing."

John nodded. "I know, my friend. The others will see the truth."

They worked in silence for a good while until John told him it was time for the ceremony. The military service was to name Mr. Standish the captain and head of their protection.

William cleaned up as best he could and decided to join the rest of the people.

Governor Carver stood and held up his hands. "Welcome, everyone. We are here today to honor—" The man blinked several times, and his jaw dropped. Several moments of silence passed.

William turned to see what the governor was looking at. Up their lone street strode an Indian.

Gasps were heard behind him, followed by complete silence.

The native man was tall with long black hair and a clean-shaven face. Most astonishing was that he was naked except for a span of leather with fringe about his waist.

Several of the women gasped and looked down at the ground. No one was accustomed to seeing that much skin, and wasn't the man cold?

He carried a bow and arrows, and he walked right up to them. "Welcome, Englishmen."

"Why, he speaks English!" One of the elders moved forward.

As the men moved in toward the Indian, William stepped back. The conversation was broken and stilted.

The people didn't trust him right now, and they had been hoping to connect with the natives since arriving. It would be better for everyone if he just went to work on his house.

He walked back to his little plot and went to work with the clay.

The process was time consuming, but if he worked hard, he could finish this wall today while it was still light.

"I guess you're not fascinated with our new guest?"

William shifted his gaze from the wall to his betrothed. She stood at the corner of what was supposed to be their home. "I figured I would stay out of the way."

Mary Elizabeth stood with her hands behind her back. "May I help?"

The sight of her—so sweet and beautiful—made him smile. "Of course." And it made his heart ache.

"You haven't said much lately, William. I'm worried about you." She worked twigs and leaves in with the clay.

He shoved the thick mud in a little bit harder than necessary. "There's nothing to worry about." But there was. She hadn't thought it all through like he had.

"Don't you want to talk about it?"

"Not particularly. It's in their hands. I will have to wait for them to decide what my true intentions were, and then they will decide my fate."

"They will see the truth. I have faith that God will work all of this out."

He let out a heavy sigh. "But what if they don't? That's the part you refuse to acknowledge. Do you still want to marry a man who's been accused of spying? On your own people?"

"William, it's not going to come to that."

"Mary Elizabeth, you've got to face facts. This could very well go in a direction that neither of us wants. Everything I've worked for could be lost. But what's worse is I could lose *you*."

She stomped her foot. "You are not going to lose me, Mr. Lytton."

"You can't know that." Shaking his head, he knew what he had to do. "Where would we go if they find me guilty? How would we survive? It's not possible."

"With God *all* things are possible."

Her optimism made him want to believe her. But the nature of people had proven she was carrying around false hope. He knew the people had been hurt a lot. But he'd also seen his share of misery. People let him down every time.

"William? What's wrong? Please talk to me." She laid a hand on his arm.

"I'm sorry, Mary Elizabeth. Truly, I am. But I think our betrothal needs to come to an end."

After shedding a bucket's worth of tears and walking along the beach for hours, Mary Elizabeth asked to be taken back to the *Mayflower*. Only a few sick were left on the ship, and they were hoping to finish moving everyone by the end of next week. The least she could do was to help pack up their belongings. It would give her something to do with all her frustrated energy since she knew that sleep would be long in coming.

How could William hurt her like that? It didn't make sense, and it wasn't like him at all. Besides, she didn't believe it. She knew that he loved her.

Climbing aboard the ship that had been one of her seafaring homes for eight long months, she realized that it was on this ship that she'd fallen in love with handsome William Lytton. On this ship, she'd grown to be strong and brave.

On this ship, she'd lost her Father and her best friend.

The good had come with the bad. Just like this awful situation for William. He'd wanted to do the right thing. She knew that.

But she also knew her future was with him. No matter what happened. How could she convince him?

Taking the steps down to the gun deck, Mary thought of their first meeting. It had been on a set of steps just like this. And William had reached down a hand for her. His touch had ignited a flame of new life for her—and she never wanted to go back.

"Mary Elizabeth." Mr. Bradford stepped aside at the bottom of the companionway.

His voice startled her and brought her back to the present moment. This time, the steps held her broken heart. "I'm sorry, Mr. Bradford. I guess my mind was on other things."

"Would you like to talk about it?"

"I'm sure you're quite busy. I wouldn't want to delay you."

He sat on one of the steps. "Actually, at the moment I'm not." He looked around the dim and dirty area. "This will be my last night to stay here. My house is finished thanks to help from your William, and I was just gathering up the remainder of my things."

William had helped with Mr. Bradford's house? Her mind fought the urge to cry and scream all at the same time.

"Now tell me, what's on your mind?" He folded his hands on his knee. "Is it the Indian visitor today?"

"Oh my, I completely forgot about that!" She covered her mouth for a moment and then let her hand fall. "No, it's not that, although I'm sure David will want to tell me all about it. I'm actually worried for William."

"Ah yes, I see."

"He tried to end our betrothal today because he says that I haven't thought through what will happen if the town finds him guilty of spying."

"And have you?"

"Well, no. I hadn't until he brought it up, but it really doesn't change anything. I love William, no matter what. I don't believe that he's done a thing wrong, and I will stand by that."

Mr. Bradford nodded.

"But it's hard for me to understand why he would want to push me away in all this. And it exasperates me."

"Have you thought of the fact that William may be doing this because he thinks it will protect you in some way?"

She frowned. "Well, no. Not really."

"That's what strong, Godly men do. They protect the people they love. By sacrificing themselves and ultimately their own happiness."

"So he'd rather be miserable and just let me go?"

"If he thinks it's best for you."

"But how does he know what's best for me if he won't listen to me?"

He sighed. "That's the tricky part. Men are good at convincing themselves that they know what's best. We are the protectors and providers. But my wife, Dorothy—God rest her soul—reminded me that God gave the woman to be a helpmeet, and that meant that I had to learn how to listen to her wise counsel rather than always try to fix it all. It took years for her to teach me, but she was a very patient woman."

Mary Elizabeth stared down at her hands. Maybe he was correct. Her relationship with William was so new, she didn't understand a lot or truly understand how it should work. But how could she get William to see? "What do you suggest I do?"

"Pray."

She nodded. That should have been her first response.

He laid a hand on her shoulder and stood. "He loves you, Miss Chapman. Of that you can be assured."

While her heart knew the words were true, it still hurt. Would William turn his back on her forever?

The air was finally getting warmer. Maybe Mary Elizabeth wouldn't make him wear his heavy cloak everywhere now.

But she probably would. She didn't want him to get sick. That was what big sisters did.

The fact that she'd allowed him to stay with Mr. Alden in the new town the past few days was pretty impressive. She'd helped move the rest of the people from the ship and would come on the last shallop today.

David couldn't wait to tell her all the exciting news.

As he stood on the shore and watched the smaller boat make its way in, he thought about William. His sister's future husband hadn't been too happy lately. The governor had yet to decide what to do about the accusations Peter had made, but there wasn't any foundation for them to find him guilty. William was a good man. And he loved Mary Elizabeth.

The shallop reached the harbor, and they began to unload. It was pretty interesting to think about. They were finally all ashore. No longer living on the *Mayflower*.

More than fifty of the passengers had died, and Master Jones had lost half of his crew. It was a sobering thought.

"David!" Mary Elizabeth ran toward him. She hugged him tight. "I've missed you."

"I've missed you too."

She kissed his cheek. "So I hear you know all about our visitor?"

"His name is Samoset." He puffed out his chest. "I talked to him, and he let me look at his bow."

"Did you now?"

"Aye. And he knew some English words."

"I heard that."

"Well, did you know that he stayed the night?"

Mary Elizabeth's eyes widened. "No. I didn't know that."

"Yes, with the Hopkins family. Then he went back to the Wampanoag people—they're the ones that live a little ways away—and they came back to trade the next few days."

"That's exciting news for the colony, isn't it?" She lifted a few blankets from the pile at her feet. "So where are we staying?"

"William is giving us his house right now. He's going to stay with John Alden in the common house. A lot of people are sharing since there's only seven or eight houses built."

"That's fine. I'm sure we will do just fine. And once William and I are married, we should probably offer a place to stay for John, don't you think?"

"Sure." David shrugged. He didn't care too much, as long as he didn't have to live on the smelly ship anymore. "Hey, you know what else Samoset told us?"

"What?"

"That this place used to be called Patuxet. But a few years ago all the people died. There was a really bad plague."

"A plague? What kind of a plague?" Mary Elizabeth had that worried tone again.

"I don't know. One of the ships brought it over. It killed a lot of people, Samoset said. All the way up north to his tribe."

Mary Elizabeth slowed her steps. "So there's a lot of Indians around here?"

"Aye. He said the Wampanoag wish to be good neighbors, and it must have been the Nauset that attacked the men on shore that night."

"Oh." Her brow was all wrinkled.

"Don't worry. Samoset said they don't want to kill us anymore."

The plan hadn't gone as Peter had hoped.

And maybe he hadn't thought about what would happen if they all agreed that William *was* a spy.

What would they think of a new company employee then? Or would he be able to convince them that he was trustworthy since he'd discovered the man who wanted them to fail? He would be up front about it from the beginning instead of hiding the secret away. The people had to respect that.

He'd have to send word back with the *Mayflower* to his cousin. Maybe his family could pull some strings and get things expedited.

The worst part was that he would just have to wait and see.

And he hated waiting.

But he still had the money. No one had even thought to ask him for it after he'd confronted William with the journal.

Maybe he would just keep it. He'd earned it, after all.

Thursday, 22 March 1620/1

Mary Elizabeth woke to the sound of birds chirping and singing. For the first time in eight months, she'd slept on dry land—not on a ship. And it was wonderful.

Stretching on her bed, she looked up at the roof. William had done a good job with the thatch. It was so thick she couldn't see any holes, which would be good for when it rained.

Another thought sent a thrill through her. She stood up. All the way. Stretching her arms above her head, she still didn't touch the ceiling. No more crouching and bending to fit into the short space of the cramped deck they'd lived on. Laughing out loud, she covered her mouth so she wouldn't wake David. She'd never been so thankful to stand up straight. And inside.

Amazing what a few months of hardship could teach. To find joy in even the smallest matters.

She wanted to accomplish so many things today. Work in the garden. Unpacking all the possessions that had been stored in the hold for all these months. And goodness, she'd love to make some bread if she could scrounge up the ingredients. They had foodstuffs stored in some of the barrels that were now in the common house, but she couldn't remember how much flour they'd rationed.

Before any of that, Mary Elizabeth wanted to speak to William. This had gone on long enough, and now that Mr. Bradford had explained the "why" behind William's behavior, she was ready to talk to him about it and convince him that she would love him no matter what.

Tightening the strings of her shift, she prayed for guidance. Certainly the Lord would bless her efforts to honor her future husband by sticking by his side.

She put on her green shirtwaist and adjusted the laces at the shoulders. She'd lost a good deal of weight between the hardship of the voyage and sickness. Holding out her hands in front of her, she noticed her wrists appeared exceedingly bony. It wasn't the greatest appearance for a bride-to-be, but she'd just have to eat more in the coming weeks.

Slipping on the matching green skirt over her shift, she hoped the extra effort would impress William. He hadn't seen this dress on her before. Would he appreciate it?

Doubts filled her mind as she walked to the common house. She wasn't normally a confrontational person. Other than her spat with the sailor on board the *Mayflower*, she'd never confronted anyone. Ever.

She took a deep breath and entered the common house. Now or never.

William sat in the corner with John as they broke the fast over a barrel.

"Mr. Lytton, could I speak to you for a moment?"

His head snapped in her direction. "Of course." Standing up, he nodded to John.

"Thank you."

William took her elbow and walked her outside. "You look lovely this morning." His blue eyes seemed sad.

Unsure of the best way to handle it, she went straight to the point. "William, I can't let you end our betrothal. I've made a commitment to you, and you can't brush me aside so easily." She twisted her hands in front of her. "I understand you are trying to protect me in some way, but this is not the way to do it."

His face turned toward the hill where the cannons now sat. The muscle in his jaw twitched. "I can't risk your well-being along with my own—"

"But isn't that what marriage is all about? The two—side by side?"

"We're not married yet, Mary Elizabeth."

The words stung. She fought back tears.

"Until we know the outcome of their ruling, I can't even consider putting you in a scandalous situation. Your reputation is on the line along with mine. That's not fair to you or to young David."

"But it's not true! You aren't a spy. You haven't done anything wrong." Tears slipped out from under her lashes.

William took her hands in his own. "I love it that you think that, Mary Elizabeth, I do. It lifts my heart to the heavens to know that you believe in me. But I have to do this. It's for the best." He squeezed her hands while he gazed at her. Those blue eyes burning with sorrow.

Then he let go and walked away.

Mary Elizabeth stood in the middle of their street and cried.

CHAPTER 31

The hurt look on Mary Elizabeth's face stuck with William all morning. And he was the one who'd put it there. It was bad enough that people didn't trust him anymore and half of them thought he was a spy, but now he'd tossed her aside. A little more of him died with the thought. It didn't matter that he had to do the noble and right thing by her. That he had to protect her reputation from tarnish. He'd never get that look out of his memory.

After leaving her in the street, his decision became even clearer. He'd have to pack up his belongings and leave with the *Mayflower*. Mary Elizabeth would stand by his side no matter what, but if the people rejected him, didn't trust him, then her reputation would be linked with him. What future did that give her? And little David?

It didn't take him long to pack his things. All that was left was to secure passage with the master. It was best this way. The people of Plimouth could carry on and not have to worry about who to trust.

As he left the shelter of their fort—the fenced-in little group of buildings—William headed to the trees. The little colony of Plimouth would be having their ceremony for Captain Standish today, and while he wanted to be a part of it, he didn't think the people wanted him. Since he couldn't be much use anywhere else, he could at least chop some wood to make furniture.

The walk gave him a chance to pray. *Lord, this isn't going the way I'd planned. But I want to trust You. I just don't know if I'm doing the right thing. I didn't feel like it was wrong to take the job, but I should have listened to Your prodding and shared with my friends.*

Everything had changed. But he wouldn't trade his new relationship with the Lord for anything. He just wished that he could change some of the other circumstances.

They were finally all living in the new settlement. It should be a time of rejoicing, yet William's future wouldn't be here.

As he smashed the ax into a large tree, it felt like all his hopes and dreams were smashed as well.

Discouragement tried to strangle him. *Lord, what do I do?*

With each swing of the ax he prayed. Over and over and over again.

The verse from 2 Corinthians came back to him. " 'We *are* persecuted, but not forsaken; cast downe, but we perish not.' "

The words soothed his anguish a bit. And so he said it again.

" 'We *are* persecuted, but not forsaken; cast downe, but we perish not.' "

He swung the ax again and decided to quote every verse he'd memorized. If he couldn't think on anything but the doubt and discouragement, he would change that by thinking on what was good—God's Word.

As a second tree fell, William looked back toward the settlement. Breathing hard, he leaned on his ax. God was in control. He knew that and trusted in it. He'd have to leave his fate in the Almighty's hands and simply do the best he could. Even returning to England.

Would he ever get over Mary Elizabeth? No. The thought of her brown eyes made him want to cry. He'd never loved anyone but her. And there wouldn't ever be anyone else.

Movement down by Town Brook caught his attention.

His eyes widened. Indians!

And not just one like the other day. There were at least forty—no fifty!—men.

The ceremony for Captain Standish should be taking place now. Were these men readying an attack?

William picked up the ax and wound his way through the trees to get a better look.

What if he was the only one who could warn them? Those natives looked like warriors. They could kill everyone in a matter of minutes.

He couldn't let that happen.

Mary Elizabeth waited outside the door. Peter had gone in, and eventually he would have to come out. And when he did? She'd be waiting.

The ceremony would start any minute, and she wanted this over with.

The door opened, and Peter stepped out.

Mary Elizabeth stepped in front of him.

"Excuse me, Miss Chapman."

"I don't think I will, Peter."

His smile looked pasty. "I'd like to go to the ceremony." He offered an elbow. "Would you like me to escort you?"

"No. I would not." She placed her hands on her hips. "But I would like to know why you still have William's money."

His eyes shifted around and then stared at the ground. "I don't know what you're talking about."

"Yes, you do." John Alden exited the house behind Peter. "It's right here. Along with a few other things that don't look like they belong to you."

Running as fast as he could, William took a longer trek back to the fort by going around the back side. If he could just warn someone, maybe they could prevent a disaster.

When he made it to the assembly, he noticed Mr. Bradford standing near the rear. "Bradford!"

Several people looked in his direction, but he didn't care.

"Yes, William?" The man turned to him.

"There's Indians at the brook."

"How many?"

"At least fifty." By this point, half the crowd had turned to stare at William.

Governor Carver stopped his speech and walked toward him. "Where did you see them?"

"They're across the brook. I don't know what they're intentions are, but I felt I needed to warn you all just in case."

Their leader furrowed his brow and then rested a hand on William's shoulder. "Thank you. You did the right thing. Let's hope they are the Wampanoag that Samoset told us about."

As William caught his breath, he noticed Mary Elizabeth with David and John across the crowd. She smiled at him.

His heart ached to go see her, to hold her hand. But he knew he couldn't.

"Samoset!" Governor Carver's exclamation made everyone turn the other direction. "Welcome!"

The tall native man walked straight down the center of their street again, and this time he had a friend. They carried some skins and fish and didn't seem to be bothered by all the staring.

"We're glad you came back." Governor Carver smiled and bowed.

Samoset nodded. "This. . .Tisquantum."

The governor moved closer. "Do you know anything about the men at the brook?"

He nodded again. "That. . .Massasoit. Sachem of Wampanoag."

"And he's here for what reason?"

Silence covered the crowd as they all waited for the Indian's response.

Samoset poked Governor Carver in the chest. "You talk."

Mary Elizabeth paced inside the common house. Edward Winslow had been sent with Tisquantum back to meet Massasoit to deliver a message that the people at Plimouth wanted to be friends with the Wampanoag. They would trade with each other, protect each other, and be at peace with each other.

Winslow stayed at the brook with Massasoit's brother while the sachem and twenty of his men came into town. Governor Carver, Captain Standish, and Elder Brewster were all in a house, speaking with the chief at that very moment.

And so everyone waited.

As much as she wanted to have peace with the natives, she had another matter of urgent business. She couldn't wait for this meeting to be over so she could speak to Governor Carver about William.

The door to the big room opened, and the governor walked in with Massasoit. "We have a treaty!" Mr. Carver smiled.

The crowd clapped and cheered while Massasoit raised his eyebrows and simply nodded.

Mary Elizabeth had to admit the man was quite striking and an imposing figure. Thank the Lord a treaty had been reached.

Elder Brewster brought forth a parchment. "I shall read you all the terms." He cleared his throat. "One: That neither Massasoit or any of his, should injure or do hurt, to any of our people. Two: That if any of his, did hurt to any of ours; he should send the offender, so that he might be punished. Three: That if anything were taken away from any of our people, he should cause it to be restored; and we should do the like to his. Four: If any did unjustly war against Massasoit, we would aid him; if any did war against us, he should aid us. Five: He should send to his neighbors confederates, to certify them of this, that they might not wrong us, but might be likewise comprised in the conditions of peace. Six: That when their men come to us, they should leave their bows and arrows behind them. Likewise, when we visit them."

The men in the room all nodded.

Mary Elizabeth did too. It sounded like a wonderful peace treaty.

Massasoit turned away and left the building. Everyone watched as the noble-looking man walked down the street with his men.

Governor Carver held his hands up again. "I do believe we need to praise the Lord for this historic event today."

Amens were heard throughout the room, and people began to

talk over one another. The excitement of having so many Indians in their midst was thrilling.

Mary Elizabeth walked up to the governor. "Mr. Carver, I think it's high time that you and the elders discuss William Lytton and the accusations against him."

Peter walked forward, his head ducked.

"I believe that Peter has something to say to all of us."

The room quieted.

The man who'd accused William stared at his shoes. "I should probably tell you that I had planned on accusing Mr. Lytton from the beginning of the voyage."

"Why would you do such a thing?" Elder Brewster moved toward the young man.

"Because I wanted the job that had been offered to him. It was only after I saw Mr. Crawford offer him the job that I came up with the plan. If I could tarnish his reputation, then you all would believe that he was a spy and out to see us ruined."

Mr. Bradford also moved forward, his brow deeply creased. "What made you come forward today?"

Peter glanced up at Mary. "Miss Chapman came to me and said that if I didn't tell the truth, she would. And she would. . ."

"Yes, go on," Governor Carver pushed.

He sighed and ducked his head again. "She would present the evidence that I have been stealing from you all. She said I deserved the opportunity to confess first."

CHAPTER 32

The room erupted in a jumble of words. Maybe it was better for William to exit now. He could grab his belongings and go speak to Captain Jones. Even with Peter's confession, the people would still consider him a spy and would feel betrayed by him. There wasn't any other course of action for him. But at least people knew the truth now.

As William walked toward the door during the ruckus, John caught his arms. His friend whispered in his ear. "You aren't going anywhere."

Governor Carver raised his arms. "Please, everyone." He turned to Peter. "What have you stolen?"

Peter ducked his head and laid the items out in front of everyone. William felt sorry for the young man—something he wouldn't have felt before he came to know his Savior.

Several gasps were heard, and William spied the coin pouch he'd been given by Mr. Crawford. Oh, if he could only go back and tell people the truth.

Governor Carver worked to get everyone's attention. "Settle down, settle down. We need to conduct ourselves in an orderly manner." He turned to Peter. "What do you have to say for yourself, Peter?"

Peter apologized and confessed to everything—his plan to accuse William and stealing from the others.

"Mary Elizabeth?" Governor Carver turned to the beautiful woman William wished he could marry. But that dream would have to die.

She tried to convince everyone that he was a good man. Then John Alden vouched for him. Several men spoke up next of the good work William had done and how he'd helped others. And Mr. Bradford reminded everyone that William had warned them all about the fifty warriors that showed up unannounced.

Peter walked up to him and returned the pouch with the money.

William looked out at the crowd. These people that he'd lived with and worked with for all this time. They might not trust him, but he could at least do the honorable thing. He held the bag aloft. "I know that my actions have made many of you distrust me. It was never my intention to spy on anyone or to be dishonest in any way. So in an effort to ask for forgiveness, I'd like to donate these funds to put toward the debts owed by the colonists. This should help." He tossed the bag to Governor Carver and strode toward the door.

The governor asked for other testimonies so they could vote.

William couldn't bear to see Mary Elizabeth any longer. His departure would be best for all of them. If only he'd learned this lesson earlier—before he'd lost his heart to her. He snuck out of the common house and headed to the stream. His future was in God's hands. Exactly where it should be.

The brook was beautiful this time of day with the sun shining down on its clear water. It made William think of being washed clean.

The rustling in the grass made him look across the brook. Captain Standish escorted Peter and looked to William. "This young man would like to speak with you, Mr. Lytton."

"I know you probably hate me after what I did, and I don't blame you. But I'd like to ask for your forgiveness, William." Peter's hands had been bound once he'd admitted to stealing. While William wanted justice done, he hated to see that.

William stood and faced his one-time accuser. "You are forgiven, Peter. Just as Christ has forgiven me." He turned to Standish. "What will happen to him?"

"Master Jones has agreed to take him back to England. The company will decide what to do after that."

He turned back to Peter. "I wish you well, Peter, and do not wish any harm to come to you." At one time, he wouldn't have been able to say those words. But God had done a mighty work in him.

A call from the fort reached his ears. William looked out across and saw John Alden waving his arm in the air.

"You better go. We will be right behind you." Captain Standish nodded.

William walked back to the little town. Dread lodged in the pit of his stomach. He'd have to find a way to say goodbye to Mary Elizabeth and David. The thought made his stomach turn.

John shook his hand as William reached the fort. "They've voted."

"And?"

"Well, you have to go inside and hear from them."

They walked toward the common house, and the crowd met them outside.

Governor Carver came forward. "It was unanimous, William. There are no charges against you."

Relief flooded his chest, and he felt like the weight of the world had been lifted off his shoulders.

"It's quite unfortunate that we've put you through this difficult time." Mr. Bradford came forward and shook his hand. "We're all very grateful that you have been part of our community, and we'd like to ask you to stay and *remain* a part of our community."

William blinked several times. Had they known he was leaving? "You want me to stay?"

Faces around the room were filled with smiles.

Mr. Bradford clapped him on the back. "Of course we want you to stay!"

John Alden was the next to come forward and whispered in his ear. "They knew you had packed to go, and that impressed many of the offended—that you would sacrifice your future for their trust."

William looked around the room again.

Elder Brewster came forward. "There is no hesitancy in our trust of you, Mr. Lytton. Rest assured."

The words touched his heart, and he let himself look for Mary Elizabeth. She stood in the back with David, a teary smile on her face.

John put a hand on William's shoulder and shouted to the crowd. "Looks like it's time to have a wedding!"

William walked to Mary Elizabeth as the crowd hushed. "Are you willing?"

Her eyes sparkled. "Aye, William Lytton. Always and forever."

Tuesday, 3 April 1621

The day was warm in the gorgeous sunlight. Mary Elizabeth walked down the beach toward the long sandbar and thanked the Lord for all that He'd done and provided. After so many months of hardship and devastation, they were looking forward to a brighter future.

Many trials were sure to be ahead, but most of the colony was beginning to rest in the fact that the worst finally seemed to be behind them. Tisquantum had stayed in their little town and taught them about planting corn and using fish as fertilizer to help it grow. Word traveled quickly around the native peoples, and Tisquantum was a wonderful asset to have as a translator. It didn't take long for the people of Plimouth to come up with a nickname for the tall and strong native man in their midst—Squanto.

He'd also been very handy teaching everyone—women included—how to fish in the brook. Mary Elizabeth thought of her conversation with Mrs. Hopkins aboard the ship—and no matter how much fish she ate, she would be grateful.

When she reached the sandbar about a mile down from their settlement, Mary saw David and William already there. She placed her hands on her hips. "Are you two plotting against me?"

"Us?" William put a hand to his chest and looked down at David. "We would never do that."

"Are you ready to race, Mary Elizabeth?"

"I just walked all the way down here. You could at least be a gentleman and let me catch my breath."

"You're just worried because you're going to lose."

She eyed her little brother. "I may be 'old' and a girl, but I'm still fast."

"How do you know? It's not like you ever run anywhere." David shook his head like she was out of her mind.

Mary Elizabeth laughed. It was true. She hadn't run in a very long time. But this was for David, and she'd do anything for the little imp. "All right. Do we have any rules?"

William stepped forward. "I'm so glad you asked, milady." He bowed. "This log right here marks the start line. There's another one way down there for the finish line. That's where I'll be waiting to see who crosses it first." He winked at her. "Now there will be no pushing, no shoving, no tripping, no biting—"

David started giggling.

"Honestly, William." Mary Elizabeth shook her head but couldn't resist smiling up at him.

"All right, there will be no cheating. How's that?"

"Run in a straight line. Win. I think I've got it." She nodded.

"Are you ready for me to head down to the finish line?"

"Yes!" David jumped up and down.

"Good. You'll know when to start when you see my arm lower, like this." William raised his arm high and dropped it down.

"Well, you need to hurry before anyone sees what we're doing. I don't think I want to be seen the day before my wedding in a footrace. I'm supposed to be a proper young lady, you know."

William's laugh was his response as he ran down the sandy bar.

David and Mary crouched down a little as they waited for the signal.

William dropped his arm.

She took off. Halfway to William she realized she should have made David wear a heavy skirt to make the race fair. But she pressed on.

William held out his two hands as they drew near.

Her feet pounded the sand, and she crossed the line of finish.

"Mary Elizabeth wins!" The shout made her laugh and raise her arms in triumph.

As she turned around, David barreled into her and tackled her to the ground. "You're pretty fast for a girl."

Breathing hard, she hugged her little brother. He wouldn't be little for much longer, and she would treasure every moment she had with him. "You're getting pretty fast yourself, little man."

He crossed his arms over his chest. "I guess you're not as old as you look."

William's laughter followed them the entire walk home.

Wednesday, 4 April 1621

The deck of the *Mayflower* no longer held crates of chickens and pigs or other animals. It had been swept clean for the festivities of the day and now held the survivors of their first winter. As she looked around at the faces, she realized how wonderful it was to be a part of this group. Through joy and sorrow, they had triumphed. They were here today for a very special reason.

Mary Elizabeth's heart thumped in her chest. Today she would marry William.

Dressed in her finest dress of red wool, she checked her sleeves and the tucks of her skirt. She closed her eyes for a moment and breathed a prayer for peace and calmness for her spirit. She hoped that Mother, Father, and Dorothy knew that God had brought her a wonderful husband.

A tug at her arm made her open her eyes. "Are you ready, Mary Elizabeth?"

"I am." She looked at her younger brother. So handsome in his blue breeches and coat. "I'm so proud of you, David."

"As I am of you. I'm glad you're marrying William. He's a Godly man and he loves you. And he's a lot of fun."

"He is fun, isn't he?" The smile that stretched across her face felt like it might reach her ears. "And you're correct: he loves me. I love him too."

"As long as you're happy." Such grown-up words from little David. Time was moving far too fast. If she blinked, he might be grown and gone.

"Very much so."

"Well then, let's get you married." David took her arm and walked her to the center of the main deck.

Mr. Bradford stood there with William and smiled. "You look lovely, Mary Elizabeth."

"I agree." William winked at her.

Mary Elizabeth's stomach tumbled over itself as Mr. Bradford talked about the holy union of marriage and how it represented Christ and His bride—the church.

William's eyes were riveting. She could spend the rest of her life just gazing into their blue depths.

After reading some scripture, Mr. Bradford looked at her. "Are you ready?"

"Oh, yes." She determined to stay focused this time. Of course, who could blame her for being focused on her husband-to-be?

Mr. Bradford had them repeat some simple vows and then took William's hand and her hand and raised them in the air. He placed them together and quoted Matthew 19:6 in a loud, booming voice, " 'Let not man therefore put a sunder that, which *God* hathe coupled together!' "

Cheers broke out around the small crowd, and William took her hands in his. They walked to the longboat together where two sailors would row them ashore while the rest would return in the shallop.

William climbed down into the boat first, and he reached up for her. She couldn't take her eyes off his as she found her way in the small craft.

When he placed his hands on her waist, she placed her hands on the side of his face. This man was hers. And she loved him with all her heart.

He leaned in with a twinkle in his eye. "I love you, Mrs. Lytton." Before she could respond, he captured her lips with his own, and Mary Elizabeth didn't think anything in the world could be better than that.

EPILOGUE

1 August 1665

The wildflowers in William's hand put off a heady scent as he looked out to the harbor. Mary Elizabeth was sure to love the bouquet he'd brought her. In his old age, he was getting to be quite the romantic. The thought made him chuckle. Twelve children and forty-two grandchildren might get a kick out of hearing William Lytton was a softy.

A massive ship in the distance showed off her great sails as she entered their beautiful bay. Forty-five years ago today, he'd left England. For where and to what was uncertain at the time, but he was ever so thankful he had climbed the gangway to the *Mayflower*.

They'd suffered great losses, and it had taken much more than the original contracted seven years to pay off their debts, but they'd survived through all the ups and downs of life. He'd come out victorious with his God and his bride.

He snuck in the door to their kitchen and crept up behind Mary Elizabeth. Wrapping his arms around her, he whispered in her ear, "I love you."

Mary Elizabeth turned around and gasped. "Flowers! You dear man." She hugged him and whispered back. "I love you too."

Her eyes were still that beloved shade of deep brown, but her hair had turned gray under her cap. It was very becoming.

Taking her hand, William led her to the door and then out onto the path where they could see the harbor. "Forty-five years ago, I started a journey. It hasn't been easy, but I feel very blessed. I found

God. And I found you."

"Aye, my love. We are very blessed." She sent him a wink.

All around them, life bustled and bloomed. What had started out as eight meager buildings became a town full of buildings and activity.

Their congregation had grown, and so had their family.

Mary Elizabeth had been faithful at his side through it all.

And whatever the future held for their little colony and this brave New World, he couldn't wait to share it with her.

His *Mayflower* bride.

What could now sustain them, but the Spirit of God and His grace?

May not, and ought not the children of these fathers rightly say, "Our fathers were Englishmen which came over this great ocean, and were ready to perish in this wilderness, but they cried unto the Lord and He heard their voice, and looked on their adversity," etc.

"Let them therefore praise the Lord, because He is good; and His mercies endure forever. Yea, let them which have been redeemed of the Lord, show how He hath delivered them, from the hand of the oppressor.

When they wandered in the desert wilderness out of the way, and found no city to dwell in; both hungry, and thirsty, their soul was overwhelmed in them."

"Let them confess before the Lord His loving kindness, and His wonderful works before the sons of men."

–William Bradford, *Of Plymouth Plantation*

NOTE TO THE READER

It's exciting to trace our lineages back. Many people are able to trace their family history all the way back to the *Mayflower*—I've had fun tracing my roots to 1659, Virginia, Colonial America.

I found it interesting in my research that the majority of Americans think of the *Mayflower* as the actual beginning of our great country. And it's true. The settlers that landed at Plymouth Rock and established Plymouth Colony are the foundations of this great land.

Take for instance, John Howland. His escapade falling overboard really did happen. How he managed to grab the topsail halyard is truly a miracle in and of itself. The most interesting tidbit to me about his whole story is that he ended up having ten children, eighty-eight grandchildren, and now almost two million of his descendants live in the United States. (Several presidents of this great country are in his line—including Franklin D. Roosevelt, George H. W. Bush, and George W. Bush—as well as many famous people, such as Alec Baldwin, Humphrey Bogart, Christopher Lloyd, and Sarah Palin.) That's incredible. Imagine what would have happened if he had been lost to sea that day.

Then there's John Alden—hired as the cooper on the ship and given the option to stay in the colony or return to England. He chose to stay and marry Priscilla Mullins. His line extends down to Dick Van Dyke, Orson Welles, Marilyn Monroe, former Vice President Dan Quayle, and Henry Wadsworth Longfellow. The lines of William Brewster and William Bradford are just as fascinating, as well as the lines of all the other passengers who lived through the great ordeal that was the *Mayflower* and her journey.

It was shocking to me to discover that out of all of the *Mayflower* passengers, only five adult women survived that first winter. Only five. Astounding, isn't it?

While we know the dates the *Speedwell* and the *Mayflower* left Leyden, Southampton, Dartmouth, and Plymouth, the rest of the dates for the voyage aren't exact. When dates weren't known, I used my own discretion and creativity with the time stamps. It's also important to note that during this time period, the Julian calendar was still in use—unlike the Gregorian calendar we use today. This makes for about a ten-day difference. The new year didn't start until March 25 (instead of January 1 like it does now). But to keep this consistent with history and to keep from confusing you as a reader, I've shown the year as 1620/1 starting in January.

It may be shocking to know that these strict Separatists—so staunch in their faith—drank beer for their staple beverage and considered it good for their health. During this time, beer was a brew watered down so that the alcoholic level was 0.05–1.0 percent. Strong enough to kill any bacteria in the water but drinkable by all—including infants and children.

The profane sailor's torment of the Separatists and his subsequent death are true events, although we don't know exactly when it happened, nor is he named (the nickname I gave him is purely fictional). According to William Bradford's *Of Plymouth Plantation*, "There was a proud and very profane young man, one of the seamen, of a lusty able body, which made him the more haughty; he would always be contemning the poor people in their sickness, and cursing them daily with grievous execrations, and did not let to tell them, that he hoped to help to cast half of them overboard before they came to their journey's end, and to make merry with what they had; and if he were gently reproved, he would curse and swear most bitterly. But it pleased God before they came half seas over, to smite this young man with a grievous disease, of which he died in a desperate manner; and so was himself the first that was thrown overboard; thus his curses light on his own head; and it was an astonishment to all his fellows, for they noted it to be the just hand of God upon him." So this unnamed man went down in history as the first to die on the *Mayflower*.

The story of the four More children is tragic, but how fascinating that Samuel More paid for their passage to give them a chance at a new life away from their mother's reputation and their own as illegitimate children.

Several sources state that Mr. Reynolds—the master of the Speedwell—sabotaged the ship so he wouldn't have to make the trip to America and potentially starve to death. A couple of sources state that the ship began leaking immediately (or that Reynolds complained of it leaking) after departing Holland, while others show that the leaking began after their departure from Southampton. Since the *Speedwell* after this adventure was "trimmed" and made many other voyages, it was believed that she was "overmasted and too much pressed with sail." William Bradford wrote in his journal, *Of Plymouth Plantation*, that once they returned to Plymouth, England, the leaks were never verified or truly found, but they kept taking on water. "No special leak could be found, but it was judged to be the general weakness of the ship, and that she would not prove equal to the voyage." He also wrote, "But it was partly due to the cunning and deceit of the master and his crew, who had been hired to stay a whole year at the Settlement, and now, fearing want of victuals, they plotted this stratagem to free themselves, as was afterwards confessed by some of them." How different would our history be if both ships—the *Speedwell* and the *Mayflower*—had journeyed to America on time with all the people who set out? Would they have reached their intended destination earlier in the year (which would be the area of modern-day Manhattan)? Would there have been as much death that first winter? We will never know, but the Saints and their expedition to the New World is indeed fascinating—not only for the beginnings of our great country, but also for the beginning of democracy because of the Mayflower Compact's impact on government over the years. Its influence on the framers of the Constitution alone is astounding.

Since our hero—William Lytton—is a fictional character, please note that he was not historically one of the forty-one signers of the

Mayflower Compact, but for the sake of the story, I had him sign. There also was obviously no espionage—there's no record of anyone being hired by the company to keep a journal or records or to spy on the Planters.

While there are many resources on the history surrounding the *Mayflower*, the best source I found was through Caleb Johnson and his fabulous website: www.Mayflowerhistory.com. You can find a complete list of the passengers and the crew (the ones that we know the names of) on his site, as well as much other information about this historic event. Mr. Johnson also granted us permission to quote from his edited version of William Bradford's *Of Plymouth Plantation*.

Acknowledgments

No book ever just happens. So I'd like to thank those who have been so instrumental in bringing this novel to fruition.

First and foremost to my Lord and Savior, Jesus Christ. This is all for You.

Second, my amazing husband, Jeremy, who puts up with crazy author research and deadlines. I love you more than I could ever express. After more than a quarter of a century of marriage, it just keeps getting better, and I'm looking forward to spending decades and decades more with you. You are amazing.

Third, Becky Germany. What fun to be a part of this series! You are wonderful. Thank you. And to my agent, Karen Ball—what a journey we've been on! Thank you for your wisdom and guidance. Becky Fish, you were a joy to work with! Thank you for your diligent work even in the midst of wedding and eclipse craziness!

Fourth, my beloved crit partners: Kayla Woodhouse, Becca Whitham, and Darcie Gudger. You're all so brilliant and very unique in your insight—each book has been better because of you.

Fifth, to all the team at Barbour. Thank you!

Sixth, to Caleb Johnson, *Mayflower* historian and an incredible help during the writing of this book. Thank you so much. www.Mayflowerhistory.com

Last, but definitely not least, my readers. Thank you for journeying with me on yet another wonderful historical novel. I couldn't do this without you!

Kimberley Woodhouse is an award-winning and bestselling author of more than fifteen fiction and nonfiction books. A popular speaker and teacher, she's shared her theme of "Joy Through Trials" with more than half a million people across the country at more than two thousand events. Kim and her husband of twenty-five-plus years have two adult children. She is passionate about music and Bible study and loves the gift of story.

You can connect with Kimberley at www.kimberleywoodhouse.com and at www.facebook.com/KimberleyWoodhouseAuthor.

Continue Following the Family Tree through History with. . .

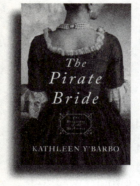

The Pirate Bride by Kathleen Y'Barbo

Pasts Collide in New Orleans when a Treasure Goes Missing

The last time New Orleans attorney, Jean-Luc Valmont, saw Maribel Cordoba, a Spanish nobleman's daughter, she was an eleven-year-old orphan perched in the riggings of his privateering vessel proving herself as the best look-out on his crew. Until the day his infamy caught up with them all, and innocent lives were lost. Unsure why he survived but vowing to make something of the chance he was given, Jean-Luc has buried his past life so deep that no living person will ever find it—until a very much alive and very grown up Maribel Cordoba arrives on his doorstep and threatens all he now holds dear.

Paperback / 978-1-68322-497-6 / $12.99

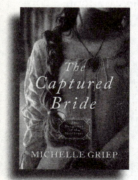

The Captured Bride by Michelle Griep

A War-Torn Countryside Is No Place for a Lady

Mercy Lytton is a lady like no other. Raised among the Mohawks, she straddles two cultures, yet they are united in one cause—to defeat the French. Born with a rare gift of unusually keen eyesight, she is chosen as a scout to accompany a team of men on a dangerous mission. Yet it is not her life that is threatened. It is her heart. Condemned as a traitor, Elias Dubois faces the gallows. At the last minute, he is offered his freedom if he consents to accompany a stolen shipment of French gold to a nearby fort—but he is the one they stole it from in the first place. It turns out that the real thief is the beguiling woman, Mercy Lytton, for she steals his every waking thought. Can love survive divided loyalties in a backcountry wilderness?

Paperback / 978-1-68322-474-7 / $12.99